W

WHITESANDS

Johann
Thorsson

CANELO

First published in the United States in 2021 by Bloodshot Books

This edition published in the United Kingdom in 2024 by

Canelo
Unit 9, 5th Floor
Cargo Works, 1-2 Hatfields
London SE1 9PG
United Kingdom

A CIP catalogue record for this book is available from the British Library.

Print ISBN 978 1 83598 067 5
Ebook ISBN 978 1 80436 665 3

Cover design by kid-ethic

Cover images © Shutterstock

Look for more great books at www.canelo.co

Printed and bound in Great Britain by Clays Ltd, Elcograf S.p.A.

1

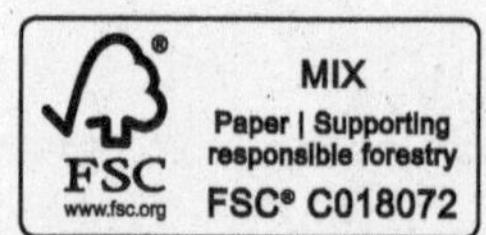

To one it happens, in the time of his youth
that his end becomes a woeful
tribulation to men; the gray prowler on the moor,
the wolf, shall devour him, and his mother,
will mourn his death, which is beyond man's control.

—The Fates of Men
Exeter Book

Prologue

Still Chasing Leads

The October rain ticked on the shoulders of his trench coat, and Homicide Detective John Dark stood outside a nightclub and felt like a ghost. The rain made the city seem smaller, gave it a reflective sheen that distracted the eye. It also made the city feel colder than it was. In the rain, all big cities are the same.

Outside the club, the young huddled together with bland looks in their eyes, attention always on their phones. The dull bass of the music from inside thudded like a heartbeat against the soles of John's feet.

"You a cop?" the bouncer said, a little loud to be heard over the rain and the music and the chatter of the people waiting. His voice was raspy but a bit high, the voice of an eighty-year-old woman with a thing for whiskey and cigars.

"Hey!" someone from the line yelled. "Back of the line, cop."

John couldn't not dress like a cop. Once he had made detective he had eased into the Fifties-style private detective wardrobe and hadn't been able to shake it since. Or wanted to. Tan coat, gray hat and a good pair of shoes.

John danced a bit on his toes, hands deep in the pockets of his coat. Heavy drops of rain banging loud on his shoulders and the brim of his hat, the night both dark and cold. The bouncer could take a step back and allow John to get a little room under the marquee, out from the rain, but didn't. Out of spite or inattention, John didn't know and didn't care.

The bouncer saw him for what he was, of course. John didn't do undercover work, that was never his thing. He had an eye for clues and motive, a good sense for human fallibility and drive, but no real knack for deception and subterfuge.

"Yeah, I'm a cop," John said. "But that's not why I'm here, no one's in any trouble. There's a man who works here I need to speak to. Not as a cop."

"Don't know him," the bouncer replied.

"I didn't—" John said and stopped himself. The downside of John's intelligence was that he often had little patience for stupidity in others. Being recognized as a cop was often the quickest way to shut mouths and doors but in this case he welcomed it. He wouldn't need to flash a badge and since he wasn't on Emily's case, officially, there would be nothing for him to deny. Inside was the best lead he'd gotten for months: a bartender who might be among the last people to have seen her. The lead came from an Instagram photo taken on the night she went missing. In it, she was standing behind the bar with the bartender, in a pose that could only be described as intimate. Missing for two years now and all he had to go on was a post on social media from that night. All other leads cold and dead.

He was about to use his charm on the bouncer when his phone rang.

"You go right ahead and answer that," the bouncer said and let in two kids from the front of the line.

John turned away from the bouncer and took out his phone. A drop of rain slid down the screen, drawing a line of distortion along with it. It was his partner, Monique.

"Yeah?" he said.

"We're on, Marlowe. Domestic disturbance in the nice part of town. A husband we need to talk to. Where are you?" Marlowe was Monique's nickname for him. She was easily the best cop on the force, with only the institutionalized bias of the police keeping her from being his boss. It was either her sex or her skin color. Maybe both.

"I'm downtown, chasing a lead," he said. Monique knew what he meant when he said chasing a lead. She sighed and John could practically see the look of pity she had on.

"Well, get to three five three Sycamore, John, and hurry."

He had been hoping their shift might end early. His life had gone downhill so fast in the last two years he was hoping he'd get that final prod to force him into a choice; what did he really want to do with his life? This close to fifty, however, maybe that wasn't the best of ideas.

"I'm coming. A few words with a guy and I'm on my way," he said and hung up. He turned his attention back to the tall man in front of him.

"Trouble with the wife?" the bouncer asked and grinned, showing a missing tooth.

"Look," John said and handed the bouncer a twenty-dollar bill. "I just need to talk to the bartender for five minutes. He's not in trouble, and I don't care about any violations I might see. I just want a few words with him, personal."

The bouncer looked at the twenty-dollar bill as if seeing money for the first time. "I might just have taken my eye off the door for a minute, if they ask."

John took the hint, walked past the big man and pulled open the heavy door to Freckles and was promptly swallowed by darkness, the smell of stale beer and the booming bass of the music playing inside. The club was one floor down, and as he descended, John thought he was walking down a monster's throat. Right into the belly.

-

In the two years following the night Emily disappeared, Detective John Dark had become less trusting. Now, John was certain that everyone he met was in on a conspiracy to keep her hidden, as if the whole world knew where she was but had collectively decided to let him suffer. And always that voice at the back of his mind, whispering: "If you were a real detective you would have found her by now."

John walked down a poorly-lit maroon-carpeted flight of stairs and through another set of double doors. He had just a few minutes in which to find the bartender and talk to him before he had to rush to the address Monique gave him.

This better be worth my time.

John pushed his way through the throng of bodies, people thirty years younger than him, girls barely dressed and guys all dressed the same. Lights from phone screens competing with the club's own lights, half the kids in the club still looking for something else to do. The modern malaise of kids caught in the net of social media and dating through apps; the constant worry that there was something better somewhere else. He passed a girl wearing a loose yellow dress, sequins reflecting the blinking lights. John felt like a tree, surrounded by dancing pixies. He made his way up to the bar in the center of the club.

"Hello?" he called out to a girl serving drinks. "Hey hey," he said.

"Yeah?" she said, leaning across the bar. She had short dark hair, brown eyes and a nose ring. Smiled politely but gave off a strong "I don't have time for anyone's shit" vibe. Good for her, John thought.

"I'm looking for a bartender, guy, blond hair, one crooked tooth."

The photo in question, John's "lead", was an Instagram image posted by a friend of a friend of Emily's. A lead twice removed. All this time later and the friend had just recently contacted John and told him about it. Had just seen the photo herself. Something about a "memory" John didn't quite get. In the photo, Emily was behind the bar, twerking against the bartender who was smiling a crooked smile with a crooked tooth.

John had already called in all the favors he had at the department, pulled all the strings and torn at every single lead until most of the cops in town had given up on both him and the search for Emily. After this long, she must be dead, right? So John went on searching for himself.

If you were a proper detective you would have found her by now.

"Blond, no," the girl said to him. "But you might mean Steph, he has a crooked tooth, hang on."

She served someone a beer and made her way around the bar. It was in the center of the club, with racks of bottles on shelves around a single wall. The shelves were lit from beneath, giving the bottles on display an eerie look. A rainbow of bottles of formaldehyde awaiting body parts. After a while she reappeared, pulling a guy along and pointing at John.

He tensed up as he saw the bartender, ready to jump over the bar and chase the fucker down if he ran. But the guy didn't run. He shrugged and walked over to John.

He didn't do it, John thought. He didn't have anything to do with it. John's split-second ability to read people kicked in and pushed the rage back down. Made room for hope. But instead of relief, John felt hope-turned-rage rise up in him. He was mad at the force for not doing all it could to find her. Mad at himself for not being able to find her and mad at whoever took her.

The bartender wore a black T-shirt and jeans. Short black hair, not blond, but it most certainly was the guy from the photograph and suddenly John was nervous. You talk to all sorts of low-lives, interrogate murderers and chase down the worst of the city's criminals and then a skinny bartender makes you nervous.

"My name is John Dark," he shouted over the noise. "I work for the police department." Showed him the badge. "That's not why I'm here though. I just want to ask about someone who might have been here."

"Sure, man," the bartender said. "How can I help?" he called over the music.

Someone bumped into John from behind and pushed him into the bar.

"Hey," a preppy teenager said to John. "You done buying a drink old man?"

John turned to look, his eyes like loaded guns and the kid went to find a better spot at the bar. John turned back to the bartender.

"Your name?"

"I'm Steph," he replied.

“Short for Stephen?”

“No. Greek. Short for Stephanos.” Conversation clipped to a minimum, a sort of club-vernacular to be heard over the music.

“I’ll make this quick, Steph.”

John didn’t like that this was rushed. Didn’t like that he should be rushing towards a crime scene right now instead of this.

If you were a proper detective you would have found her by now.

He pulled out his phone, found the Instagram photo and showed it to Stephanos. “Do you remember this evening? This girl?”

He took a look at the photo.

“That’s me, sure. Don’t know who she is though. When’s it taken? Old, right? I haven’t been blond since a year ago.”

“June, two years ago. June fifth.”

Steph shook his head, bit his lip. “Sorry. Who’s the girl?”

“Nothing about her? The hair, the tattoo under the ear? Nothing?”

The music changed, slower beat, less noise. So John heard the rest clearly.

“Girls ask to come behind the bar about two, maybe three times a night, man. They tip better, after, that’s why I allow it. I flirt and take their orders fast and they leave a hefty bit of green, usually.”

“Who else was here that night?” John asked. He looked at the clock. He needed to finish this up. He still had a job to do.

"Look man, I'm sorry I can't help," Steph said and turned to leave. John jumped, grabbed his arm and pulled him back. Steph pulled his arm free. "What the fuck?"

John looked him in the eye. "She's my daughter." Spoken far too loud. "Not a junkie. Two minutes."

Steph looked at him. John knew the look he needed to show him and he did, the father in a desperate search for his daughter look. Wasn't hard to do. He showed the photo to the bartender again.

"Please," he said.

Steph took hold of John's phone and looked at the photo. Shook his head a little.

"Look man," he said. "I'm the only one still working here since then, apart from the manager, maybe. You're asking about something from two years ago. No, I don't remember her."

As he moved to walk away John reached over the bar again and grabbed his arm. Steph turned, looked annoyed. John handed him his card.

"Please. If you remember anything."

Steph looked at him. Took the card and stormed off. John's phone vibrated. A text from Monique.

"*Someone got it wrong. It's a Homicide case John. Get. Here. Now.*"

"Christ," John said. He put his phone back into his coat and walked out. Ran through the rain to his car.

He got in and just sat behind the wheel. Shaking. Shaking with anticipation and frustration at another useless lead. He gripped the steering wheel, his knuckles white from the tension. John felt wrung and used up, angry at the world. There was nothing left of him but grief and the drive to find his daughter no matter what.

Slowly, he pieced himself together, breath by breath. John picked up a thick manila file from the passenger seat, held together with string and hope. Inside were newspaper clippings, photographs of Emily and people she was with that night. A map of the city with her possible movements that evening drawn in in different colors.

A missing person's file made with obsessive care, and it was the single most important thing in John's life. He flipped through it, as if hoping to suddenly discover the missing piece he needed to find her. To find himself. A habit as much as anything else now.

He put it back and turned the key in the ignition. It was time to go to work.

Chapter One

Detective John Dark parked his unmarked Chevy Malibu by a curb in the nice part of town and looked at the scene of the crime; the home of Michael and Ellen Stillwater.

The house, like all houses on the street, was two stories of suburban materialism, decorated now in the flashing blue of police cars. Two patrol cars were parked in the gravel driveway next to a maroon SUV and an ambulance. The radio was playing one of his favorite songs but he'd heard it so many times that it didn't register anymore. Getting old meant your favorite music was now on oldies stations. John took in the scene. Neighbors stood outside in their yards, husbands with their arms over their wives' shoulders. They were people who still cared what happened to the people in the community. Or maybe they just wanted a better look at the drama.

John stepped out of the car as the last notes of the song sounded on the radio. He pulled his coat tighter against the October rain drumming on his hat and his shoulders. He took a deep breath and walked towards the house.

Monique was waiting for him. She wore a dark raincoat and had her hair in a strict ponytail and was hunched over a little notebook trying to protect it from the rain as she jotted something down. She tucked it into a pocket and paced towards John as soon as she noticed him. Monique had broad shoulders and dark eyes that always seemed to reflect a certain disappointment with the world. Her eyes held an obsidian fire and when you had Monique's attention, you had it completely.

"Moreno," John said. "What are we—"

"Where were you?" she interrupted.

"I'll tell you later," he said.

She looked at him, like she knew. She knew.

"Call came in as domestic disturbance," Monique said, speaking fast and low, as if sharing a secret with him. "O'Reilley had no one but us to put on it, I guess. Or didn't realize that this was actually a homicide case. If she'd known from the start that some rich lawyer had killed his wife I'm not sure *we* would be here."

John nodded and looked at the house.

"So what?" John asked. "They're letting us in from the cold now? Maybe we *should* just let someone else take this." He looked back towards his car. If someone else took this, he could go back and put some pressure on the bartender. Get better answers.

"What? No," Monique replied. "Let's go in and get started. A proper homicide case, John. *Homicide*, not helping an old lady with a flat tire or administrative fucking detail. I need this, John," she said. "*You* need this."

John was still looking at his car. He could almost see a ghost of Emily in there, waiting for him to tell her that it was alright. That he hadn't forgotten about her. That one day he would find her. It took willpower to turn back to Monique.

"What do we know about him?" John asked. His car stood empty under a streetlight. Emily still lost somewhere.

"He's a lawyer out in L.A., travels a lot for work. Name's Michael Stillwater. Nothing but a few speeding tickets and an old shoplifting incident on his record. Upstanding suburban white guy, for all his record tells, though maybe not perfect."

As if on cue, two officers led Stillwater out of the front door, hands cuffed behind his back. Blood streaked his chest, vivid against the white silk shirt he was wearing. Shoulders slumped, eyes wide open, scanning the faces around him. For a moment the scene was frozen in the flashing blue of police lights: a man being led out of his nice suburban home in handcuffs, disbelief all over his face, stern police officers leading him forward. Rain making everything glisten.

From long experience, John could judge the seriousness of any crime scene by the tension in the officers' shoulders. Breaking up a party meant cops showed up, nice and relaxed with shoulders loose. Breaking up a bar fight gave them a little more bob, like boats on choppy water.

Murder scenes tended to put starch in all shoulders, pull them up and back and now, here, all shoulders were stiff as coffins. John watched as an officer pushed the husband into the back of a police car.

"What?" Monique asked, looking over to John, who hadn't moved or spoken as he watched Michael Stillwater being escorted from his house into a police car.

John had no answer for Monique. He was looking at the husband, surprised to see no defiance in him, just confusion.

He didn't do it, John thought.

The suddenness of the realization was unbidden and unwelcome. His instincts were coming alive; Stillwater's unexpected expression sparked his homicide detective's insight to the forefront. Ten minutes ago, he hadn't wanted to be here. All he'd wanted for the last two years was to look for Emily. To bring closure to that wound, one way or another. But now he was intrigued.

"John?"

"What? Yeah, let's take a look," he said to Monique and they walked towards the scene of their first homicide case since Emily Dark disappeared two years ago.

-

Forensics made them put on blue shoe covers just outside the house before they walked in. The foyer was neat, though there was a messy bouquet of roses and a pizza box on the floor. What really drew the eye, however, were the leaves and bark that littered the floor and made a trail from the yard into the house. The trail of leaves led from the foyer to a staircase to the second floor.

As they walked in John saw a kitchen to the left, all black marble and dark wood. A living room to the right that seemed designed to impress visitors more than anything else. The sofa was large – black leather that appeared new and unused, a coffee table with a stack of books arranged in the center.

Under any other circumstances, the house would be unremarkable, a domicile in which a well-off couple lived mundane lives, if not for the trail of bark and leaves.

An officer John knew walked towards them from a room at the back of the house and cleared his throat.

"Officer Palace," John said.

"Detective Dark, Detective Moreno," he said and paused. He seemed confused as to why *they* were at the scene of a murder. He collected himself and spoke. "All the ground floor windows are closed and unbroken. The front door itself was locked and we've found nothing indicating a forced entry. I'd say it was just the two of them in the house."

"What's with the leaves and debris on the floor and the staircase?" Monique asked.

Palace didn't immediately answer. As if privately giving the scene the respect it deserved. He seemed surprised at the question.

"You don't know?" Palace asked. "You haven't seen the body?"

"No, we just got here," John said. "Why?"

"He did something to the body," Palace said. "I've never seen anything like it."

John looked at Monique, who raised an eyebrow. John thought of the streaks of blood on the man's shirt just before he was pushed into the police car.

"What did he do?" John asked, trying to imagine what he could possibly have wanted with branches from a tree in his yard.

"Nothing sexual, nothing disgusting. Just… strange," Palace said.

"Did they have a housekeeper, anything like that?" John asked.

"What? No, they have no live-in help. As far as we can tell, it was just the two of them."

"Thanks," he said.

He then turned to Monique. "Take a look upstairs?" he asked with more dread than usual.

He wanted to see it before checking out the rest of the rooms. He wanted to get a feel for the case, a sense of things to look for.

"Yeah."

They went up the stairs, blue plastic shoe covers crinkling as they walked. The upper floor had hardwood flooring, dark and expensive. The lighting was minimal, just a few LEDs at ankle-height, giving the hallway a futuristic feeling without giving it much in the way of useful light. A forensics tech, Miller, was examining the banister outside the bedroom, looking for prints or residue.

"Can we go in?" John asked.

Miller took down his face mask.

"Yeah," he answered. "Just watch where you step."

"I've been to this rodeo before, you know," John said.

Miller's reply was unspoken but John saw it in his eyes. *Not in a while, you haven't.*

John opened the bedroom door, and for the first time in his career, he gasped.

The room looked more like modern art than a murder scene. The body of Ellen Stillwater had been carefully arranged on the bed, naked, feet tied together at the ankles with what looked like coarse green wire. After she died, she had been placed on the bed with her hands upwards above her head and out, so she now formed a sort of Y.

There were multiple stab wounds in the torso and around the heart. Messy. Streams of blood had been tossed up onto the walls as she had been stabbed again and again, furiously. The blood trailed down the walls like bad graffiti, a shining streamer of crimson on an otherwise pale painting of boats on one of the walls. And then the madness of the scene – two branches had been attached to the top of her head and then added to; two became four became eight and so on, up and outwards from her head before climbing up the wall and expanding. Antlers of branches made into wings of leaves that spread open across the wall.

"This must have taken hours," John whispered, taking in the scene and then the atmosphere of the room, the body. The blood. "He must have been so angry with her," John said.

Ellen Stillwater's dark hair was slick with blood and combed back carefully. Her eyes, a fine brown that reminded John of polished wood, were staring upwards with fright and disbelief. Her mouth was open as well, with a single drop of blood on a tooth. That's the image John would remember at the end of the case. Not the antlers, not the spatters of blood, but the single delicate still-red drop of blood on a perfect, white tooth.

The flower of a single rose lay just above the wounds near her heart. John stepped further into the room and realized that the wiry string tying her feet together was rose stems, thorns sticking into her ankles.

The room smelled like a forest after rain. Mixed with the stink of death.

"He tied her up *after* she died," he said, pointing to her feet. "There's no sign she was struggling, her feet would have been cut up more."

"Why do… *this*?" Monique asked. "What is he doing? Killing his wife and then arranging her like this, like what, a deer?"

"He was found there." John and Monique turned to see the forensics officer, Miller, in the doorway, pointing at a location against the wall by the bed. Bloody handprints on the slick white walls. "He was sitting there, rocking and humming. I heard that when the first officers came he asked them if they were going to catch whoever did this."

"That's a little bold," John said. "Hey."

"Yeah?" Miller answered.

"No footprints in the blood apart from the husband?"

"No. Nothing we found indicates anything other than that they were alone in the room. The house was locked when the first officer got here. They had to unlock it themselves. The husband didn't answer the door, even though *he* called 911."

"And the knife?" John asked.

"Kitchen knife, found there," the tech said and pointed to a bloody spot on the floor. "It appears to fit an empty space in the kitchen knife stand."

"Okay. Thanks," John said.

John approached the body, careful not to step in any of the blood. He looked at the antlers the killer had made. He pinched the bridge of his nose.

"What are you thinking?" Monique asked.

"Nothing yet. Only... It still seems a really unnecessarily brutal way to kill your wife," John said.

"Is there a non-brutal way of killing your spouse?" Monique asked.

"What I mean is, if he had planned it he would have used a gun or poison, something quicker and less messy, and then tried to hide the body. If it was a crime of passion, like he found out she was cheating on him, whatever, and killed her in a jealous rage it seems a little odd to..." he gestured with his hand at the blood-spattered room, "do this."

John leaned close and pointed at her hands. "Look at this. No defensive wounds. He surprised her."

The body, apart from the blood spatter, looked peaceful. As if she might stir awake at any moment, lick the drop of blood from her tooth and say that she just had the strangest dream.

"Well, you don't usually expect your husband to stab you to death, either," Monique said.

"Hack," John said, then looked at Monique. Sorry he used that word.

John paced. He walked around the bed and traced the branches as they grew into antlers. Not affixed to her head but placed, maybe as a crown but far too elaborate. He tried to envision the time and patience that went into making them. Moving the branches, cutting them down and nailing them to the wall. And then he looked back to the wounds on Ellen Stillwater's body.

"Look," he finally said to Monique. "This is not one thing. This is *two* things."

"What do you mean?" Monique asked.

John, once he got into the force, had risen quickly through the ranks. He had a no-nonsense way of talking to people that made even the hardiest of dealers feel they could trust him. *This* cop was okay. John also *felt* crime scenes as much as he looked at the evidence. And what he felt here was all wrong.

"The murder itself, for one. The wounds are not from a stabbing, but from a furious and messy attack. There's so much anger in there. Did the husband seem angry to you?"

"No, but angry people don't stay angry for long."

"Okay, but then there's the second part. There's love here. A delicate love. He wants her to be seen as pretty. She means a lot to him and it matters to him how she is seen. The way he combed her hair. The rose on the heart, the care that goes into the antlers. He sees her as fragile, *after* he kills her so savagely. It's two things, and I can't reconcile them."

"Yeah. Well," Monique said. A hint of a smile played on her lips. She might as well have said; *Glad to have you back, John.*

"Forensics has him now. Once they're done we'll get to ask him about this," she said, her gaze lingering on the ritualistic scene before them.

John looked at the scene, at the blood on the walls and the woman on the bed. Looked at the branches stuck to the bed and wall, fashioned into antlers that made this into a tableaux of art and horror. He turned and walked down the stairs and out of the house, thinking only that this was not going to have a simple answer. Why would someone go to such lengths and then call in the murder themselves?

Chapter Two

The offices of Gamma Pharmaceuticals were in a dull, square toad of a building. The third floor was wedged in the middle, above the entrance and the dining hall but below the nicer offices. It was on this third floor that Daniel Hope sat in a cubicle, staring at a computer screen. He was looking at lines of grey-on-black code, trying in vain to find the parts that were broken. It was a slow process, tedious, looking through the endless commands and routines, most of which he had not written himself, and Daniel wasn't making much progress. The medication he was on helped him interact with his coworkers and kept the world in place, but it also made his mind a log-jammed river on a winter morning.

He stood up and stretched and walked around on the faded carpeting that covered the floors, carpeting that, through some textural magic, swallowed up most of the common office noise. Around him, his colleagues' faces were faintly lit up by the glare from computer screens. Faces in the dark, staring blankly at near-blank screens. Minds for hire, working into the night to make money for someone else.

A fan whirred in the distance, stirring the air above their heads.

Daniel was working on a dose-correcting program that Gamma Pharmaceuticals was going to sell to hospitals to help with drug dosing for long-term patients, a system that would potentially save millions of dollars in nurse salaries in hospitals all over the country. Why have people, fickle unreliable people, work around the clock doing menial tasks that were better handled by infallible and unfeeling programming? Sure, there was a good possibility that nurses would lose their jobs, or at least part of their hours, but Daniel felt that the patients' gain outweighed that factor. It would end wrong or missed drug doses, end patient suffering, and ensure proper healing.

It would also make Gamma millions, none of which Daniel or the other programmers would get. Daniel wasn't directly employed at Gamma, nor were most of the others in the office, but worked through a temp agency. The hours Gamma hired them for were just enough not to have to pay for health insurance, which was actually quite a bit of money in his case, due to his "condition." Luckily the state picked up *that* check.

The last few weeks and days had grown increasingly tense. Daniel had noticed more hurried whispers, more shouting behind closed doors and an increase in overtime requests. He hoped he wasn't imagining anything. Schools of tightly-suited men would exit the large elevator, swim in unison toward the large meeting room and leave, hours later, stern-faced, glistening and silent. Afterwards, Miguel Relnez, the office manager, was stuck alone in his own little private hell of an existence.

Something in the code didn't work, and deadlines were approaching. Daniel had been reading through and updating the program for weeks now with little progress. The only solace he had was that none of the others working on the same thing seemed any closer to a solution than he was. It wasn't *his* failure.

Two of his coworkers, Stephen and Jessica, also brought on through the temp agency, stood by the drinks fridge in the corner. The fridge was only waist-high and it illuminated their knees well but cast up an eerie light. It appeared as if they were cardboard cutouts, placed there to give the appearance of normalcy at the office. "Look, people work here. They converse and enjoy refreshments. All is well! All is well!"

Daniel walked towards them. Not wanting the drink, not wanting the conversation, just wanting to remember that feeling of "everyday" that so eluded him. Just wanting that one thing that his illness had pushed so far out of reach that it had nearly fallen out of recall; just fitting in.

He was self-conscious as he approached them, worried what they thought of him. They seemed to float now, something about the light from the fridge made it seem as if they were just legs and faces. Office ghosts. He thought of what he would say, every word mulled over. There was little natural in Daniel's conversation now, at least as he experienced it. He always felt as if he were outside of his own interactions, staring at them in real-time and judging them as they happened. Aware of every word and action.

"Hey Daniel," Stephen said, freeing him from having to interrupt. They both looked at him, disembodied hands holding small plastic bottles to their floating office-worker ghost-faces. "Making any progress for our dark overlords?"

"I am not," Daniel replied, relieved to see that today was a good day, conversation-wise. Today his mind gave up the words easily.

"Jessica was just saying..." Stephen paused and glanced around into the darkness. "...how she heard that the code was now two months late. And that's just the prototype."

Jessica looked at Daniel, waiting for his reaction. She had short, dark-red hair with a single striking purple lock. Pretty, but carried and dressed herself in a way that made it seem she didn't care to be. Wore dresses she made herself from vintage band T-shirts, color long faded so all that was left were band names in varying shades of gray. She favored a dress featuring the cover of Megadeth's *Rust in Peace* album. Stephen wore the same dull shirt and khaki-pants every day. Either that, or he had a few shirts of the identical pale-blue color. Daniel imagined a closet with rows of the same outfit, and thought he remembered hearing how Steve Jobs and Mark Zuckerberg did that; wore the same thing every day because it meant that they had fewer decisions to make in the morning.

"They are losing something like a hundred-thousand dollars every day," Jessica added. "Every *day*."

"Why don't they hire more people?" Daniel asked, hoping he hadn't been lost in thought too long.

"They are, that's the thing. So, the rumor is that there's a whole other office, just like this one. A Gamma alternate-office. It's like, you know, the same company but different for tax or profit reasons, has another department working on the same thing. Competing with itself. Cannibalizing itself."

"How many people work at the other place?" Daniel asked and then wondered why he asked that. What would they think of his question? Would Jessica think it stupid? Always questioning his own words as he said them, overly self-aware.

"Probably the same as here," she said. "I think it's a bit, you know, bizarro. To think that there's an office of people like us, working for the same company, on the same thing. Maybe, right now, there are three people standing around a fridge of off-brand soda in the other building, talking about *us*."

The idea made its way through Daniel's maze of a mind. He wondered if that meant there was another copy of him, identical, in that other building. A shot of adrenaline as he wondered if he should have known about this. Was it his fault? Were they watching… no, he thought. That's not you thinking, that's the—

"Anyway, we hear they are either going to push us harder until we complete the thing before that bizzaro-office, or fire everyone if we don't. Of course, they're not going to pay us more or add us on as full-times," Stephen said. "That would be too much. You'd think that a company that makes billions annually would be able to afford to hire permanent people and, you know, pay for our healthcare and benefits. Fuckers."

There was a moment of silence. Daniel felt pressure to say something, as if it was an unspoken rule of the office that it was now his turn to speak. He couldn't shake the image of the identical office competing with them for the code. How could he not have known before?

He remembered having *ambition*. He had imagined graduating, getting a job at the bottom and then climbing, climbing higher and faster. Setting goals, improving himself and sticking to a plan until he, Daniel Hope, looked out over the horizon from the top.

He had stumbled before even starting, tripped up by a force stronger and more devious than any seven habits could account for. No staring into mirrors chanting self-empowerment mantras, no daily meditation and mindfulness, no $10,000 Dale Carnegie course could get him on the path to success now. An anchor was pulling him down, holding his ambitions and dreams in place.

Grounding Daniel for life. It had little mercy, cared little for hopes and dreams and normalcy. A tricky, invisible anchor.

All his coding at Gamma was laced with the self-doubt of his condition, as all his actions in life were. As everything he thought was marbled with distrust, as all sounds were to be questioned and all decisions to be taken with care. Daniel made his way slowly in the world, and didn't want to disturb anything.

"Anyway, I better get back," Jessica said. "I want to get *something* done before I go home."

Daniel wondered if the conversation ended because he didn't pick it up, and hadn't been able to think of anything to say. Every conversation now a maze of social rules and etiquette that he had to focus on single-mindedly to keep up with, that same focus robbing his contributions of any ease or grace. A runner having to think, at every step, which foot came next, right or left.

"Yeah, we wouldn't want to disappoint Relnez," Stephen scoffed. "Hey," he added. "You guys going to that thing later?"

Daniel didn't know what the thing was, he never did. He didn't use Facebook, which was where most of these "things" were usually planned so he tended to miss them. Facebook, with its never-ending stream of little nuggets of interaction felt not like a newspaper that you could scroll up your screen but a wall that went *down* into his screen and if he just stood up on his toes and peered he would see how far down it went, but of course it went down forever and if you leaned too far you could fall in, fall down the never-ending wall of vanity disguised as news and—

"Daniel?" Stephen and Jessica were both looking at him. "You all right, you zoned out a little there."

"Yes," Daniel said. "Yes I just—"

"It's going to be at the Fridays on Lafayette, you know it?"

"Yes," he said, hoping that was the right answer. He was still, in his mind, pulling back from the Wall, the image so clear in his head of a giant tower of a wall rising up from the edge of a cliff. He couldn't fit that and "Fridays" and "Lafayette" into his mind as well.

"Well, maybe we'll see you there, yeah?"

"Sure," Daniel said.

They walked away from the little fridge on the floor, back to their computers. The fridge light illuminated their calves and then they were just the backs of two people walking away, no outlines or substance.

Daniel shivered but allowed himself a thought. *They asked me to join them.*

He walked back to his own workstation, only to find Mr. Relnez there waiting for him, looking upset.

Chapter Three

Emily Dark left home at around eight p.m. on a Friday evening in June and never came back. She was going to meet her friends, Toni Shepherd and Shawnette Maye, both nineteen years old. Emily had admitted to her mother that they would be going downtown, the pretense being that Shawnette was meeting a boy whose brother was at Harvard and so might help them with their applications in the fall. Lonei hadn't believed them, but on remembering how she herself had been at nineteen, had let it slide with a grin.

It was a decision that haunted her every day.

Lonei said she could stay until one at the absolute latest and when Emily wasn't home by then her anger started to sour into worry. She texted Emily and Toni, whose number she had. The response she got from Toni was that she had gone home earlier and that Emily had mentioned staying over at Shawnette's house.

Lonei was not one to call people's homes in the middle of the night (if only she had, or asked John to have an officer take a drive). Something in Toni's voice had soothed her into a false trust. The girls had gone home together and were sleeping. Emily would get an earful in the morning.

Lonei crawled into bed that night at 1:13 and fell asleep next to John.

After checking in on Emily's room in the morning and finding the bed empty, she called the Maye's at nine o'clock sharp to talk to Emily, knowing she would be waking her up.

Debra, Shawnette's mom answered.

"Hello?"

"Debra, it's Lonei, is Shawnette there? I need to ask her about Emily."

"Hang on Lonei, I'll go get her up."

"Well, Debra, you best put her on the phone right quick," Lonei said. Her voice broke, the words "right" and "quick" coming out as sobs. She felt the world hold its breath in the long moments it took to rouse Shawnette and get her to the phone.

"Hello?" Shawnette said, her voice raspy from a night spent in poor sleep.

"Shawnette? Where's Emily?" Her voice, fallen into the dark pit of an empty stomach.

"Who this?"

"Lonei Dark, Emily's mom."

"Oh hi, Mrs. Dark," Shawnette had said that morning, tone rigid and formal. "I don't know where Emily is if she ain't with you. Maybe with Toni?"

"No honey, she ain't at Toni's."

"Well I…" hesitation. Something she didn't want to say.

"What," Lonei said, trembling. Heart beating wingless and frightened.

"She ain't home?"

"No."

"And she ain't at Toni's."

"No."

"I just…"

"What, Shawnette?"

"I left her at McDonald's. I… I went for a ride with a boy, we drove and he took me home. Emily said she'd be fine and I should just go. That's the truth, ma'am I swear. I left her at the McDonald's and she said she'd be fine. I thought she would just go home."

"Well, she isn't home and her phone is off."

Lonei's fear, contagious. Crossed the wire and infected Shawnette.

"Mrs. Dark, I'll help you find her. I'll call some people. We'll find her."

"Shawnette. Now talk truth to me. Does Emily have a boyfriend we don't know about?"

"No ma'am. She ain't seeing nobody now."

Lonei woke John and John, seeing the look in her eyes and her quivering lip felt for a moment helpless as he heard the words, "I can't find Emily."

Sleep sluiced off him.

"What do you mean?"

"She went out last night and she ain't back. Neither Toni nor Shawnette know where she is."

"When did she go out?"

"Eight," Lonei said.

"With Toni and Shawnette?"

"Yes."

"And she's not with either of them now? Could she have come home and left before we got up? Maybe to the gym?"

"She… she could," Lonei said, hoping but not believing it.

-

The CCTV footage from McDonald's confirmed Shawnette's story. They were there from 12:40 until just after one, when a young man, later identified as Michael Washington, picked her up. Emily stayed behind, finished her fries and left at 1:05.

She was not seen on any camera after that.

Her phone was tracked until just before two a.m. It was still for a while at a location that John later determined was a bench on a sidewalk. It was close to a bus stop and a taxi stand and it was assumed she was waiting for either one. Then her phone moved east and further south, away from their house and went silent. Whether the battery ran out or the phone was deliberately turned off remained unknown.

Nothing was known about where Emily Dark might be. No one was found who was around the sidewalk bench at that time. A bus driver said he remembered seeing a black girl sitting on the bench, sure, but nothing more. Any number of black girls could have sat on the bench at that time.

As if all black girls were the same black girl. And one had just vanished before everyone's eyes and the only ones still fighting for her now, two years later, were her parents.

Chapter Four

The Chief of Police, Samantha O'Reilley, asked John to close the door behind them as they entered. She was dressed as if for a funeral that morning, wearing a black dress and nice shoes. John sat down on a leather couch against the office wall, as outside the window the sun was peeking up over the horizon to see what the world looked like this morning. If the humans had survived another night without it.

The walls of the chief's office were decorated with a few photos of hunting trips. Moose up in Canada, reindeer in Finland. No photos of kids or a husband, though John knew she had both.

"Look," O'Reilley said and John thought he knew what was coming. He glanced over at Monique, who seemed to be holding her breath. "This is bit of a mess. I put you on this Stillwater thing because despite everything you are good detectives. No complications, just look at the evidence, see if you can find any more of it, and then have a few words with him. From what the men at the scene and forensics have told me it's pretty simple. Should be a good warm-up as you get back into the groove."

John leaned forward just as Monique spoke. "Yes, chief," she said. Eager to get back into the nitty gritty.

"John," O'Reilley said, and sighed. "Look. I'm putting you back on homicide but I need you to really *be* back, right?" A moment of silence as the reason for him being put out in the cold passed through their minds.

If you were a real detective you would have found her by now.

She sighed. "Just wrap this one up and we can get you on to bigger cases. Real cases."

Monique stood up and opened the door. She seemed tense, as if expecting to walk into a trap.

"John," O'Reilley said. "Again. I'm sorry about your daughter. We'll help if and when something new comes up. Don't think we don't care."

"Who is he friends with?" John asked.

"Sorry?"

"Stillwater. Who is he friends with?"

"Detective," she said. The three syllables sound like the clicks of loading a gun. "I'm letting you and Moreno back into the department despite bridges burned. And you question my motive?"

"I'm sure he—"

"And I'm sure, Detective Moreno, that Dark can tell me what he meant."

John felt the world shimmer. Knew the shape it ended up in depended on what he said next. "Sorry Captain. I didn't mean it like that. Surely though, there's a deeper reason to me and Monique being on this than just a newfound mercy on your part."

"Goddammit, Dark. Moreno, close the door."

Monique closed the door and shot John a look he'd remember for the rest of his life.

"Look," O'Reilly said. "Despite everything, you are good detectives. Yes, Mr. Stillwater does have friends in high places who are already asking me to get this taken care of. Your rosters are pretty light these days so I figured you could put your full weight behind this and that… is… all."

"Who is he?" Monique asked.

"Stillwater? Just a lawyer with friends, that's all. They have the simple interest of keeping this from becoming a media circus, so just finish it fast. And I mean fast. Overtime if you need it, full department resources."

Full department resources. Something John had been promised when Emily disappeared. Something he knew had a shorter lifespan than you might think.

"Sure," John said. "We'll finish this."

"Detectives. There is nothing behind this request but the desire to keep this tragedy out of the media. Really."

She seemed sincere. John couldn't help but admire her, despite everything that had passed between them in the past years.

But his thoughts were ever bent towards Emily. Always Emily. Since walking into the Stillwater house, however, he hadn't been carrying his guilt as consciously as before, had allowed his mind to dwell on other things. Upon realizing this a worry settled in place, immediate thoughts of people judging him for not caring enough. As if that could ever be true. He stood up, and took the weight of Emily with him.

"Talk to forensics, talk to Stillwater, and get everything to the D.A. as quickly as possible. Then we'll talk about your next case."

They left O'Reilley's office, Monique with a new lightness to her steps, John with nothing but a sense of dread and guilt.

Chapter Five

Mr. Relnez was an iguana of a man. His head and neck sliding together without an edge, disappearing into a suit that Daniel sometimes imagined he molted out of at night, ending every day by discarding the suit-skin, crawling into bed naked, pale and slick, only to grow a new suit by morning. And now he stood there, grinning his thin-lipped iguana-grin, asking for Daniel.

"Yes?" Daniel said.

"Could I have a word, in my office?" Not waiting for an answer but already walking, melding with the odd lightlessness of the office.

Daniel followed, worried that he was about to listen to *that* speech again. A boss, with a tilted head asking him to pack up his things and find work that better suited his temperament. That he would again be told he didn't fit, didn't match the corporate ideals or team dynamics. Telling him that the company appreciated his efforts and they would of course give him good references and assist in any way they could. Anything, that was, except keeping him on the payroll despite his illness. Anything except just a little understanding.

As he followed Mr. Relnez down the hallway he became aware of the fact that the only sounds were clicks of keys on keyboards, sighs and creaks of chairs. He felt like he was being led to something. The light coming into the office from the evening-turning-into-night outside seemed slow, as if strained and made lethargic passing through the slim curtains, with little brightness to give, only the most subdued illumination. He smelled nothing. He wondered, not for the first time, why they didn't keep the lights on.

His slippers dragged on the carpet, he wished he'd dressed better this morning, that he didn't always let himself slip into the stereotypical lazy-programmer outfit; jeans, a clever T-shirt and an unbuttoned shirt.

As Mr. Relnez sat down behind a turtle of a desk he gestured for Daniel to close the door and take a seat. Daniel sat down in one of the uncomfortable chairs across from Mr. Relnez. He looked at his boss, a man younger than he was, all attitude and little actual computer or pharmaceutical knowledge, and wondered why their positions weren't reversed. The answer, of course, was already there.

Mr. Relnez, hair slicked back across a smooth skull, with premature grey showing by small ears, smiled again. It was a nervous smile, the smile of a man about to say something uncomfortable, not the confident grin of a lizard about to lick a fly off a stone.

"Daniel," he said, followed by a long pause, even by Daniel's standards.

"I...," again a pause. Shorter this time. "We at Gamma Pharmaceuticals have a reputation in the field. Guys like us have been pushing the industry forward—"

Daniel looked out the window behind his boss. The city seemed to stretch out unceasingly into the night. The lights were so bright against the autumn darkness and Daniel lost himself in thought, wondering what the people living in all those buildings did. How could so many people live in—

"Daniel?"

"Yeah, sorry." All too often when people were talking, Daniel found himself not just zoning out but losing himself completely, especially when he was nervous. For a moment, he was *there*, floating over the city.

Mr. Relnez had gotten up and walked over to a bookcase.

"We have come to a make-or-break moment for the company, Daniel. The shareholders are losing their patience and we are running out of time with the product."

Daniel sat up, conscious that he had been zoning out and suddenly feeling hot. He focused on Mr. Relnez, who continued talking.

"We *need* this program to ship, not next month or next quarter, but next *week*. I've sweet-talked us past deadlines for the last time. I can't keep us afloat by myself anymore." He sat down again. Straightened a magazine on his desk, looked at something on the computer screen.

"I'm sorry to ask you for this. I know about you." He shifted in his chair. "I... the agency told me about your, erm, thing, of course. Your unfortunate illness. The medication."

Daniel felt the chair sink a little into the carpet. He sat there with the anchor in his hands, on full display, pulling him down, down again, pulling the chair down into the floor.

Mr. Relnez *knew*.

"But I also happen to know one of your former professors."

Daniel was waiting for Relnez to use his illness as an excuse to fire him. Never stated outright as the reason, of course, that would be somewhat south of full legality, but always the true cause.

"And *they* told me about the brilliance hiding in the mess, to use their own words."

The brilliance hiding in the mess. Daniel was gifted, and there had been a time when there was no mess to hide the brilliance. As soon as he had fired up DOS as a boy to poke around the family's computer a fire had been lit. At first it was just to try to find a little extra RAM to get a computer game going, but there was no turning back. He *got it*. He read up a bit and just understood how computers worked, the logic behind them. He finished high school with mostly good, yet unremarkable grades and went to college. Computers and math, *that* he understood. People were strange and you couldn't really trust them or their emotions. But computers, yeah. They just did what he wanted. So when he got to choose his own classes, when he finally got to talk computers and math all day it was like he was a hungry tiger let loose. He was set to graduate with a higher grade than his school had ever awarded.

That's when he started noticing the people following him around.

Cars parked outside his apartment building would suddenly drive off when he approached. Any time he made a phone call there were odd clicks and static so he knew they were listening. The girl he was with at the time knew something was wrong, she kept telling him to get help, but she just didn't hear it the way he did. Or maybe she was with *them*? They put a camera in his fridge so they always knew what he was eating and that was how they got the tracking bugs into his stomach. He put all his electronics into the shower and turned it on, full blast; phone, computer. TV.

He was going to cut the tracking bugs out with a knife when the girl he was with, his beloved Stacy who, despite everything, *still* had his heart, finally had enough and, sobbing and heartbroken, called the police. He might have mentioned cutting the bugs out from her stomach as well, he didn't remember.

Daniel was arrested and diagnosed, mere weeks before graduation. Given an anchor that he would never shake off. Schizophrenia.

He had to take counseling for a while and then drugs forever. Luckily, they told him, he didn't need to be placed in a home since he hadn't actually hurt anyone, and the drugs and therapy seemed to work well.

He finished school with good marks, mostly because of his first two years. He got a job placement through an agency, but people balked at his social lethargy, felt uncomfortable being around a crazy person. Daniel needed the work, so he did computer work that was simple and easy, bouncing around workplaces. Gamma Pharmaceutical, however, had had him on their radar before. And once here, they kept him on because even with the medication slowing him down he was no worse than most of the other programmers. Maybe even slightly better.

"I'm going to ask you for a favor," Mr. Relnez said.

"Yeah," Daniel said, uninterested in the conversation, already thinking of the walk home in the rain. He enjoyed the rain.

"I'm going to ask you for something, but I'm going to have to ask you to never mention it to anyone."

"Sure," Daniel said. He wanted this conversation to be over.

"We're struggling. We're going to have to let a lot of people go unless we get that program working. It will not reflect well on me," he said. He stood up again and walked over to the bookcase. He put his finger on a book with a drab green cover, faded almost. "How would you like to work from home for a few days, Daniel?"

Remote work, it was all the rage in start-ups now. Daniel didn't care either way. When he was in front of a computer the rest of the world just dialed itself right down anyway, didn't much matter where he was.

"Sure," he said. "If that'll help."

Before the diagnosis, Daniel had a good group of friends. Had Stacy. Had Friday nights and Sunday afternoons. Now he just had endless solitary hours. He also knew that sometimes he made people uncomfortable and he suspected that, more than anything, was the reason Mr. Relnez wanted him to work from home.

"I'll have them send over a new computer. The best, whatever you want. We'll stock your fridge and everything, just so you can focus on the work, right? I'll even get you a big bonus at the end of the year."

Miguel Relnez walked over to the window and looked out, his back to Daniel.

"And, Daniel, this is the important part. I'm going to need you to stop taking your medication while you work on this."

There it was.

"Sir? If I do that—"

"Don't finish that sentence, Daniel. It was just a thought I had, never mind it. Your wellbeing is of utmost importance to Gamma. It's just that, we've been getting some complaints about your behavior lately and, well, your code isn't as good as it used to be."

Lies. Daniel got along well enough with the other guys, though he didn't socialize with them after work. Alcohol was off limits to him, drug-interaction and questionable decision-making did not go well with schizophrenia. Daniel had read everything he could, of course, and managed to convince himself that there was no cure. Medication kept it at bay but slowed him down.

Violin virtuosos, child prodigies who were on the cusp of worldwide fame as they were diagnosed with schizophrenia and prescribed the drugs Daniel was on, they were later just passably good, the violin a constant and unused reminder of what they used to be.

Suicide was common.

"I'm just saying that most of the others have finished their parts of the program, we just need your code now. You wouldn't want to be responsible for the whole project falling apart, would you?"

It was a threat, intricate but still clear enough that Daniel knew that he would be blamed for GP's failing now.

Daniel thought of the anchor he was holding, thought that maybe he was better and the pills just kept him down. Maybe he never had schizophrenia, not really. And it was tempting.

"I'll do it," he heard himself say. It was almost as if the sentence had been waiting all along, as if Daniel had just needed permission or a reason to *try* skipping the drugs for a few days.

After all, what was the worst that could happen?

Chapter Six

The Reid Technique for interrogation was first used on 21 December 1955, in Lincoln, Nebraska. It was developed and used by a polygraph expert named John Reid, to elicit a confession from a man named Darrel Parker for his wife's murder. Parker was convicted by a jury, almost solely based on his confession, and on 2 June 1956 he was sentenced to life in prison.

Success using the Reid Technique hinges on the suspect being worn down, mentally and physically. Food and water are always "on the way" and will arrive as soon as the suspect just admits to a little something connecting them to the crime. The interrogator will pretend to empathize with the suspect. "It's okay. I understand. I get angry at my wife too. And sometimes we all want to be single again, right?"

Mr. Reid subsequently started a company, John E. Reid and Associates, and made "The Reid Technique" a registered trademark. The technique consists of three phases, where a confession is elicited from a suspect through an assumption of guilt. It is mostly used when the police themselves are sure the suspect is the guilty party. Questions become tricky. "Did you do this because you caught her cheating or was it accidental?"

John Dark, unlike most other detectives, did not like the Reid Technique and avoided anything resembling it when interviewing suspects. To him, it was no different from asking "Have you stopped beating your wife?"

Detectives had used The Reid Technique to get the false confessions from the now-exonerated Central Park Five. Darrel Parker himself, the first suspect convicted based on a Reid Technique confession, was fully pardoned after a death-row inmate named Wesley Peery confessed to the murder, decades later. Darrel was awarded $500,000 in damages.

John had no plans to coerce a confession from Michael Stillwater using the Reid Technique. He was just going to talk to him like he would talk to anyone else. Like he always did.

The brass handle on the door to the interrogation room was cold in John's grip. He was standing in a basement hallway in the police station. Behind him, above him, the sounds of phones and footfalls and murmurs, the day-to-day rumblings of a police station's digestion, him standing in the bowels. He took this moment to collect himself before the interrogation, gathered his thoughts for the performance he was about to give. The questions were as much part of a play as anything else. It was in moments like this that he felt out of his league. An imposter. At any moment someone would come along and say, "Sorry John, you're not cut out for this. The professionals are here now. We'll handle it." He supposed everyone felt that way at one time or another in their careers. He just wished it didn't happen so often. On the other side of the door, Michael Stillwater, having been escorted into the room moments earlier by an officer, sat alone.

John sighed just before opening the door.

Here we go, he thought.

The room was a simple and sparse concrete box with a table, folding chairs and a long mirror on one of the walls. They kept the temperature in the room just below normal, something about people being more likely to tell the truth if they felt a little cold. It made them think of the comforts of home and perhaps more willing to cooperate to get there.

John had, during the course of his career, conducted a great many of these interrogations, though it had been just about two years now since the last one. A long two years.

In this play, the interrogation play, you asked the person a few questions, starting with easy ones about their childhood or their work, things they would answer without thinking. Then, slowly, you moved over to questions about the case. John would hand the lead over to Monique and accept it back, the ebb and flow of good police work.

You wanted the subject to like you just enough to let their guard down a little, feel comfortable so they, too, took part in the play. Asking people about themselves outside the scope of the particular criminal case was a great way to do that.

"Mr. Stillwater," John said as he walked in. He caught a glimpse of himself in the wall-length mirror on the other side of the room and thought how he needed a shave. The odd moments our ego gets a say.

Michael Stillwater turned his head towards John, eyes red-rimmed and wide with the shock of the evening's events. The look threw John off balance – the guilty have a cold emptiness in their gaze under interrogation, the innocent always stare with a sense of bewilderment and impatience. Stillwater just looked hurt, and John didn't know where that put him. He was wearing a clean white T-shirt, the clothes he had been wearing earlier now being examined as evidence. His hair, a thinning salt-and-pepper, was uncombed.

John sat down and sipped his coffee. He grimaced, the coffee cold already. Had a distinct sourness to it.

"Do you like coffee, Mr. Stillwater?" he asked, placing his cup down.

No answer. John opened the slim file folder on the desk. It contained a print-out of Mr. Stillwater's criminal record; a few speeding tickets spread out over nearly thirty years of driving.

"Mr. Stillwater? Mr. Stillwater!"

"I'm here," he said. Eyes rimmed red. This man who had just a few hours ago stabbed his wife to death, now shedding tears for her. Putting on a play of his own. "I know I'm here but I'm really hoping I'm not, you know? Maybe it's an elaborate prank." He looked around the room, as if seeing it for the first time. He spoke slowly. "Did you ever see that movie, *The Game*?"

A cold tickle at the back of John's neck.

"Mr. Stillwater," he said. "I assure you this is not a TV prank. Were your rights read to you?"

He lowered his head back down. "Yes," he said.

"And do you understand your rights as they were read to you?" John said, not for the first time in his career.

"I like coffee," Stillwater said. His voice had turned hoarse, somewhat distant. Full of regret. Like a frightened and confused child accepting offered candy.

"I'll have someone bring you a cup," John said. "I have to notify you that this interview is being recorded. Do you understand?"

"Yes, I understand."

"And did you understand your rights as they were read to you?"

"I'm a lawyer. I understand my fucking rights."

The door opened behind John but he didn't turn. Michael looked up, desperate hope glinting at the back of his eyes. Monique walked in and closed the door behind her without making a noise. She walked over and sat down next to John. Monique was smartly dressed, as she usually was. Professional in every way. John thought she would fit well in most respectable settings and could just as easily have been a politician, or a lawyer. A television journalist. Something made her become a cop though, and even though they had been partners for years John still didn't know what it had been.

"This is my partner, Monique Moreno," John said.

John used to laugh when guys at the station told her to smile more, until realizing that it was not a compliment or a helpful piece of advice but an attempt at control. It jarred him now when he heard it, and he heard it too often. She had shoulder-length curly hair and eyes that John had seen turn most shades of brown, from the near-black of dark oak to a soft tan. Always he saw in them how tired she was of the world. And always a hope that maybe, from this moment, things might get better.

"Mr. Stillwater," she said as a greeting.

John had thought he was falling in love with her, once. He did nothing about it, knowing it would go away. As it did. Still, he would give his life for Monique, and not just because they were partners. There was a shared understanding of life between them; the unfairness and the rare moments of joy.

"Yes. I understood my rights," Mr. Stillwater said, as if to make up for swearing before.

They had decided not to put on any good cop, bad cop show. This case was pretty clear and they didn't really need a confession, though it would certainly speed things along. John was mostly curious. The slight man in front of him didn't seem like someone who'd kill his wife in a fit of rage. Not that many of them did.

"And you are aware that you have the right to have a lawyer present?"

"Yes. I have a friend on his way."

"A friend?" John asked.

"He's my lawyer. I'm a lawyer myself, I know how these things work and I understand everything you've said. What I *don't* get is why the fuck I'm in here being questioned." He had looked up, looked John straight in the eye. John was surprised by the determination he saw.

"Do you wish for us to pause the interrogation until your lawyer arrives?" Monique asked.

Michael looked at them then, eyes clear, pupils like stones at the bottom of a stream. "No. I want you to find out what happened to my wife. I want to help, I want you to find the guy that was in the house and I want this interrogation to end. I want my wife."

John was taken aback. This did *not* sound like a man who had killed his wife. In fact, John got the sense that Stillwater really believed he hadn't done it.

"All right Mr. Stillwater," John said and cleared his throat. He took another sip of coffee. "You work at Napoma Talent, right?"

"Yes. I'm a talent and acquisition lawyer," he answered.

"What's that?" John asked.

"I deal with singers and actors who need to renegotiate contracts, mostly. I also find talent for bands and casting agencies."

"So… you discover movie stars and singers?" Monique asked.

"I assist in pairing together talent with talent, helping everyone get the most out of the cooperation." A rehearsed line, one spoken hundreds of times as Stillwater explained what it was he did for a living.

"Sounds complicated," Monique said.

"I'm basically a hand-holder for the stars. What does this have to do with my wife?" On the verge of tears.

"Just covering some basics, Mr. Stillwater," John said.

"I don't care about your basics, Detective," Mr. Stillwater said. "I care about finding the man who killed my wife."

You were alone in the house, John thought. *You were alone but you think you weren't.*

"Mr. Stillwater," Monique said. "Walk us through the evening, as you remember it."

Stillwater's gaze drifted from John to Monique. He then closed his eyes and turned his head to the side. He didn't say anything. John felt goosebumps.

Did this room have to be so fucking cold all the time?

"I got home at about seven," Stillwater said after a few moments, his voice an exposed wire. "My wife was already there, back from a business trip upstate."

"When was this?" John asked.

"Around six, I guess," Mr. Stillwater said.

"You guess?" Monique asked.

"She had been home for a while when I arrived, but hadn't eaten or showered so yeah, I guess six. I had bought flowers and pizza, but we never got to that."

John and Monique stayed silent. John took a sip of coffee. The pizza was still in the box, on the floor in the foyer of the house. The flowers as well, apart from a single rose taken out; stem used to bind Mrs. Stillwater's feet, the flower placed over her heart.

"When I walked in she was already a little upset. Said she thought there was someone in the house. I put down the pizza and went in to see. I thought it was nonsense. The thing is, she didn't say it like you would if you heard someone, she said she *felt* it."

"What do you mean, *felt it*?" Monique asked.

"She said she had a feeling. Not that someone had broken in, but that someone else was in the house. So I walked around and took a look but…"

John waited as Michael's gaze grew distant. "But what, Mr. Stillwater?"

"There *was* someone there," he said and looked at John, but the rest of the sentence John was expecting never came. It was as if he were realizing this just now.

"Sir?" John said.

"He must have hit me on the head or something," Stillwater finally said.

He's telling the truth, John thought. *He didn't do this.*

"Why do you say that?" Monique asked.

"I just remember getting hit with something, stumbling backwards, and then everything went black."

"Mr. Stillwater," Monique said. "There was no sign of an intruder in the house. No sign of a break-in, no fingerprints but yours. Doors locked and windows closed, glass unbroken."

Michael looked at them, shoulders slumped, head forward.

"I just…" but something broke inside him and he started crying.

John had seen all sorts of acting in this room, people trying on any number of lies. He wasn't sure what this was.

"Okay, go back," John said. "That morning, was anyone outside your house?"

"I wasn't there in the morning. I was in L.A."

"Your wife?"

"She didn't say anything about that," Stillwater said. "We didn't talk much when I got back."

"Why didn't you?" Monique asked.

"Like I said, as soon as I walked in she was nervous. Told me there was someone in the house and I went to check it out."

"What did you find?" John asked.

"I didn't see him, but I'm sure someone was there. It's… maybe he hit me over the head or something. I saw like a figure, a black figure." The last sentence, spoken as if he was just realizing it himself.

"What, like a…" John hesitated, then took a deep breath. "You mean a black man?" How it grated on him that everyone's go-to image of a criminal was a black man.

"No no, a figure ALL black, like a shadow."

"A shadow?" Monique asked.

"Yes!" Stillwater had gotten excited, as if it were coming back to him now.

"And then what?" John asked. He was surprised at the simplicity of Stillwater's answers. A person covering something up would go for something more elaborate than a simple "*I don't remember.*" A person ashamed would say less.

Stillwater looked away from John. His eyes unfocused, his voice dropped to a whisper. Pain on his face, as if he was physically pulling the words out one by one.

"And then it's like I'm in an endless ocean of cold and dark. Or like I'm at the bottom of a hole or a cave. I remember seeing a tiny bit of light, way up above me. There's no way I can reach it.

"It's maybe… like I was inside a giant puppet, like I was down in the stomach and the eyes were way up, high above me like windows on the fifth floor but I was standing at the bottom. I saw something out of the eyes but I couldn't make out what it was. Then everything shook and there was screaming."

Stillwater looked frightened as he spoke, like a child recounting a traumatic incident with a large dog.

"He must have… he must have knocked me out. Hit me in the back of the head or something. Then it's like I'm pulled up from a pool of ice-cold water and I'm in the living room downstairs and there are leaves all over the house and Ellen is dead."

John took a sip of his coffee, now tepid and greasy. There was a silence in the room for a while as John and Monique swallowed the pity they felt for Stillwater. He had clearly been in some sort of daze when he killed his wife, denial now running rampant in his mind. Good cops go with the evidence, not the story. And so far, the evidence didn't back up Stillwater's version.

"You like to drive fast, Mr. Stillwater?" John said after a while.

"What?" Stillwater looked surprised, maybe hoping John and Monique would run out, eager to catch a black man that killed his wife.

"You have a number of speeding tickets," John said.

"What, I… yes. What does that have to do with my wife?"

"And then there's a shoplifting charge." John didn't care. Wasn't trying to establish a criminal past. He just wanted to get a feel for Stillwater through his reaction.

"A shoplifting… it was a T-shirt I forgot to pay for. I was wearing it after trying on a few things, things I paid for. The store had this zero-tolerance policy and an overzealous security guard. I'm not a thief. It was an honest mistake."

"Okay," John said. He felt it, the truth of Stillwater's words. There was no reason to pursue any of his minor indiscretions, they didn't matter. No one goes through life spotless. "I just needed to ask. A formality."

There was a tiny grain of sand in John's brain, slowly being encased in a pearl of a headache. Or the pain of a realization. The same way he *knew* that Stillwater was telling the truth about the shoplifting charge, he *knew* that he was innocent of killing his wife. But there was no way he really *was*, given the evidence. John felt dizzy, a truth was plummeting away from him, a crack forming in the firmness on which he stood every day.

Stillwater's prints were on the knife, his footprints in the blood in the bedroom. The doors were locked. His hands were bloody and splintered from hacking down branches and then carrying them into the house.

How good a detective can you be if you can't find your own daughter?

The thought, louder now. More confident in its doubt.

"Were you hoping for a warmer welcome, is that it?" Monique asked.

"What?"

"It's just, you come home after a business trip, maybe expecting your wife to be happier to see you. Instead she's tired. Doesn't want to… you know. How did that make you feel?"

"It didn't make me feel anything, that's not how it was. Seriously, why are you treating me like I'm a fucking suspect?"

A certainty to the emotion behind his words. *Stillwater really believes his story*, John thought. The headache starting to shine.

"We're not, Mr. Stillwater. We really just need to get a few questions out of the way. Boxes to tick, you know how it is. We need to get a full picture of your evening. Is there anyone you can think of that—"

There was a knock on the door and then it opened. John knew the knock. All lawyers have the same knock and the same tired lines.

"This interrogation is over. Michael, don't say anything else."

Those lines.

"It's fine, Marty," Stillwater said.

"Hello, Detectives, I'm Martin Martinez and I will be representing Mr. Stillwater. There will be no further questions until I have conferred with my client."

John sighed.

"May I have a few minutes with him alone?"

"Sure," Monique said and got up. John stood up to follow her.

"Detective," Stillwater said. The look in his eyes gave John a chill.

"Yes?" John said.

"There's a security system on the first floor," he said. "Cameras that record everything. Maybe they caught what happened. Maybe they caught the shadow thing."

John stepped back towards the desk, closing the door to the room again.

"You have cameras *inside* your house?"

"Michael, you don't have to tell them anything," Martinez said.

"Fuck, Marty, I want this solved!" Stillwater said. "The camera records just the kitchen and the living room downstairs. In case of burglaries. Nothing upstairs."

"Outside?" John asked.

"Yes. Full perimeter. Someone broke into our house a few years ago. Ellen got really paranoid. We bought security for a fortune. In fact, most houses on the block have them, hooked up to a shared system."

Michael Stillwater looked at the chain and handcuffs fastening his hands to the table, and raised them up, palms thick with bandages.

"Not that it helped," he said.

Chapter Seven

Daniel Hope lived in an apartment partly paid for by the state, in a noisy building of other apartments paid for partly by the state. The elevator was constantly on the fritz, never to be trusted. It would open up between floors, to hastily-scribbled and unimaginative graffiti. People shouted at each other in the hallways and the mailboxes were constantly vandalized.

The stairway and halls stank of too many people in too small a space. On some days, however, the smell in the hallways was a welcoming mix of spice and people, a map of sorts that Daniel felt he could almost see. He liked the building, liked living here. Something about the chaos of the crowds made him feel as if he belonged. As if he could blend in and be protected and hidden by the sheer amount of people, the maze of stairs and halls keeping him safe.

The apartment itself was small – a bedroom, living room, bathroom, and a chicken-wing of a kitchen. He seldom used the living room; his life was in the computer in his bedroom. A new system, one supplied by Gamma Pharmaceuticals just over a week ago, now took center-stage in Daniel's life.

The new computer seemed to be powered not by electricity but by time. He would wake up just as the smells and sounds of lunch were dying down in the building. He would sometimes eat, sometimes just piss and sit down at the screen. It would then suck the hours out of the room, and as the din of people coming home from work and settling in decreased he would feel a quick pang of hunger and realize that while the computer had eaten its fill he had not. He would chew on a protein bar and drink a can of some bubbly, green-tasting energy drink, both supplied by Gamma, along with the little fridge they were stored in.

Daniel didn't turn the lights on in his apartment. He felt it unnecessary to always let everyone know if he was home or not. That was how thieves knew when to commit burglaries, wasn't it? He would sit down again, hunch over the code and the computer would suck a few more hours from the room, from Daniel himself, and then he'd stand and stumble and sleep again. Every day he was sure that he had showered the day before, though he didn't remember being wet. Where did he keep the towels?

He was getting closer. His mind had slowly turned back into a river, logs floating away one by one as the drugs left his system. Clear and quick and the code that had in the past just been a single line of focus at a time among a blur of others was now a beast he had tamed. Now, Daniel could keep thousands of lines in his head at once, and he reveled in not just making the code work but finding ways to make it work faster, more efficiently.

Gamma had sent him so much hardware that he didn't think he would ever need to go back to the office. The room, the whole apartment, his life, was unlit apart from the dull green of the code editor he was using. Lines reflected in his face, his hands seemingly disembodied as they too caught the light from the screen.

His mind was a river, now free of the pharmaceutical logs that, while allowing him to control and trust the flow, would also jam up his thoughts. The river of his thoughts flowed free and fast but wild, now and then splashing up against the shore. It flowed free and fast and the quickness was what Gamma needed and Daniel gave it to them.

He saw the faults in the code, the stiff subroutines that broke it, the unneeded calls for variables and the algorithms that, while not exactly incorrect in and of themselves, Daniel was able to tighten and speed up by factors of two, of ten, of ten to the nth.

Days of this, of his mind racing, of not eating, of not sleeping, of exiting the real world and casting off the shackles of the drugs that corralled his thoughts along and, on a whim, he ran the program against the dummy data and in mere seconds it spun back, throwing lines of patients and drug doses against the screen. Daniel paused the output and read a few lines. Patient names, diagnoses, drug names, drug doses, drug dose timing, delivery method… it was all there. In just a few seconds of running the new code.

Daniel unpaused the output stream and let it flow across the screen. He held his breath and stood up, turned his back to the screen as the light of patients and data filled the room. It was growing brighter and brighter, but the light couldn't get out of his room. Daniel rushed to the bedroom window and drew the curtains. Outside was something, buildings, a city he didn't really know anymore, but the light kept filling his room, the air growing thick and dense with it, making it hard to move.

Swimming, pushing, clawing his way through the increasing brightness toward his keyboard, Daniel's eyes watered as he pushed, frantic, towards the computer and managed to press "esc" to make the program stop running.

He wanted it gone. Sat, opened the connection and uploaded it to Gamma. Wrote Mr. Relnez a quick email. "It is done. Uploaded. Tell them to run it in batches or they'll drown in the light."

He had managed it. He had never exactly said yes to Mr. Relnez, who hadn't really asked him to do anything, had he? But he had stopped taking the pills. Yellows and reds accrued in his little medicine cabinet and his river of a mind raced, white tops tickling as the river crashed against the rocks. For the first two days he had felt no different. He worried that this meant he had been taking the pills for no reason, that he didn't have schizophrenia anymore, if ever. That he might be "normal" now, a new, more mundane kind of normal.

He also worried that it meant his special affinity for computers was lost to him. But on the third day something had indeed happened. The logs stopping up the rivers of thought dislodged, one by one by one, from the banks.

His mind had *raced*.

In two days of virtuoso programming he had the problem solved. He polished the code, tested it and sent it off. He then streamlined a few of the processes they used and restructured some of the overall architecture of GP's systems and, while he knew that he had just taken away a few of his co-workers reasons for employment, in the long run he had just saved GP a few million dollars, easily.

He went into the kitchen, triumphant but not knowing how to celebrate. But when Daniel looked into the fridge he thought the light looked a little dimmer.

Were they doing it again?

He shook off the thought and pulled out a can of coke. He had a sip, decided he was more tired than thirsty and went into the bathroom. In the mirror he saw a figure that was not himself, this person hadn't shaved for a week, and his chin was filling out. A diet of bananas, Snickers, and energy drinks would do that.

He brushed his teeth and wondered what it was that they put in toothpaste to get the teeth clean. Didn't the brushes do all the work?

He spit into the sink.

–

The following day an email awaited Daniel.

> Dear Mr. Hope,
>
> Gamma is elated. The code looks brilliant and works perfectly.
>
> Attached is our signed acceptance of your resignation. Gamma Pharmaceuticals thank you again for your contributions, and are sad to hear you no longer wish to be part of the team. We wish you all the best in your future endeavors. To compensate you for your contributions, Gamma will honor your contract for the next six months and pay you a portion of the years' bonus payments as applies. You are also under no obligation to return any hardware you received from Gamma.
>
> On behalf of Gamma Pharmaceuticals,
>
> Miguel Relnez, MBA
> Senior Vice Director of Programming

There were words in the email that repeated, and Daniel sang them under his breath. "Gamma, Gamma, wish wish contributions contributions Gamma Gamma wish wish contributions contributions." He turned off the computer and walked out of the room.

He knew he had been fired, though the letter said resigned. Clever, that. They had probably dated the resignation letter in the past and forged his e-signature. There was no way he would go fight them in court. He was also just hired as a temp, they had no need to pay him for six months. Six months of paid leave. Hush money, naturally, but still. He could do whatever he wanted.

He didn't feel empty or rejected. It was as if this was expected. What he did feel was a tiredness creeping into his bones from the floor. Black tentacles of fatigue reached out from his bed, beckoned him. He was about to let them pull him in when he heard something. He had the sudden and strong feeling that there was someone in his living room. Heart racing, Daniel listened. He thought he heard a rustle, like the sound of pages in a book being turned. And then a sigh.

He took a few steps towards the living room and heard it again. A paper-on-paper sound. There *was* someone in his living room. Daniel stepped forward, wondering if he had left the front door open. Maybe a wind was flipping pages in a book on the table. The sound came to him scratching and slow across the floor and he felt he saw it and smelled it, as if it wasn't just sound but festering emotion and hesitant decay.

He walked into the living room, heart rattling somewhere in his body like loose change in a pocket. He felt light. Frightened. Silly.

The man sitting in the recliner didn't look up as Daniel entered the living room. A chill pricked Daniel's skin, cold long needles. The man was wearing a winter coat and a long brown scarf. He looked to be about forty-five, older maybe, something about him made it hard to tell. He seemed to be settling in, like rabbit in a burrow, trying to find a comfortable spot in its bedding for a night.

The man looked at Daniel and then continued trying to find the right position in the soft leather chair. But he slowed and then looked back at Daniel. A look of genuine surprise and apprehension crossed his face, and then his jaw fell.

"You… you… you can see me," he said. The voice was strong and direct, contrasting the mousy overall look of the man. "How can you see me?"

"Who…? Get out of my apartment," Daniel said. His voice was hot and bright, surprising Daniel with its confidence, as if someone else were speaking through him. He wanted the man gone, sure, but like most people he mostly disliked confrontation. Would avoid it at all cost.

"What?" the man said, regret evident on his face. "Yeah yeah sure. I was just cold. It's always so cold out there." He stood up without making a sound. No crease as he pushed against the leather, nothing as he walked on the creaky floor.

"It's just," he said. "It's so cold outside, and I've been there so long. Alone. There's no one that—"

"Get out!" Daniel shouted, voice bright and forceful.

The man backed towards the door. He kept his eyes on Daniel, as if trying to memorize his face and, without slowing, walked right through the door without opening it. He was just suddenly not there.

A chill took over Daniel Hope's body as he walked back into his bedroom, the same thought swaying in his head as he undressed and went to sleep.

"You are sick again Daniel. You are sick again."

Chapter Eight

If he kept his eyes closed for any period of time, an image entered John Dark's mind – his daughter at the bottom of a well, a mental image he couldn't shake. It's Emily superimposed over the girl from *The Silence of the Lambs*, standing at the bottom of a well while her captor looks down at her, sneering.

He knew it was an unlikely scenario; a man like that would have killed her by now. She was still alive, he told himself. A man like that would have skinned her, eaten her, something.

He hated these thoughts, but couldn't shake them.

He'd seen too much.

-

There was a particular case that came, unbidden, into John's mind, mixed in with worries of Emily. A memory of details that pulled his thoughts to the darkness. A case that ended with them saving a few girls from a prostitution ring. (God, don't let it be that). The women were kept in a single room in a small apartment. Men, white, middle-aged, pudgy men, came in and examined them in the beam of a harsh flashlight and would pick one from the bunch, the way you pick fruit at the grocery store. Some of the girls started to damage their faces to keep from being picked but their captors punished them for that by breaking their toes, removing toenails. "Captive whores don't need pretty feet, after all. No stretch of pavement to walk."

Tricked into the city with the promise of a fancy job, silly girls from out of state or, more often, undocumented climate change refugees who were now thoroughly disillusioned, their lives ruined.

Like drugs, prostitution was a fight that you would never win. There was always the demand for it. That didn't mean you stopped fighting.

The memories and images meant John didn't sleep much. Emily was ever behind closed eyelids, waiting. She called out to him in the dark, and John would wake up with a start to a world of guilt and hopelessness. He jumped at every phone call, every time the doorbell rang. Every time he opened the front door he hoped to find her there but was always greeted with heartache. Every phone call was a phone call he didn't want.

When he caught himself laughing he would snap it shut. Clipped laughter as he thought *What if someone saw me laugh? Would they think I no longer cared about my daughter?*

And so the days passed. Mirthless, one after the other.

Chapter Nine

A candy bar landed with a thud in the vending machine drawer, pulling John back into the world. He had been dozing, unfocused and as close to sleep as he got these days. A uniformed officer fished for the candy bar and then walked away as she unwrapped it.

John and Monique were sitting in a windowless corner of the police station that was referred to as The Gallows. Just two vending machines in a corner of a broad hallway, green linoleum floors and yellow walls. The light from the vending machines gave the corner an artificial feel, like they were on the set of a TV series. John heard a humming but couldn't tell if it was from the vending machines, the industrial lighting chasing away all the shadows or if it was just something in his head. The hallway smelled of sterilizer and cheap floor wax and somewhere down the hall a ventilator had a loose fan that rattled every now and then. He pulled at his shirt collar.

There was always a pot of mediocre coffee on a table by the vending machines, and somehow there always seemed to be one more cup to be pulled from it. Some police-station magic. Two beat-up chairs that didn't match had been left there at some point. Comfortable and stylish, they clashed wildly with the rest of the corner and no one remembered how they got there.

The Gallows had become an informal lounge, a place within the police station that somehow managed to take the tension out of the shoulders of any cop who found five minutes in his day to spend there. A home for deep breaths and cathartic sighs.

Due to its proximity to the forensics lab it had also become the spot where forensics would present their results to investigating detectives. Informally and unofficially, of course, but everyone knew that this was where the cases were made. Detectives felt relaxed here, and would arrange to accidentally meet the forensics techs when they went to get a drink or a candy bar. Now, John and Monique waited for the results from the lab. The informal first results, not the tidy ones the D.A. would get.

Someone had brought a box of donuts earlier and, surprisingly, there were still a few left. Monique's phone rang just moments after they sat down and she swore in Spanish as she looked at the caller ID. She answered reluctantly, looking at John first. Spoke in hurried Spanish, of which John understood just a few words but her tone told him it was just a mild annoyance. She stood up and walked down the hall.

John took a donut, one with a thick blue glazing that was starting to sweat. It tasted of nothing, but the sugar felt good. Suddenly realizing he was hungry. Anthony Smith, the forensics guy assigned to the Stillwater case, walked towards John. Anthony was a slim black man who wore no-nonsense glasses at all times and if you allowed him to he would talk endlessly about the benefits of veganism, especially for the African-American metabolism.

"Hey man," John said and sat up and bumped fists with him. "What's good?" When he sat back down, he sat looser.

John was glad Anthony had their case; something about a full professional conversation with another black man where race was completely irrelevant felt like a blow against white privilege. Somehow felt safer and more relaxed and John felt it allowed him to get his best work done.

"Hey man," Anthony said back. "I'm good, you know."

"What do you have?" he asked Anthony.

"Should we wait for Moreno?" Anthony asked, pointing at Monique at the end of the hall.

"No no, it's fine, she'll be here in a minute," John said.

Anthony stood with his back against the wall and took a look at the donuts.

"Who puts that shit in their body? Cancer feeds off sugar, you know. Don't feed the cancer."

"I don't have cancer," John said, putting the last part of the blue-glazed donut in his mouth.

"You don't know," Anthony said.

"I..." John started but thought better of it. He wasn't going to prove to Anthony that he didn't have cancer, much less argue that donuts weren't the crap he knew them to be. "Stillwater case, what do you have?"

"You sure you don't want to wait for Moreno?"

They looked down the hall at her. As she noticed them she raised a hand and made a "go on" gesture and continued talking on the phone. A light in the hallway behind her flicked on and off.

Anthony shrugged and opened a file folder. "All right then. So, this is about as straightforward as they come. Michael Stillwater's prints are on the murder weapon, a kitchen knife retrieved at the scene. And not just, like, partial fingerprints in a couple of places like we sometimes get, I mean this guy was *gripping* that knife. We're talking fingerprints and palm-prints and DNA, and her blood on the blade mixed in with his palm-sweat. No doubt, Michael Stillwater stabbed his wife with that knife, that evening, and he was *mad*."

"Mad?" John asked.

"Yeah. Wounds are deep, and there's a lot of them. A bit of hacking, notches on the ribs as he stabs and hits bone so he stabs again. He was angry at her for something."

John noticed that Anthony dropped all professional pretense. No "The victim was stabbed..." Already using a "he." Already assuming Stillwater's guilt.

"Coroner says Ellen Stillwater died from being stabbed; internal bleeding, loss of blood, organ failure, shock; take your pick."

"Did you place anyone else in the house?" John asked, looking to make sure Monique was out of earshot.

"No reason to think anyone was. Footprints in the blood are all his. Hey," Anthony said, slipping from his professional voice into a more colloquial one. "Why you think he did the body up like that?"

A question asked off the record, a sheer curiosity thing.

"Not sure. Ritualistic fantasy maybe, I don't know."

"What?"

"What?" John asked back.

Anthony looked at him, but let it go. "Michael Stillwater had his wife's DNA all over; his hands, his hair, his clothes. In the form of blood, that is. His wife had just a little bit of a defensive wound in her right hand, otherwise it doesn't seem like she fought back much."

"Windows broken, door forced?"

"Not that I know," Anthony said. "No drawers opened or anything. No shoe prints in the yard around the house."

Monique joined them. She pulled her credit card out and swiped in the vending machine. "Go on, I hear you," she said as she punched her choice in the machine's keyboard. The machine whirred and dropped something into the slot.

"Look," Anthony said. "It don't often come much plainer than this. Michael Stillwater stabbed his wife to death. He then went out and hacked some branches off the trees in his yard, dragged them in and arranged them on her head. Her blood is on the branches, all neat and tidy with his fingerprints dug deep in. His hands are cut from the branches, from dragging them into the house and arranging them. Lots of little nicks and splinters."

He took out a photo of Michael Stillwater's hands, palms out. They were cut and splintered, bloody and raw.

He closed the slim folder and handed it to John.

"What's the guy like?" Anthony asked. "You talked to him, yeah?"

"Pretty normal," John said as they looked through the photos taken at the scene. The formality of the photos making the Stillwater house into just another crime scene. No warmth or personality, just evidence and cold facts. Still, something left a splinter of doubt in John's mind, something that he wanted to pick at but knew he should just leave alone.

"He's a normal rich white guy," Monique said, taking a bite of a Snickers bar. "A normal rich white guy who just up and killed his wife for no reason and put branches on her head."

"Some sort of satanic thing, like you said John?" Anthony asked.

"He doesn't know," John said, almost in a whisper.

"What?" Anthony said.

“Stillwater, he says he doesn’t remember any of it,” John said.

“John thinks the guy must have had an episode,” Monique said.

“What, sleepwalking?” Anthony asked. “I know a guy whose girlfriend, well ex-girlfriend, used to do that. Get up and go to the fridge in the middle of the night. Once she even got on top of him.” He made a show with his hands, to better express himself. “You know? Now, my friend doesn’t object to this, I mean, he’s a guy and well, we’re simple like that.”

Monique had stopped chewing and John leaned back in the chair, hat in hand.

“She’s on top just riding away and my friend he’s just getting into it when she wakes up. She’s startled and slaps him and jumps off the bed all ‘What the fuck’s going on, Tyrone?’ and he’s trying to explain but she ain’t hearing it. Took him two hours to calm her down.”

“Now Officer Smith,” Monique said. “I’m just going to assume you didn’t just imply that our victim was stabbed repeatedly and decorated with branches by her husband… *sleepwalking*.”

“No, I just. It’s a thing. Anyway, it’s all in there. Tech guys will have the security footage for you soon, maybe it’s even ready now.” Anthony pushed himself away from the wall. “Also, you guys have to eat something real one of these days.”

They watched as he walked away. The files in John’s hands would be formalized and presented to the D.A. As it was, they would probably be more than enough to charge and convict Stillwater with the murder of his wife. All that was left was to see the security footage from the Stillwater house, though John doubted that it would help Mr. Stillwater in any way. The whole thing creeped him out. He'd seen plenty of murders, even from domestic disputes, but they were usually stupid, drunken murders. One shot, or one blow to the head with something heavy. Not this elaborate staging of the body afterwards. It was almost like it was meant to send a message. But what message? To whom?

"John," Monique said.

"What?"

"Don't make this into a mystery to solve."

"I'm not," John said, thumbing through the crime scene photos in Anthony's report.

"John."

"I'm *not*. I just want to give Stillwater the benefit of the doubt, you know."

"What, you think he *didn't* do it?"

"No, that's not it," John said. "That's not it. I just get the sense that Stillwater really thinks someone else did. Not, like, to throw blame around, but because he *really* thinks someone else was in the house."

"Well," Monique said. "The security footage should be ready for us. Let's go take a look at what went down at the Stillwater *casa*."

Chapter Ten

The gentle buzzing in the bedroom was not, as Daniel feared at first, a headache but a fly. It flew in an "8" pattern around the room and soon Daniel was seeing its path written in the air. The fly left a trail of shimmering silver as it flew, a nearly invisible line. But it was there. It was the first time Daniel remembered seeing a fly leave a trail. He couldn't remember hearing about them doing that before.

Maybe it was some sort of dust, like on a moth's wings. Maybe the fly was leaving a trail as a sort of mating ritual. Maybe this just meant he was sick again.

He sat up and wondered what time it was. Wondered what he should do that day. Was there ever anything ever to be done again? Now that his work at Gamma was over he should probably find himself something to do. Doctors warned him against idleness, saying that it might lead to anxiety and depression.

He made coffee, though he wasn't sure why. A clock he didn't remember buying hung on the kitchen wall, innards shaking and moving, hammering out the time but as he looked at it he didn't seem to know how to read it. Found it hard to decipher what it really meant.

Dark coffee slid down his throat. And then he saw that man again, standing in his living room. A silhouette against the world. Hands up, palms outwards, he seemed to be searching for something to say, now that Daniel had spotted him.

Who was this, why was he here?

"Who sent you?" Daniel asked. "Did Gamma send you? I already gave them the code."

"No one, I…" he stopped. Seemed surprised to hear his own voice. A tear ran down his cheek.

Daniel gripped his cup tighter, knuckles white. The man looked disheveled, but his clothes had an odd quality to them. White shirt in need of ironing and a black tie, but the look was made motley by a thick green winter jacket. The clothes seemed slightly blurred, like he was looking at an out-of-focus photograph. The man's face as well, would, from time to time, drop out of focus, as if he were suddenly looking to the side. Slipping around in time.

Was it like this before? Did people look like this all the time? How much was lie and what was real? How could he tell the difference?

"I want you to leave," Daniel said, not because of the fear we all feel at the unexpected, not worried that the man might hurt him. He just didn't like the thoughts the man's presence forced up.

"I will. I will. I just…" He lowered his head and slowly shook it side to side. He drew a deep breath. "I think I died." Emotion and confusion clear on his face and this frightened Daniel, somehow got through to him. "I think I died, and I'm so alone now."

Daniel didn't know how to respond to that.

"Go, or I call the police," Daniel said, hoping it would frighten the man into leaving. Then suddenly worried. The police, were they watching this already?

"You are confused," Daniel said.

"I'll leave," the man said. "I'll go but, but you… you see me? You hear me?"

Seeking a validation that Daniel couldn't give. The man sat down awkwardly into a deep recliner, the same one he had been sitting in when Daniel had seen him a few days before. Relief took the tension out of him. He now seemed uncoiled. Less dangerous.

"I used to live here," the man said. "My wife and I, this was our first apartment together."

Daniel stepped towards the man, stood with feet apart. Still held on to the coffee cup, ready to throw it.

"I can't help you," Daniel said. "I don't know you and I have problems of my own." The most generic of responses. Everyone has problems of their own that they think negate the urgency of others. Everyone can help. Daniel was distracted for a moment by this realization, and his mind cascaded down a river of philanthropic logic. There is always someone who has less than us, so if everyone just gave something it could flow downhill until all was even. Until everyone had the same. Why didn't they? He felt like he had just discovered a great potential truth, a way to change the world but couldn't grasp it. Too big for one mind. His mind too dynamic to hold on to it.

He thought of clothes he had thrown away, food uneaten. Money spent on frivolous things. He thought of—

"They shot me."

"What?" Daniel heard the stupidity as he said it. Felt like someone else had spoken. The man seemed unhurt.

"It… I fell into the street. I fell or… was pushed. I was at the store and these guys. We argued and there were flashing lights and a person saying something. But after a while I was standing at the tree in my yard. I stood and the world rushed by."

Daniel sometimes thought the past was a construct inserted into his mind. So quickly did his life seem to have passed in retrospect that he wasn't sure he had actually lived it. How could he verify it?

"Yes, yes, I know."

Was he talking about the way we remember the past? How we can play our memories over in our heads and make the past spin by in seconds? "You mean the past?"

"No," the man said. "I mean that if I did nothing the world rushed by. Maybe that's what happens to most people. Maybe that's what's supposed to happen. We die and heaven is that we get to see our loved ones grow up and prosper. We get to stay on for the show."

The thought of heaven as an afterlife show seemed odd but logical. A neutral end with a reward of sorts. Didn't need a divine explanation. Not heaven as a place you go but heaven as a thing you witness after death.

"Why didn't you?" Daniel asked.

"Why didn't I what?" the man asked.

"Why didn't you just watch the show?"

His eyes lost focus and the man disappeared for a moment. Faded in and out of the world. The cold feeling down his back that this wasn't real. Once he had faded back into being, the man looked at Daniel. Shouting, a man's voice and a woman's voice. A door slammed. Was he hearing this in his ears or his mind?

"We argued. We argued and I said the most awful things to her, you know? I don't ever swear, especially not at my family but I was afraid I was going to lose her and I just wanted to hurt her, wanted *her* to be afraid of losing me. So I called her a cunt and slammed the door. I stormed out and something…"

Daniel saw it as *he* saw it. Saw the man's wife, his house. The slamming of the door and then the lights and a shouting match in a corner shop that ended with a gun going off—

He dropped the cup of coffee. It fell with a crash to the floor and Daniel saw the blood but the blood was just coffee. Just coffee.

But he *knew*. He felt the man's desire. Tried not to let it in, not to let it become part of him.

"I just want to tell her I'm sorry," the man said. "That's all. It's like a splinter or a… puzzle that I need to complete before I can pack it away. Like an itch under a cast."

"Why me?" Daniel asked.

"What?"

"Why are you here, why me?"

The man didn't seem to understand the question. Lost in thought. Daniel heard a child crying and then stop. Silence and then a whisper of wind that turned to a blaring alarm and the sense of falling. Clouds passed by and there was utter chaos, screaming. His heart sped up. Daniel was witnessing what the man was thinking. Somehow his memory and feeling, so raw and vivid, was being transferred or experienced by Daniel as well.

The cabin of an airplane. Fire, smoke. Fear.

"I was in an airplane crash once. The plane lost power just after takeoff and we crashed into the trees at the end of the runway. I broke my leg in three places but managed to hop out of the wreckage as it caught fire. People were screaming and there was smoke everywhere. I couldn't help anyone. I could have died there."

Daniel feels the fire, smells the gasoline. Hears the screaming.

"I decided to change my life after that. Decided to do things I wanted to do, tell people what I really thought without hiding behind the stupid things I imagined society wanted me to be. But now… now I'm just a spectator."

"What do you want with me?" Daniel asked.

"I died," he says. "I was at the store and some guys shot me and I died."

Daniel just looked at the man. Wanted to ask him to leave but didn't.

"I need your help," the man said. "I need… will you talk to my wife for me?"

"My help?" Daniel didn't think he was in any position to help anyone.

"You see me. No one else does. My wife drives past me on her way to work and doesn't hear me. Our daughter plays in the yard sometimes and it is the most exquisite form of torture. I see her. I can watch her but if I get close I feel the pain of a longing love. I can't touch her.

"They can't hear me or see me but *you* can. I need you to tell my wife I'm sorry."

Daniel, however, had a better idea.

He put on a coat and said "Come with me."

Chapter Eleven

There was very little glory in a police officer's day-to-day work. The popularity of shows like *CSI* gave most people rather lofty ideas about police work, especially when it came to the evaluation of evidence. But in reality, it just took clever insight and a lot of combing through the mundane.

John and Monique sat side by side in front of a single computer screen like kids in a classroom completing an assignment together. They hunched over John's desk, gloomy orange sunlight easing its way in along the sides of the windows. The office hummed with activity; phones ringing, police officers shouting at each other and belting out belly laughter at dirty jokes thrown across the room. Doors shutting, chairs scraping the floor and the incessant background of indecipherable radio chatter. The room smelled of uniforms that needed cleaning and millions of cups of coffee.

If used in court, the video they were about to view would be presented on a large screen, big enough for all members of a jury to see clearly. Now, however, they were shoulder to shoulder in uncomfortable chairs, supplied by the lowest bidder, trying to get the picture to play on the department's antiquated computer terminal.

"It's right click and 'open with'," Monique was saying. "And then you select the video player."

John did as she said, but his mind was elsewhere. He had his hand across his stomach, shoulders slumped. He leaned forward and looked at the screen, seeing mostly their reflection in the black. Then a flicker of static and they were looking at the video recorded the evening Michael Stillwater allegedly stabbed his wife of eleven years to death.

The footage was clear, recorded in good quality. No static, no twitchy jumps. It showed a view over the bottom of the staircase, the hallway in front of the front door leading into the kitchen, and the very end of the living room. Anyone coming into the house through the front door would be seen, as would anyone entering or leaving the kitchen, anyone coming down or going up the stairs.

The recording started at three o'clock the afternoon of the crime, so John and Monique had a bit of viewing ahead of them. They could, of course, skip right to the time Michael Stillwater claimed he got home, but they had to see if there was any evidence of a person entering the house before that, as Michael Stillwater claimed his wife had said as he got home.

John and Monique existed and worked in their own bubble in the department. John had burned through all of his goodwill in the weeks after Emily went missing. The department's worst-kept secret was that Monique had anonymously supplied the narcotics unit with leads she got from her daughter. The leads were good, of that there was little doubt, but they also always seemed to help a certain gang her daughter was affiliated with from time to time. Fruit of a poison tree, garnered from a whispering snake. The apple of her mother's eye.

"Well, this is just riveting John, I have to say. Should I get popcorn?"

They had been looking at the Stillwater house recording at eight-times normal speed. Two hours had gone by in fifteen minutes. There were formalities involved, of course. Video evidence could be viewed at eight-times normal speed at first, to develop oversight and establish a timeline of events. Said events then had to be viewed at normal speed and logged to be admissible as evidence. Veer from this, and it might be argued that the police did sloppy detective work and the evidence deemed inadmissible. The glamorous life of a detective.

A long silence followed as they waited for the clock to reach six p.m., which was the time Ellen supposedly got home. They needed to keep their eyes on the screen though, to see if anyone was in the house before then.

"Did you ever go on a second date with that DMV guy?" John asked. The question hung in the air. He had asked in a stilted manner, as if reading it from a card to a stranger. It was like he had just remembered to ask her, after being reminded by someone else, the way a teenager is made to ask their grandparents about their day.

"No," Monique said, not taking her eyes off the screen. She was holding a pen, waiting for something to give her reason to write a note. "The guy was soft. All he wanted to talk about was movies and the weirdos who show up at the DMV. I get enough weirdos here and I don't care about movies."

"Well," John said. "They can't all be German horse-trainers." He was referring to Monique's sometime boyfriend, a man whose principal quality was that he spent most of his time in Germany. John didn't see how that was a plus but Monique assured him it was.

"Dating is a young person's game now. It's all apps and shit, booty calls on order through the phone, done without talking. What happened to just getting drunk and picked up at a bar?"

John had no reply. He had met Lonei at a cabin during a weekend getaway. A setup if there ever was one. A friend of his invited him, and the friend's girlfriend brought a single friend of hers. This had been before he started at the academy, when people still tried to get him out of his funk. The cabin was big and full of dust and creaks, up in Colorado. His friend and the girlfriend had gone for a walk, leaving Lonei and him alone. He tried chivalry upon seeing she was cold, got her a blanket and made an attempt to start a fire. The kindling didn't catch and John had never started a fireplace-fire in his life. She laughed at his attempts and he let her.

There had been something there though. Conversation was easy with Lonei and upon returning, his friend found John talking and smiling with her. He later remarked he had never recalled seeing John so laid-back.

Lonei confided in him that she was leaving the States in a few months to go to culinary school in Italy with another friend. Remarked how she was glad she didn't have a boyfriend or much of a family holding her back.

The following day, while out on a walk in the pouring rain, they kissed. A spontaneous kiss they both felt coming, that they both privately thought was a bad idea. To this day, John remembers it as if he watched it happen to someone else. Lonei had stopped walking, moments after their hands had brushed together between the umbrellas. The woods around them were heavy with a silence only broken by birdsong, the rain pouring down.

She had looked at him with a bit of anger in her eyes. "What are you doing to me?" she said. "You can't even light a fire."

The fire had become a joke for them that weekend. Something they had already referenced dozens of times. Now, she was standing across from him with a flame in her eyes. John took a step closer and they kissed, umbrellas on the muddy ground as he held her and they kissed, the sort of deep kiss in heavy rain you only see in movies, only imagine happen in movies but it seemed so natural there.

He would run that memory through his mind at times to remind himself how good life could be. It came to him at odd times, surprising and warming, like sunshine breaking through a storm.

It had been a while since his mind visited that kiss.

"John," Monique said and pointed at the screen.

It showed 6:07 p.m. and there was movement by the Stillwaters' front door. Right now it was just shadows and movement but it then gathered into Ellen walking out of the foyer. Ellen Stillwater had her hair tied back in a ponytail. She was wearing dress pants and a white blouse that was loose on her. She placed a small suitcase on the floor as she stepped out of the foyer. She sighed, the kind of sigh one has to let out when finally arriving home after a long bout of travel. She walked into the kitchen, out of the camera's eye.

"What's that?" Monique asked.

"What?"

"You didn't see that? Wait, I'll rewind it."

Monique clicked back thirty seconds on the recording. The screen was exactly the same; just a view of the Stillwater's foyer with the kitchen and the living room off to either side. John kept his eyes on the screen.

"It's… it's nothing," Monique said after the counter went past the time she had stopped the recording.

"What did you think you saw?" John asked.

"I don't know, just… movement. Something."

"I didn't see anything."

"I know, John. I just said I thought."

The recording rolled on, silently. The only indication that time was passing were tiny bursts of static every now and then, and the clock, ticking away the final hours of Ellen's life.

She came back into the frame. She picked the suitcase up off the floor and walked upstairs, out of frame again.

"Stillwater said he got home at around seven, right?" John asked.

Monique said nothing.

"Monique?"

"There it was again!" she said and pointed at the screen.

John looked but saw nothing. He kept looking as Monique rewound and waited as the recording passed the point she had been waiting for.

"Fuck," she said.

Ellen Stillwater appeared on screen again. She ran down the stairs and stood there with her phone in her hand. On the footage the phone appeared as a square of white light. She looked back up the stairs. Something about the way she carried herself told John that she was straining to hear something.

"She's shaken," Monique said. "It's like she heard something."

John didn't reply. He watched as Ellen's thumb hovered over the screen. He wanted to cheer her on. *Call for help*, he thought. As if this was live and not a recording. As if he were cheering on a teenager in a slasher flick to not make the stupid choice they always made.

He knew how this one ended.

"So she heard something," Monique said.

"Looks like it," John said. "Or saw something." John noted the time. A chill went through him as he watched the screen. It reminded him of a ghost movie he had watched with Orlando and Emily a few years ago. A couple moved into a house and the husband, sensing something odd going on in the house, set up a camera to record everything and the whole movie had that security footage look to it.

John rubbed his hands together.

"You don't feel that?" he asked Monique.

Ellen was pacing by the stairs. There was a moment she seemed startled, and then she ducked her head, as if trying to see something at the top of the stairs.

"You'd think that if people are splurging on in-home cameras they would get a set for the second floor as well," Monique said. She spoke without sarcasm, no little joke at the end of that sentence.

On the screen, Ellen was startled as her phone suddenly rang. She answered it and paced around the hallway as she talked.

"Might have installed mics as well," John said. "We know who called her?"

"No," Monique said as she made a note of the time of the phone call.

"How long until Michael gets home?" John asked.

Monique looked at the timer in the top corner of the screen. "Just under half an hour."

"So she waits for him, even as she thinks someone might be in the house."

Ellen was walking slowly now, no longer pacing, just walking as one does on any normal phone call. Whoever she was speaking to was having a calming effect on her.

She walked into the living room, off-screen.

They were watching this at normal speed, but wouldn't have time to review the whole evening, minute by minute.

"We need to get this done," Monique said, as if sensing what John was thinking.

"She's spooked," John said. "There's no question there. She's spooked *before* Michael gets home."

"Who's prosecuting this?" Monique asked.

"Not sure. Does it matter?"

"Well, yes, John, it matters. It's a question of years in an institution if they get him off for temporary insanity, or life in jail. I'd say it matters."

"Sorry, I…"

"What?"

"Stillwater just doesn't strike me as the man who kills his wife, out of nowhere. He certainly seemed, if not innocent then at least confused and angry."

"John, don't. Men kill their wives and get off too easy, is what I say. The statistics alone are a reason to evaluate the sentencing of the last twenty years, John. And don't get me started on rape."

"He didn't rape her," John said. He heard the click of a landmine under his feet.

"That's not what… even now, even to you I have to uphold the honor of women?"

"What do you mean 'even to you'?"

"You've been on the streets, you've seen the truth. You're smarter than most guys I know and… dammit John, you're on *our* side and even then I have to… there she is again." Monique pointed at the screen.

Ellen had finished her phone call and stood at the base of the stairs again, head down, looking upwards and trying to see something on the second floor. She had her phone in one hand and the other was wrapped around her midriff. She backed away from the stairs, into the foyer, closing the door behind her.

"She calls Michael about now and they have a three-minute conversation," Monique said.

A few moments passed, broken only by an officer coughing loudly somewhere behind them.

On the screen, the foyer door opened and Michael Stillwater entered the house. Ellen stayed in the foyer but could be seen on the screen, half in, half out. Michael went into the kitchen. Ellen said something, her lips moving.

"Sure there's no audio?" John asked.

"No audio."

Michael came back into view, having checked out the kitchen to his satisfaction, and went upstairs. After a while, a few minutes at most, Ellen took a step into the house, as if responding to being called. She took a few steps in.

"She's saying something," Monique said.

Ellen walked slowly towards the stairs and then walked up to the second floor. She would not be seen again.

"Mark the time," John said.

Time passed on the tape but nothing could be seen. John reached for his cup of coffee but knocked it over.

"Shit," he said, and got up to find something to clean the spilled coffee up.

"There!" Monique said and John ignored the spill to take a look.

On the screen, Michael was walking down the stairs. He took the steps unhurriedly, walking as if held up by the shoulders.

"Why is he walking like that? Did he get hurt?"

They watched as he walked down the stairs and into the kitchen. His gait was stilted and awkward, like an actor doing Frankenstein's monster. Then he was back on screen, walking out of the kitchen holding a knife, and he walked upstairs, one step at a time, as if each time having to remember to lift the leg and move it.

Minutes passed, and the sun outside the station, seeing this, decided that it had had enough, and set.

Michael came back into the frame, walking down the stairs again.

"John, his hand."

Even in the grainy black-and-white of the screen they could see the blood on his hand.

"Why is he walking like that?" Monique asked.

Michael walked out of the house. From the timeline the forensics team put together he would most likely be going to the garage to get a saw. There were bloody handprints on the garage door and in quite a few places in the garage. Tech said the only thing missing was a saw.

"He touched a lot of things in the garage," John said.

"Yeah."

"If I were going to get something in my own garage, I'd just go and get it. But the way the blood was spread in the garage it's like he was looking for something. Why touch so much? It's almost like he doesn't know his own house."

"Don't even get started on something like that, Detective Dark," Monique said.

According to the timeline, Michael Stillwater should have been outside now, sawing down branches. And sure enough, after a long while he appeared back on the tape, dragging a few branches into the house. He pulled them up the stairs, trailing leaves in his wake.

He did this three times as John and Monique watched.

"There's no one else in the house, John," Monique said.

She hadn't needed to. The evidence, and there was quite a bit of it, put Michael Stillwater at the scene, in the bedroom.

"He's calm," John said, almost under his breath.

"What?"

"He's… he's so calm. Going outside to get the branches. Ellen's wounds tell us that he was furious at the time he killed her. Why is he so calm there?"

"Let it go, John," Monique said. She stood up and paced behind him.

"Fuck," Monique then said, as if realizing something. "Neither the defense nor the prosecution is going to want to use the tape."

"What do you mean?" John asked, not taking his eyes off the screen.

John's strength was sniffing out motive. Knowing people and what drove them. Monique's was an uncanny ability to play out the cases as they might go in court. More than once John had listened to her reason out how a case they were working on would go in court, predicting the prosecution and defense tactics. More than once she had been spot-on.

Michael reappeared on the recording. He walked down the steps in that strange gait. It was as if his body were connected to strings. He "dropped" into each step of the stairs, as if feeling heavy. As if he were a marionette being made to walk.

"The tape has Ellen at home," Monique said. "She's worried about something in the house *before* Michael gets home, right?"

"Um, hm," John said.

"That's great for the defense, maybe there *was* someone there. But it's *all* they have. The prosecution has Michael come home, go upstairs and then call out to Ellen to join him. Then this, this, shit with the branches. Defense doesn't want to show that, it's clear evidence he killed her, and prosecution doesn't want to show Ellen spooked before Michael gets home. They'll say there was probably someone in the house before Michael."

"Fuck," John said.

"Right?"

He pointed at the screen. Michael was coming back into the house with more branches from the yard.

"So what *do* they have?" John asked.

"Who?"

"The defense," John said.

"They have Ellen calling him. They have a phone call from Ellen to Michael moments before he gets home. They will say she called him to tell him that there was someone there."

"But nothing else."

"What?"

"There's nothing else for them, right? No breaking and entering, no prints apart from Michael's, nothing usable on the tape."

"John, what are you fishing for?"

"And no evidence that he's being forced to do this at gunpoint."

"John?"

John turned and looked at Monique. On the screen, grainy and silent, Michael Stillwater walked down the steps for the last time that evening, stilted and odd, and went into the living room. In a few moments the tape would reach the time he claimed his memory of that night started.

"Michael Stillwater said he didn't kill his wife. He looked us in the eye as he said it."

"Yeah? So?"

John stared at the screen and then pushed his chair backwards and sat still for a few heartbeats. His hands cupped, elbows on his knees head down.

"I believe him," John said. He raised his head to look Monique in the eyes. "I believe him."

Chapter Twelve

John and Monique entered O'Reilley's office with a certain hesitation. Would the completion of their part of the Stillwater case mean they'd be put on normal beat work again? John sat down on the ratty couch while Monique stood by the door.

O'Reilley was dressed in a pantsuit with her hair down loose to her shoulders, a look on her face as if she were straining not to bare her teeth at them. A tiger, combed and camouflaged as a Chief of Police.

"Dark, Moreno," O'Reilley said by way of greeting.

"Chief," he said.

"Chief," Moreno said as she closed the door.

"So, how did the interrogation with Mr. Stillwater go?" Not one to stand on ceremony. No chit-chat, not this morning. Not with them.

"The report is—" Moreno said.

"I don't care about the report, what's your take?"

Moreno cleared her throat.

"He did it. There's really no getting out of it. The doors were locked, there's no sign of break in, no other prints on the knife or anywhere in the house, for that matter. I'd say he meant it do it too, I mean the way he dressed up the—"

"I saw the photos." O'Reilley said, interrupting Moreno again.

"Stillwater sticks to his story, says he didn't do it," John said. "Weirdest thing, ma'am, is that if I hadn't seen the body and been through his house... if I'd only been present for the interrogation, I mean, I wouldn't have made him as a killer and would probably have thought he hadn't killed his wife."

"Moreno?" O'Reilly prodding for clarification. Her way to get you to talk was to fill conversation with prodding and uncomfortable silences.

"The guy is consistent in his answers," Moreno said. Not backing John up, not contradicting him. "He sticks to his story of not remembering any of it. He reads true."

"He's a lawyer," O'Reilley says.

"I'm not saying he didn't do it, chief. I'm just saying he seems to believe his own words and that he doesn't have the tics of a liar."

John worried his words carried less weight than did Monique's. There was a difference in the depth of the value they gave Stillwater's words, though. Monique saw the surface only, that he was claiming he was innocent to avoid jail time for a crime he obviously committed. John read Stillwater as a man confused and afraid, certain that someone had knocked him out, killed his wife and then made the body out to look like a deer. An elaborate setup. To John, Stillwater's words carried the terrible weight of actual truth.

"Dark?"

"Sorry?" John said. He had been asked a question but hadn't heard it.

"Your take on why he did that to the body after he killed her?"

Ellen Stillwater flashed across his mind, a drop of blood on that bright white tooth. John stayed quiet for a moment, considering his words carefully. What to say? How to say it?

"The body is arranged and then decorated out of some sort of love. It is done very deliberately and with care, not the rage in which she was killed."

The chief had her hand on a piece of paper on the desk, something she had been glancing at as Moreno had spoken but she now gave John her full attention. For a moment he felt as if he were looking at a photograph. O'Reilly framed by the large window behind her, showing the city as it rose from slumber. The seriousness of O'Reilly's expression, the impatience in her eyes and the hard line of her mouth. Computer screen and framed photos on her desk mere black rectangles to John.

Still life at the station.

"It's not remorse," John continued. "It's not him trying to make up for what he did or trying to fix her after the anger dissipates. It's as if it was planned."

O'Reilly stood and looked at John. The world outside was becoming brighter but none of the light seemed to get through the window into the office. As if the glass behind her was a painting of a city in the morning. Framed and hung, giving the office the semblance of a view, but no light or life.

"It certainly seems planned to me, Detective," O'Reilly said and sat down. She sighed. "Look. I didn't expect to see the two of you in here again discussing a case. You let me down." She looked at John and he did not look away. "You let me down and you dragged her into it with you."

John wanted to shout and throw things. Wanted to raze the city to the ground to find his daughter. Wanted to cry at his wife's feet and tell her he can't do it. He can't find her.

"I was—"

"I know, John. I know. I'm sorry."

"He didn't drag me into anything, Chief," Moreno said. "Just… for the record."

O'Reilly stood back up and looked out the window. For a moment, all they heard was the chatter outside the closed door, the murmuring of a police station in the morning after a busy night.

"It seems like the world is changing," O'Reilley said. "There's more crime and less money to fight it. And we need to fight it, every day we need to fight it and keep it back or we lose, Detectives."

She turned to face them again. There was a desperation in her tone, as if she had received bad news she wasn't sharing. It reminded John of the stretched tension of walking in on his mother and father arguing. The forced smiles and the fake platitudes.

"I need you back, Detectives. Tie off whatever loose ends you have with the regular beats and finish the paperwork. The department has been running on just a few souls but goddamnit Dark, Moreno… I never said this and I should have. Before Dark's daughter…" She was having difficulty putting it into words. A conversation no one knew how to have with John. A conversation he himself didn't know how to have without feeling rage and guilt and shame.

If you were a real detective you would have found her by now.

O'Reilley had the look of someone who had just managed to stop themselves from saying something they would later regret.

"Look John. I know how you must feel about all this, but we need you back. The two of you, however you do it, have the best read on people in the department. Sure, there are officers who are better at investigating the scenes or digging up the tiny detail that cracks a case, but it pales in comparison to your ability to focus on the cases where we can convict. And it's those numbers the Mayor's office looks at."

Moreno shot John a look. While O'Reilley maybe saw it as numbers and conviction ratios, John and Monique knew it was John's gut. He saw a person and after as little as a few words he knew if they were guilty or not. It was that single trait that made him rise to detective as fast as he did.

"Now," O'Reilley said. "Finish up this Stillwater case, it sounds about as open and shut as they come, and I'll get you fully reinstated into the squad. No more breaking up frat parties or tracking stolen cars."

John cleared his throat.

"Yes, Detective?" O'Reilley said. She seemed tired. John knew she had expected them to thank her and tell her they promised to be good and that they would never again misuse their authority or the resources of the department to search for their missing children.

"I'm not sure Stillwater killed his wife," John said, looking down at the floor.

Outside, the sound of a passing police car, sirens on. It passed and left them in the heavy silence. The sun was beginning to heat up the room.

"Would you repeat that please, Detective Dark?" O'Reilly said, indicating that John should really, please, say anything other than what he had just said.

John looked at Moreno and then at O'Reilley.

"I don't think Stillwater killed his wife. Or, rather, I'm certain he believes he didn't."

"What are you saying, that he's insane? Isn't he a what, celebrity lawyer? John, you better be certain about the next words you say to me."

"What I'm saying is that when we talked to Stillwater he was consistent and adamant that he did not kill his wife. His story didn't change and if anything he was confused and surprised at the situation he found himself in."

"'*Situation he found himself in*'? Fuck, John. Didn't you hear a word I just said? Close this case, close it fast and you're back in the department. Don't start second guessing right away, John. Moreno, what's your take on this theory?"

Monique stepped into the middle of the room, hands behind her back.

"The crime scene, the murder weapon, the security footage. His clothes, her body, her blood all over him. I'd say there's really little reason to even consider any other scenario than Stillwater stabbing her to death and then making the body and the room into, well, whatever you want to call that."

"Well then," O'Reilley said.

"However," Monique looked at her feet and then back up at O'Reilley. "I agree with Dark that Stillwater really does believe that he didn't do it, and John is usually right about these calls. Usually."

"What does the evidence say?" O'Reilley asked. A rote question, one of her go-to lecture questions for new recruits. Usually followed by the lesson itself – "Always go with what the evidence tells you, not the suspects or the witnesses. Their testimony is for making sense of the evidence, not the other way around." But not this time. This conversation had gone somewhere she hadn't expected and she wanted it back on course.

"The evidence says Stillwater killed his wife," Monique said. "The security footage does too, though it also makes his wife's claim that someone was in the house plausible as well."

"A claim we only have from him," O'Reilley said. "Don't make this more difficult for yourselves. Don't try to make this case something it isn't. Get the evidence and your report to the D.A. If you can get a confession from Stillwater, that is great, but we don't need it. I suggest you go find a desk and then take the rest of the day to move your things."

"You can't just—"

"Goddamnit, John, just close the case." O'Reilley said in a way that really meant, "Now get the fuck out of my office."

They did.

Chapter Thirteen

Home was an oyster shell with the pearl missing. A nice enough house on a cop's salary, a single-story square block of wood and sheetrock made pretty with two trees in the neat front yard and a maple in the back. The top of the maple reached into the sky, the few leaves that still hung on in the late autumn looked gray. It was almost like a child's drawing of a house, though John imagined a child might give it more color.

Four people had lived in the house, in a more mundane but genuine happiness than John would have thought possible. A happy family in a generic home on a normal American street. Now it was just three of them trying to keep it together, trying not to fight and resent each other. All conversation forced, all interactions tense. A strung bow with an arrow missing.

John was looking over the file he had on Emily, the file that lived in his glove compartment. It was the heaviest thing he had ever held, it was the center around which his world rotated. He took out the map on which he had tried to draw out the possible ways she might have gone, though only one of them made any sense – the one tracking her cell phone. Going east and then south, moving fast. Her phone stopped sending a signal at exactly 1:17 p.m., though whether it was turned off or the battery died was unclear. The theory being that either she was in a car heading out of the downtown area, or that her phone had been stolen before something happened to her. Or during.

"Where are you?" John asked. He had asked this before, in this car, looking over the file.

He got out of his car. The nights were getting colder. He smelled food being grilled somewhere, and trees. No one was about, but there were lights on in most of the houses on the street and smoke from barbecues rising from a few backyards. There was a silence he didn't like, and then he thought the silence had been growing louder over the years. For some reason it was only now, standing in front of his house, not really wanting to go in, that he realized what it was; the constant insect buzz of his youth was going silent. Or maybe he was growing old and just didn't hear those notes anymore.

He felt a pang of guilt and shame as he walked up to his front door, always bracing himself for words from his wife, though she had only said them once: "Shouldn't you be out there looking for her?"

After the frenetic first days after Emily's disappearance, Lonei had receded into herself, and John had worried what would happen to her if he left. Lonei surprised him by rebounding quickly from her funk, full of angry energy. She started a website, *Where is Emily Dark?*, which soon became a hub for people looking for missing children. They got a slew of leads from it in the first days and weeks, but now the leads they got were like drops of water in the desert – loud and pointless, evaporating quickly into nothing.

They had only had sex once since Emily disappeared, a quick passionless few moments that hadn't succeeded in taking their minds off their missing daughter.

John opened the front door and went in. He put his keys in his pocket and hung up his coat. Orlando was sitting on the living room couch. It was just a year until he was as old as Emily had been. Headphones pulled his attention to a phone held sideways, his default state in the last months. John had no idea what it was he watched. Orlando was lithe and tall, with long bones and little muscle. Stretched and taut but without filling. A string of spaghetti in a hoodie. He carried himself much as John had as a teenager but had an anxious sensitivity that John had never had.

John said "Hey – hey, son," but Orlando didn't seem to register anything. A concentrated effort to make his father notice him not noticing him.

Orlando's world had collapsed not when his sister went missing but when his father the detective couldn't find her and bring her back. What did this mean about the world, about Orlando's safety? Did he now see his father as just another cop to be avoided?

In the kitchen, Lonei stood and stirred a pot. Gumbo by the smell of it. It was the only thing cooked in the kitchen now, a hot stew to power her through another evening spent online.

John wondered, not for the first time, if he would ever not find her beautiful. She had been pretty when they met, heartbreakingly so when they got married. There was a looseness to the way she carried herself now, and all the affection she had once shown him was hidden. No impromptu embraces, no kisses on the back of his neck, no words of romantic love. Just that look in her eye. They swam now, her beautiful brown eyes, swam in a salty sea with a shore that was always rimmed red.

"Hey," John said as he entered the kitchen.

Lonei said it back and then added "You were gone long."

"Nothing new," he added, answering the question she no longer had to ask. "I went to the club again to talk to the bartender, but he didn't remember her, didn't know anything. He was telling the truth."

John was making the rounds again. Seeing if there wasn't a stone somewhere that he hadn't turned over. Something he had overlooked. The night of the Stillwater case he talked to the bartender at the club Emily had been at the evening she disappeared. The week before he tracked down and talked to the guys driving the buses that night. Again. Memories clouded over fast.

Lonei's laptop was open on the counter, browser open to the comment section of her website. Notes and printouts covered the kitchen table, along with a few yellow legal pads, half-filled and then discarded. It had become a shrine of sorts. Lonei slept in fits and, upon waking, rushed into the kitchen to sit in front of the laptop.

They were just barely keeping it together, barely managing to stay civil with each other. All conversation was strained, every inflection of the voice over-interpreted.

"I got put on a case," John said. "Homicide."

Lonei turned to look at him but didn't reply.

"Anything new here?" he asked, gesturing at her laptop. He felt as if he should touch her, show some affection, but the thought was now already in his head and anything he did would seem stiff and forced. Worse than doing nothing.

"What's the case?" she asked.

"Guy killed his wife," John said. "Did it in a locked house and then went out to his yard a few times to get…"

John paused. There was always the question of how much of the outside world to bring with him into the house. "He did some things with the body. It was all recorded on the security system cameras. Well, some of it. But he says he didn't do it, that it wasn't him."

"Don't they all?" Lonei said, as if it was so obvious she didn't understand why he was even mentioning it. There was an edge to her voice. There was always an edge to her voice now.

"Yeah, I guess."

John got himself a glass and filled it with water. Looked out into the evening gloom and felt his brain trying to make sense of things. He needed sleep. The water tasted metallic. He thought of water purification plants and wondered what it was they actually did. Envisioned large pans of inch-thick water being strained by people in those radioactive hazmat suits using rakes. He put the glass down, half-empty.

"Traffic is down to nothing," Lonei said, referring to the website. "Nobody cares anymore. All it is now is people asking *me* to help find *their* missing kids or wives."

John imagined Lonei's thoughts.

If you were a proper detective you would have found her by now.

Wondered if she actually ever thought that, decided she probably did. Many times a day.

"Orlando?" he asked. Orlando had been missing a lot of school now, a problem they had yet to really tackle.

"He's going to school tomorrow," Lonei said in a voice meant to carry into the living room. Then, to John, "He is losing touch with his friends. He hardly even plays computer games anymore. There was a point I thought we'd lost him, too. When he'd sit there all those hours playing that game with the guns, but now he doesn't even do that. At least then he spoke with his friends, through that headset thing."

John's phone had vibrated as she was talking. He picked it up and looked at it, not understanding what he was seeing at first. Brain needing sleep, thoughts moving like a slushy through a straw.

It was a text from a number John didn't have registered.

"*I remembered something. Call me. Steph.*"

His thoughts became glacial. He understood the words he was seeing but he didn't connect them with anything. The lack of sleep was getting to him. Was Steph someone he should know? But then, dawn on the Serengeti. A lion disturbed the pond and the animals fled in droves. Steph was the bartender at that nightclub.

"John?!" Lonei said. "Goddamnit, John, you have another child and he needs you, right? Could you put that phone down for a single minute and remember that there's still people here, in the house?"

John kept his eyes on the phone.

"I have to make a call," he said.

"Goddamnit," Lonei muttered and turned back to the gumbo.

John walked out of the kitchen as he called the bartender. He disliked talking on the phone in front of Lonei, a mix of the need for secrecy around his job and also the fact that she would quiz him after each personal call. Not out of a sinister curiosity or jealousy, she just seemed to want to be sure he wasn't forgetting to tell her some piece of news he'd heard on the phone call, like a deceased relative or an invite to dinner.

"I remembered something. Call me. Steph."

John walked into Emily's room without meaning to. It was immaculately tidy, a result both of her neatness and the obsessive care that was paid to turning over every single thing in search of clues to where she might have gone and then placing them back. It didn't smell of her anymore, didn't feel like her anymore.

"Hello?"

"Steph? This is Detective John Dark."

"Oh yeah. Hey. I… it's probably nothing," Steph said.

John stood in Emily's room and looked out at the grass in the backyard and the tree and the house beyond the fence, facing back against theirs. He thought of the thin straw he was grabbing at; a bartender who maybe saw her that night two years ago, who maybe remembered a single thing about that night and who would maybe give John just that little bit of rope he needed to hang himself.

"Your daughter, if I'm remembering the right girl and the right evening, was, I think talking to a guy. Yeah? Strange guy who used to hang out at the bar some nights. Don't think I ever heard his—"

"What was that?" John asked. "You – I missed that last thing you said."

"What? I never heard his name? That's the last thing I said at least."

This would go nowhere.

"He was a religious guy. Or, like, had a thing," Steph went on. "There's… after you came here he just popped into my head. He talked to a lot of girls, always just girls, at the bar."

"That's not unusual is it?" John asked. His heart was broken and he had set himself up for too many people to step on it in the last two years. Had allowed himself to believe too many things he shouldn't. Had made a fool of himself and the department by believing things he shouldn't.

"No, I guess not," Steph said and laughed, a small laugh. A polite laugh at a funeral, cut off. "This guy though he, uh, he was different. Wasn't there for... you know. He'd sit and *talk* to the girls, yeah? Not chat. Not give them lines and drinks in the hopes they'd go somewhere together, but actually talked to them. I never caught much of what he was saying but I know he was talking about, like, a religion."

"What, like a Mormon in a bar?"

Steph said nothing for a while, maybe realizing he was being silly. John worried he was maybe being too cynical.

"Yeah, but you see, I remember him talking to *your* daughter that evening, the girl in the photo. I remember because I found something he gave to her that night."

What was this? How had they missed this? Emily sat and talked to a man that night. Why hadn't her friends mentioned it? Had they?

"Detective?"

"Yeah, I'm here."

I'm falling. I'm furious. I've never been so tired in my life, and I have miles to go before I sleep.

"So, did that help?" Steph asked.

"You... what is it you have from that night? You said you had something."

"Oh yeah. He would leave behind a bunch of these flyers. Like advertising his religion. Like that *Watchtower* the Witnesses keep passing out, about all the rest of us going to hell and burning forever unless we stop drinking and fucking and all that."

"What is it?" John asked. He needed sleep. Needed a break. Needed to find Emily and then cry forever.

"It's a pamphlet. A brochure. But it has no info on it, no address, I checked. Just this weird nonsense. *Are you ever unsure how your thoughts and deeds will be weighed when the day comes?*" Steph seemed to be reading from something.

"We should meet," John said. "When can we meet?"

"Soon. I'm free the day after tomorrow? Buy me lunch somewhere?"

"Okay," he said. "I'll call you with a place, the day after tomorrow. Lunch."

"Yeah, sure."

"And I can reach you at this number? This is *your* phone?"

"Yeah," Steph said and hung up.

A single thread at which to pull. The only thing they had now. John went back into the kitchen.

"That was..." he said to Lonei. "That was a guy I talked to last night. He remembers Emily."

"The homicide case?" Lonei asked, confused.

"No, that came after. I talked to him at the nightclub, Freckles."

"Freckles," Lonei said. "She was at Freckles from just after eleven until about twelve thirty, when they went to the McDonalds." Lonei knew the timeline of that evening better than he did. Officers worked cases for years and didn't know the timeline as well as Lonei knew Emily's.

"Yeah," John said. "This guy I just talked to is the bartender at Freckles. He remembers Emily talking to an odd guy. Has a pamphlet he's going to give to me."

"He said that?" Lonei asked. She had a spark to her eyes now. "He said he remembers Emily talking to this guy and that he gave her something?"

"No, he didn't say he gave her anything. He said the guy was at the bar a lot. Talking to girls but not like, sleazy. Just creepy. Talking about his religion."

"Mormon?"

"He didn't know. Said it was something not popular."

"Mormonism's not exactly popular, John."

"No, but it's, you know, regular. It's a known thing. Mundane."

"So?"

"So?"

"When are we meeting the guy?" Lonei asked.

"Day after tomorrow."

-

John took a shower, moving slowly and peeling his clothes off as if he was shedding them. A quick shower and then he crawled into bed and tried to fall asleep before the guilt became too loud for sleep.

If you were a proper detective you would have found her by now.

If the world were a proper place, he thought back, *she wouldn't be missing.*

Chapter Fourteen

Monique Moreno, like John, lived in a small, single-story house on a street long with single-story houses. Her yard was no more and no less tidy than most of her neighbors' yards, her porch no more and no less cluttered. All in all, her house blended in with the street. Monique's house was square, set in a square yard with a small tool shed in the back.

Monique got home after a long shift, bone-tired but feeling somehow alive nonetheless. She was back in homicide, back doing real work. Even if just the one case, it was a step in the right direction. A step to getting back on course. She had thrown her lot in with John when Emily went missing, without hesitation. They had left their caseload to others as they ran after leads, though in the rush and the madness they had overreached – ignored the rules and the best practices of police work. It was personal and they were racing against a clock and the statistics they knew all too well. It had been a slow car wreck as they went further and further, squeezing CIs and calling in favors. Paying with favors owed. Ultimately paying with their positions and status without getting any closer to finding Emily. In the end, Emily remained missing, Monique and John reprimanded and demoted.

John would have done the same for her.

Monique opened her front door, already asleep in her mind. She stepped inside but instead of the expected sigh of finally being home she gagged and covered her mouth. A pipe in the bathroom must have burst and sewage backwashed into the house, she thought. It was the clear and unmistakable smell of piss and shit and as she walked in she saw what it was.

"Goddammit!" she said.

Someone must have broken in and then as a parting gift left a brick of a turd on the rug just inside the door. She folded the rug over the offending pile and walked it out to the garbage can next to the house. After dumping it unceremoniously she stood still over the closed garbage can and let out a long sigh and cursed.

She walked back in and closed the door. Her TV was gone, inexpertly ripped from the wall, leaving holes in the sheetrock where it had been attached. She had a thought and ran to the bedroom. The drawers of her night-table were out, the contents on the bed. But it was the safe she was thinking of. A single door to her bedroom closet was open, clothes tossed onto the floor and the safe pulled forward. A bulls-eye had been crudely drawn on it with lipstick but it remained closed.

Monique turned the black dial one way, then back, then forward again, the combination decided randomly at the store so her daughter Valeria wouldn't be able to guess it. Because of course this had been Valeria. Monique opened the safe and looked inside. Her will, a necklace that was the only expensive thing she owned and a few thousand dollars in cash. Still there. Monique breathed a sigh of relief and then closed the safe and pushed it back against the wall inside the closet.

She felt unclean.

She walked back into the house, which still smelled like shit, and tried to assess if anything had been really damaged. There was no need to investigate anything, she wasn't going to report this. There hadn't been a break-in, after all. Valeria still had a key.

The stupid things we do for our children.

She had been in before, of course. Monique made a habit of putting a few twenty-dollar bills in a place that was easy to find and then a fifty in a place that was not so easy, thinking that Valeria would search and leave. She didn't want her daughter doing drugs, but she preferred that to her going to jail for holding up a liquor store. Prisons were not places that punished or improved anyone, unless the person went in there with a will to change and somehow kept that will unbroken on the inside. In reality, prisons transformed petty thieves into career criminals, squeezed desperate junkies into heartless killers. They were a place for the problems that society didn't have the maturity to deal with yet. In some cases they were actual moneymakers for private companies. Modern-day slavery in plain sight, propped up as a solution to a problem.

The irony that her job was putting people into places she thought were counterproductive wasn't lost on her. That's why she wanted the job in homicide so much; at least then you knew the criminals deserved what they got. Kids stealing beer and smoking weed didn't deserve jail, they deserved help.

Her daughter deserved help, but Monique didn't know how to give it to her. All she knew was that prison would make things worse.

She called a locksmith, made coffee and, for the first time in years, turned on the radio in the kitchen, just to feel less alone. Voices filled the kitchen, voices of people who weren't there. Voices that told her that the world was slowly unraveling and then voices that told her what things she might want to buy. Monique changed the channel, and found some music.

-

"It's shit. Someone literally took a dump on the floor," Monique said as she let the locksmith in.

As she entered, she put the back of her hand against her nose and shot wild looks around the inside of the house. The locksmith was taller than Monique and had quite a few pounds on her. The uniform she wore looked uncomfortable; tight around the shoulders and chest but baggy around the feet. A uniform made for a tall man now worn by a hefty woman. Monique knew the feeling.

"Well, it's gone now," Monique said and closed the door behind her.

The locksmith lugged a big case into the living room. It made a reassuring thud as she dropped it down.

"Break in?" she asked as she looked around.

Monique hadn't had the mental strength needed to tidy up yet so the apartment looked a little torn apart. She had put some vodka in a cup of coffee in an attempt to get her head in the right place. She was so tired that the time was just a strange number now. The call to get back to work would come too soon.

"I..." Monique didn't know where to begin. How to explain her life to this person. "My daughter doesn't like me much," she said. "So sometimes she'll break in and move my things around to annoy me." The lie coming easy.

"Not my business," the locksmith said. "I'm Aida, by the way," she said and extended her hand. Monique shook it. Aida had a reassuring grip. She could probably throw a good punch.

"Lot of women locksmiths?" Monique asked. She quickly recognized it for the shit her male colleagues would ask. "Sorry. I haven't slept."

"No no, I get it. We try to send women if the caller is female. Apparently there had been an issue with a guy, this is before I started, he made copies of the keys and would, you know, visit the women. But, I shouldn't tell you that, sorry."

"It's okay," Monique said.

"So," Aida said. "You want your locks changed?"

"Yes, I..." The world on her shoulders seemed so heavy again. The lack of sleep was making her raw, all emotion unprotected. She'd felt the hope that her life might just be getting back on track with the new case and then this. A literal shit on the rug to pull you back down.

"My daughter is missing," Monique said and then corrected herself. "Or, not missing. She's sick. Drugs. She tried drugs at a party and then she just slowly drifted away from me and I..." and Monique threw the coffee mug against the wall, shattering it. Coffee splashed and dripped down the wall as the shards spun on the counter.

"Sorry," she said, crying. "Change the locks."

"Yes ma'am." Aida said. "The house – just the front and the back doors?"

"Yes," Monique said.

"I think I've been to one in this neighborhood before."

Aida went to the back door and then out to her car to get the right locks. It took her all of twenty minutes to change the two locks. She placed two keys on the kitchen counter and a hand on Monique's shoulder.

"Locks are done. I'm sorry about your daughter. My father, he… I understand."

Aida left, pulling the door firmly closed behind her. Monique wished she would have offered to sit on the sofa while Monique slept. A guard of sorts. She showered, brushed her teeth, undressed, dragged herself into bed. She was too tired to cry and she hoped she wouldn't dream.

The phone woke her up, of course, but the light outside was different so she must have slept. She felt like her body was made of broken rocks crashing around inside a burlap sack. She reached around for the phone, found it but it kept ringing as she struggled in her sleep-daze to remember how to answer it. She would rather have missed the call.

Chapter Fifteen

John picked a Lebanese place to meet Steph and sat trying to decipher the menu. It was a rather small restaurant, only about fifteen tables but it was bright and he'd heard the food wasn't half bad. It was also cheap, something John didn't think too much about usually but couldn't ignore either. It smelled strongly of cumin, or maybe that was the only spice John could pick out of the invisible bouquet in the air. He patted the manila file in the seat next to him. It was becoming a habit, something his hands seemed to do when he was anxious.

Arabic music played on the speakers. Could be a modern club hit from Beirut or a fifty-year-old song from Syria for all he knew about middle-eastern music.

Sunshine reflected off the cars driving past.

The bell jingled as Steph opened the door and walked in. As if this were a small-town bookstore and not a busy restaurant in the city. He was wearing a denim jacket and John wondered if they were coming back or if this guy just had no style. There was no way to tell.

Hands in his pockets, he turned towards John but instead of acknowledging him, Steph looked around furtively, as if worried he might be recognized sitting in a restaurant with a cop.

He slid into the seat across from John.

"Hey," he said.

"Hey. Thanks for coming."

"Yeah," was all he said. He picked up a menu and then placed it back down without really looking at it.

"You okay?" John asked.

"Yeah, yeah. It's just… look, there's people who know that you were at the club. Well, not *you* you, but like, a cop asking questions."

"People?"

"I'd explain but there's… what's it called? Plead the fifth?"

"You're not in court and I don't care. You could be baking in the basement and selling to frat boys and I would not care. Not my thing."

John still had his hand on the file. Steph still had his hands in his pockets.

"Hungry?" John asked. "I'm buying." Teeth clenched, heart hammering. Holding back the urge to shake him and scream at him to tell him what he knew. Flimsy ice holding back a sea of tears.

"Sure."

He picked the menu back up. John examined his hands. Fingers clean, no rings. Looked at Steph's eyes, saw only clarity and health. Apathy and lethargy, while not positive traits, were hardly something to complain about. John didn't remember the last time he talked to a young man who didn't have some sign of drugs or drink.

For a moment he wondered when he last looked Orlando in the eyes.

"I'll just have the chicken wrap. That's got to be a safe bet, right?"

"I wouldn't know," John said, trying to remember why he had chosen this place.

A waitress came over. Long dark hair, dark eyes. An eagle of a nose that made her face memorable. A look of total indifference to the men in front of her. John liked her right away.

"Take your order?" The R rolled with a Lebanese accent.

"The falafel for me," John said.

Steph said nothing.

"Steph?" John asked.

"Oh. Just the chicken kebab for me."

"Chili sauce?"

"Sure," John said.

She turned to Steph.

"Not for me," he said.

"Drinks?"

"Coke for me," John said and looked at Steph. "You?"

"Yeah, just a Coke."

The waitress walked away and left them with a silence John didn't know how to fill. The crushing weight of a question he didn't know how to ask.

"So," he finally said.

Steph had taken his phone out of his pocket and was checking something. He put it back.

"So?" Steph asked.

"You sent me a text saying you remembered something."

"It's probably nothing, I mean that was two years ago. The nights at the club pretty much all blend into one these days, yeah?"

John didn't want to come off too strong. How his hopes of finding Emily were now slipping from him. What would *he* tell parents of other teens missing for two years? Console them, or tell them the statistics and encourage them to have a funeral for closure and get on with their lives?

"I'm sure whatever you know will be of help. This is my daughter, remember. I'm not a cop here, just a father."

Steph took a breath and looked John in the eyes.

"So. I think I remember seeing her."

Those words. John took off his hat, placed it on the file. Pulled up a notepad and a pen.

"Something about the tattoo in the photo you had, I remembered. The guy, he was in the club a lot of nights before that. A religious nut, he came to the club to recruit, you know, lost sheep. He told me his name once or twice but it was something unremarkable. Something like Smith or Jones, you know? He would order Sprite for himself but strong stuff for whoever he spoke to. Always girls."

"You never reported this?"

"What, a guy buying drinks for girls?"

"Description?"

"What?"

"The guy, tall, short, black, white, what?"

"Oh, yeah. White guy, black hair combed back slick. Tall, not like you but still tall. Pale, sort of bloodless, like he had thin skin that you could almost see through. Strange vibe."

"How so?" John was taking notes, writing as fast as he could.

"Well, it was like he wasn't sure how to act. He smiled at odd times, you know."

"What do you mean, odd times?"

Steph turned in his seat, looked out of the diner's window at a passing car.

"It was as if he only did it because it was something you were supposed to do. Like he had an interior voice saying, 'Remember to smile,' you know?"

"Okay, and what, did she leave with him?"

"I didn't see. I just know they were chatting at some point."

"Was she alone?"

"Yeah, this was maybe half an hour, an hour after the photo was taken."

The waitress brought them their food. Neither one of them even looked at it.

"This guy, that time I spoke to him, even as odd as he was he wasn't bad to speak to. Had a preacher vibe, you wanted to trust him even though you knew he was crazy."

"Crazy how?" John asked.

John didn't think they'd been talking long enough for anyone to make food worth eating, but here it was. Time played tricks on you sometimes.

Steph picked up his kebab and took a bite.

"He..." Steph chewed and swallowed. "Just, like all religious nuts. Like the Scientologists. They seem like nice people but they're all aliens and money. Crazy, but safe, you know? Anyway, hang on."

He leaned over and dug something out of the back pocket of his jeans. A pamphlet, rumpled and fading.

"I found one of these in the back with a lot of useless shit. It's the pamphlet he would hand out to people. Sometimes he'd leave a few at the bar and we always just tossed them as soon as he left."

John took the pamphlet and straightened it.

It was slim, printed on glossy paper. On the front was a picture of a single farmhouse at night, a starry sky in the background. A barn behind the farmhouse itself, large doors partly open and what appeared to be a candlelight inside.

Printed at the top, in all-caps: THE VESTIGIAL FLOCK

"Vestigial?" John asked.

"It means, like, what's left."

"I know what the word means, it just seems like a strange word to use."

He opened it, looking for a contact address, a name, something.

"They used to stalk the clubs. Easy marks, drunk kids you know," Steph said. "Not that, you know, your daughter was drunk or that she left with them, I just—"

The text in the pamphlet, light yellow on the starry background, spoke of the few remaining true believers of the world. Existential questions and meaningless fluff. "*Do you ever feel alone? Ever wonder why you are here? The Lord has the answers. His Messengers gather his flock.*"

John read the whole thing and found nothing concrete. No names, no addresses. It was almost like the pamphlet itself was a puzzle.

"How are they gathering people if they have no address and no contact info?" he asked.

"I… what?" Steph said.

"Never mind. When was the last time you saw the guy?"

"About a year ago, I think. Maybe they gave up. Realized that nightclubs weren't the best places to find lost sheep."

"Maybe," John said. "Did you see her leave with him? How much did they talk?"

"I don't know. I don't think they left together, but they might have. The club gets crazy busy."

"I know you need to not be seen with cops but I'm going to need you to come down and work with our sketch artist."

"What?"

"To get an impression of the guy's face."

"It's been two years man."

John felt every second of those two years. The first two weeks he didn't remember sleeping, just a frantic flash of one bad lead after another. Running and shouting. The futility of it all, how bare your life is when the comforting hood of self-delusion is torn away and you realize what it is that really matters.

"You'd be surprised what the sketch artist can pull up. Just tell him I sent you."

"No, man I…"

John looked at him. Just a kid. Whatever it was that was going on at the club was keeping him from telling him everything he knew.

"I can have him meet you somewhere, anywhere. Please?"

It would mean John would have to ask for another favor. He no longer knew how many he owed.

"Do the sketch and I'll leave you alone. Look, I don't care about what's going on at the club, I really don't."

Then he saw it. It was the smallest of small print, up along the side of the back of the pamphlet. *South Star Printers, Chicago IL.* John took a single big bite of the kebab and then rushed out, leaving Steph calling after him.

"Hey man, what the fuck?"

But John hardly heard him. He knew who printed the pamphlets.

Chapter Sixteen

It's not often something happens to you that totally changes your perspective of the world. Emily's disappearance had been one of those events. God, if he ever existed, had abandoned his children long ago and we were slowly ruining the planet and killing ourselves. There was no magic, no purpose to it all and nothing "behind the scenes." No salvation waiting if we just lived our life right.

John got a call just as he was finishing his shift. He had been going over the Stillwater case and was getting a headache from drinking nothing but bad station coffee all day. It was O'Reilley.

"Dark," she said. "You and Moreno are on again."

He suspected this would come, that them being back on homicide was just a temporary thing. O'Reilley still hadn't found it in her to let him back in. To let them back in. But John wasn't hearing her right.

"Chief. We're still sifting through everything on Stillwater, we just need a few—"

"Okay. We'll let forensics do their thing and give it to the D.A. No need to spend too much time on a case that's already over. Now, you and Moreno need to go to 554 International, apartment 442. Similar thing, I'm afraid. Guy called 911 and said someone had killed his wife. But I'll be damned if…" the chief left the end of the sentence hanging in the air.

“Ma’am?” John asked.

“Just go.”

John looked at the time. 7:42 p.m. Their shift was supposed to be over in less than twenty minutes.

“Harlen and O’Rourke are here in—”

“I want you and Moreno on this, John.”

John was wrong. O’Reilley was calling to give them another case, not to put them back on the regular beat. They really were back in.

He looked at Monique and nodded.

“Yes, ma’am,” he said and hung up.

–

“Hey,” he said as Lonei picked up the phone.

“Hey,” she said back, sensing the tone in his voice. John heard in that three-letter word both that she heard in him the need to work more and that, as usual, she was making her peace with it. When you’d been married this long and been through as much as they had, a certain reticence crept in your communication. It’s not that they wanted to talk less, it was just that they knew each other so well, knew what each inflection and emphasis in the spoken words signified, so they needed fewer words to communicate.

“There’s a—”

“I made the noodle thing you like, and you have another child here who—”

“I know.”

She didn’t answer that but stayed on the line, waiting.

“I *know*,” John said again. She didn’t blame him for Emily’s disappearance, wasn’t mad at him for not being able to find her, though she was angry. But what did get to her was that their other child, Orlando, was at risk of being lost from neglect. John wanted to get closer to Orlando, he really did.

"I'll be home as soon as we finish, I'll try to get Monique to take it if isn't too serious and then—"

"He'll be asleep," Lonei said. "*I'll* be asleep."

Again that silence. John didn't know how to reply. There was a way he spoke to his wife that was different from the way he spoke to anyone else. He often just didn't know what to say, not out of guilt but out of a feeling of inadequacy. He wanted to do right by her but felt he couldn't and instead of making excuses for it he just didn't find the words.

"I'll find her," he said and hung up.

He stood still for a moment, feeling as if he had just put on a heavy coat, wet and cold. It pulled him down, snapped a cold through his bones.

Where are you, Emily?

He thought of the last time he spoke to her, as he remembered it. It was dinner the Thursday evening before she disappeared. She talked about wanting a new phone. Something about hers not being able to upgrade an app, so she needed a new one. No personal information, never at the dinner table. Just the very mundane.

Did teenagers anywhere really tell their parents anything?

"John?" Monique said. "You okay?"

"Yeah. Yeah sorry, I was just… let's go."

Chapter Seventeen

Monique parked on the street right outside the building. Rain pounded the windshield faster than the wipers could keep up. John hesitated, hoping that the rain might let up in the few seconds they had before going in. Monique sensed his hesitation and used the chance.

"Where were you?" Monique asked.

"What?"

"On the Stillwater case, where were you? You were late."

She hadn't asked him before, which John felt a relief at the time but now, hearing the question he'd thought he wouldn't get, he wasn't sure he had a good answer for her. She had to feel he was back, all the way back, for her to be able to work properly. In all that happened as he searched for Emily, all the frantic fumbling about, abandoning reason and protocol to try to just get the fucking police department off their ass to help him look for his daughter… he had finally understood the empty stares and impatient pleading from people he had consoled in the same position. The statistics, the grim fucking statistics. If a missing person isn't found within two days the chances drop pretty quickly. After a week it is unlikely they will ever be found alive.

"*But it happens?*" the relatives of people missing would ask and then, automatically, his response. "*Yes, it happens.*"

That's what he was telling himself these days.

"I was… I got a lead, a good lead," John said to Monique. "She's in an Instagram photo from that night, with a bartender. I tracked him down and talked to him."

"John," Monique said. He wasn't sure if it was pity or a sliver of hopeful encouragement in her voice. As time passed, more and more people turned the tone of their voice and words from hope to pity. But surely Monique was still on his side.

"She's out there somewhere, Monique. I can't ignore it. I can't get past it. I—"

"Okay," she said.

"Okay?"

"Okay."

John allowed himself to remember that Monique was really on his side. The way only the truest of people can be; fully and without reservation. He tended to think the whole world was against him. It was worth taking a moment to remember that, sometimes, there were people on your side.

"So," he said, breaking the spell. "The guy admitted to killing his wife *on the 911 call*?" he asked Monique again. A sharp change of tone and subject. He hadn't heard the call himself and was having a hard time with what Monique had been telling him on the way over.

"Yes. No hint of regret, or that's what the dispatcher told me."

"Why call 911 at all then? And why are we being put on wife-killer cases now?"

A car went by, hitting a puddle and throwing water all over Monique's side of the car. She looked out the window, as if thinking about something.

"Why do these guys do anything?"

John opened the door and stepped out into the rain. He looked up at the building. It was the type of high rise where the apartments got more expensive the higher they were. Not generally the place you would expect grisly murders. Though, not much surprised him these days.

-

The elevator was oddly small for such an upscale address. They had walked in, flashed a badge and the security guard, a pudgy man with close-cropped hair and a crooked-toothed smile, stood up from the desk. He walked them towards the elevator and pushed a button for them. No one had spoken a word.

"The house was built in 1913," the security guard said as the elevator doors closed. They needed a special keycard to access the floor where the victim, Maria Ortega and her husband Ruiz lived, so the guard had joined them. "They say it's haunted, you know?"

John didn't say anything. His disbelief in all matters religious and supernatural had gotten him into many a heated discussion. He didn't want one here, now, in the tight confines of the elevator, with a man he might want to keep on his good side if he wanted answers.

"Haunted how?" Monique asked, no doubt partly to bother John.

The elevator lurched a bit and after, John heard a ticking noise. John was suddenly very aware of his reflection in the mirrors on either side. The security guard grinned, seemingly happy to answer Monique's question.

"Well, they say there's a basement that used to be a bootlegger hideout, like a hundred years ago or something. Doubled as a bar and under the bar a secret lower room used to store liquor and whatnot. Someone got cheated and there was a shootout, which ended with that someone fleeing and locking the rest of the gang in. So this guy runs out after locking the trapdoor from the outside, planning to come back in an hour when everyone's heads were cool again, only he gets shot. He was the only guy left who knew about the trapdoor and the hideout. The guys in the basement, well… they didn't get back out."

The elevator dings and opens as John imagines a bunch of prohibition gangsters starving to death. Of course, they would have shot the trapdoor open or made enough noise to be discovered. There were plenty of holes in the security guard's story. There always were.

John cleared his throat. "If everyone who knew about this died, the story would have died as well."

"Only," the security guard said and turned to them. "I tried finding a trap door, just where they said it would be. Wasn't nothing there. But I put my ear to the ground anyway and I swear I heard something."

"Which one is the Ortega's?" John said, not wanting to give this security guard any more rope to hang himself with.

"335, down the hall that way and to the right."

John saw the open door and the flashing lights of what he assumed were forensics' cameras.

"Thanks."

"There's more," the guard said as they walked into the hallway.

"What?" Monique asked.

"People hear shouts for help. On quiet nights, they sometimes call the front desk and say they hear people calling from help. Always say it's coming from the apartment below."

"Listen," John said. "I got enough to do with real-life bad people. I don't care about anything else."

"Peculiar thing though," the guard said as the elevator doors were closing. "They often say the people they hear are saying they're trapped. People who've never heard this story."

And with that, the elevator doors closed.

-

John stood in the doorway of apartment 335 and wasn't sure what he was seeing. What at first appeared, impossibly, to be snow covering most of the floor of the apartment slowly revealed itself to him as small feathers. Someone had torn apart a great number of pillows and spread the feathers all over the floor. Through floor-to-ceiling windows John saw the skyline of the city, a jagged darkness with intermittent scalpels of high-rises and skyscrapers piercing the sky.

A camera flash and a gentle push from Monique brought him out of his thoughts and he stepped further into the apartment. Marble countertops in the minimalist kitchen directly ahead matched the marble tiles visible through the cloud of feathers on the floor. The living room to the left had a shiny black grand piano looking calm amidst the chaos, a black ship in an ocean of fluffy white.

The forensics team had placed little footpads for anyone entering the apartment to step on. In the feathers they looked like stones in snow. Two steps in and John saw the blood and then the body. The loose feathers on the floor around the body had been disturbed, probably by the first people on the scene checking for vital signs.

It was a woman. An opera singer named Maria Ortega, aged forty-seven, lying face-up on the floor. Multiple stab wounds were visible around her left breast, which looked hacked. The blood on the floor around her was a shiny black, while the blood on the feathers was still a shocking red.

One of the forensics team approached them, tip-toeing on the platforms. She took down her mask. The three forensics experts in the room all wore pale blue onesies and surgical masks. Not wanting to contaminate the scene. John recognized her. Wabash.

"Hey Dark, Moreno," she said but John had his hand up, stopping her. The world was spinning.

John took a step closer.

He looked at Wabash and shook off a creeping feeling and a coldness that he felt reaching up into his feet, like chilled nails through the floor.

"You all right, Detective?" Wabash asked.

"I'm fine. I'm just—" he looked over the scene.

"He heard a ghost story in the elevator, it has him rattled," Monique said, trying to break the tension.

John put his hand up as a camera flashed, making the whiteness of the feathers sting his eyes.

"The apartment was locked when the first people arrived," Wabash said, reading from a little notebook she held. "Security guard opened it for the first responders. Husband was covered in the pillow feathers, panicky. Covered in her blood as well. He spent the first minutes screaming, trying to get the feathers off himself. He's already in custody, you can talk to him when forensics downtown is done with him."

An echo of the Stillwater case.

"Pillow feathers?" John asked.

"Yes. We have five empty pillow covers on the scene. Two appear to be from the bedroom, so he didn't accidentally cut open pillows. He wanted to get the feathers."

"Must have taken a while," Monique said, and John again heard an echo of Stillwater.

John felt like a balloon in a stiff wind, held down only by the flimsiest of threads. He held on against a realization that couldn't possibly be right.

"It's the same," he said.

"What is?" Monique said.

John noticed the feet. Bound together with rose stems. He felt dizzy.

"Look at her feet. The 911 call. It's the same."

"John they – Stillwater? Are you—?" she didn't finish that question.

This is all wrong.

Can't be the same person. Stillwater is in custody.

Wabash pointed to a low coffee table in the living room. "The knife was here." The table she was directing their attention to was silver and glass and had a dark crimson splash of blood across it with a smudged handprint in the blood.

"He says he didn't do it, of course. Guy better have a good lawyer, though I'm not sure even a great lawyer is keeping *this* guy out of jail."

"You think the husband did it?" Monique asked.

"*Think?*" Wabash said. "Guy was covered in blood and feathers, alone with her in the apartment the whole time."

John was still dazed. The idea that the two cases were connected was so strong in his head now that he had a sense of vertigo. Both times the husband had killed the wife in a locked room, arranged her body and decorated it, almost like arranging art. Feet tied with rose stems after death, thorns cutting little gashes into the ankles.

"I'm not so sure," John said, speaking slowly, each word pronounced as if not part of a sentence.

"The medical examiner has examined her and we're done with the photos so we can turn the body over to you. Judging from the way the blood is pooled and partly coagulated and dried around her torso our guess is that she was on her stomach for a while after dying."

"And the murder weapon?" Monique asked.

"Kitchen knife. There's an empty space on a sort of long magnetic strip the kitchen utensils hang from that could have been where the knife is from."

"So the body was face-down after death?" John asked.

John thought he heard a laugh then, a menacing short laugh, almost like a child's after winning a game but slow, drawn out and stretched. A hand touched the back of his neck and he turned to look at Monique but she was taking notes.

"John?" she asked.

"What? I'm fine."

"You look a bit pale," Monique said.

"It's the same. Two things – the brutal way she was stabbed, and then the gentle way she was arranged and decorated."

"This doesn't look very gentle, John," Monique said.

Maria Ortega lay on the floor, covered in her own blood and feathers. Outside, the people in the city went on with their lives, this death not slowing the pace of the world. How little we care about the lives and deaths of others. How unintentionally callous it could all seem.

"Can we turn her over?" John asked. "I want to see how she looked when he finished with her. Just before the 911 call."

"Sure," Wabash said.

They stood awkwardly over Maria Ortega and together the three of them turned her so she lay face down. The way Ruiz Ortega had most likely arranged her body after killing her.

There was a certain peace to her when the brutality of the wounds wasn't visible. What little blood was visible on the back of the body looked insubstantial, as if it had been dried off at some point. John bent down and took a look at the feathers on her arms.

She looked like a bird in flight. Her hands spread out and covered in feathers to make an angel or a swan.

"They were placed individually," he said as he examined the places where most of the feathers were. Small white and gray pillow feathers.

"There's…" Wabash looked at them. As if wondering how to phrase the next sentence. "I'm not one to tell you how to do your jobs, detectives, but if the husband *didn't* do this one I'm buying you both a steak dinner. With a bottle of wine for each of you."

John tip-toed from platform to platform until he stood right by the body. He felt like he was looking at the woman from the top of a cliff. As if he was on the cusp of something that threatened to plunge him down into a never-ending pit of darkness.

Chapter Eighteen

Darcy Chang went along to the seance with a friend, just for a laugh. Her parents, naturally, would not approve.

They didn't mind her having white friends, but made it clear that they expected this to just be a phase, that one day she would come to her senses and marry a nice Chinese doctor, perhaps Mrs. Chinua's nephew. Of course, they didn't know that Mrs. Chinua's nephew had a pretty serious coke habit or that he was quite openly gay. Darcy would like to see the looks on their faces when they found out.

Even her name, Darcy, was one she had recently taken for herself as an act of rebellion, though she didn't mind her actual name, Daiyu, that much. She longed for the day someone asked her where she was from, meaning where locally, not just trying to find out whether she was from China or Korea.

And this tonight, another small act of rebellion, another way to show to herself and to her parents that *this city* was where she belonged. She'd never even been to China and had no real desire to go. She knew the language and the stories but it all felt a little made up, a little irrelevant. A little something she didn't plan on teaching to her kids.

It was Nena who had had the idea to come. Nena was really into these spiritual things and, while the remark wasn't exactly racist, her claim that Darcy should be into it as well because, "You know, you're from China," bothered her. She didn't believe in the afterlife, much less that the deceased would stay around to give their loved ones vague advice and meaningless platitudes. Nena, however, read the horoscope every day, recommended homeopathic medication to them when they were sick, believed in past lives and was always on the verge of meeting her "Tall dark stranger."

"It'll be fun," she had said earlier that week. "We'll go for a laugh, I mean the guy's probably a faker, so many of them are."

"So why go? How much does it cost?" Darcy had replied.

"We'll go for drinks before. He might tell us something about, like, what our future holds or where our family's fortunes lie."

And so they went, just for fun. A girl's night out.

The "hall" they were now in, the venue for this sort-of-seance turned out to just be a living room in an apartment on the second floor of a house owned by The Society for Spiritual Research, a narrow off-white three-story building that stood, and stood out, between two black marble ten-story tenement buildings. The house reminded Darcy of nothing so much as a rotting tooth. The street was poorly lit and dirty, with Darcy letting out a rather clichéd, "Are you sure about this?" at one point during their walk over from the subway. Inside the living room, folding chairs were placed in five rows with a gap in the middle making a walkway from the door at the back.

"Does someone *actually* live here?" Darcy asked Nena as they sat down.

"No, I don't think so," Nena said as she looked around. "No, it's props, like at the theater."

Most of the seats were taken five minutes before the meeting was scheduled to start. People spoke in hurried whispers, as if speaking at a proper volume would scare off any spirits that might be present. Or as if they were at a funeral. A reverent hush.

The crowd filled the room and waited. Outside in the distance, the sirens of the city rang and then distance made them quiet.

Finally, a man who had to be the host walked in, the man who was supposedly in touch with the spirit world. He took slow deliberate steps down the space between the rows of seated guests, whispering, "Welcome" to people as he passed them. He was a man of about sixty with a lazy eye and a well-groomed beard. Long hands with wide palms and short fingers, which reminded Darcy of paddles. He made his way to the front of the room and, with his back turned to them, lit a few small candles on a table.

He then turned to face them. "Hello and welcome," he said. His voice was deep and low, words spoken slowly. He stood up straight and held his hands together in front of a potbelly. He wore a plaid flannel shirt, and what little remained of his receding hair was combed sideways and looked greasy. He smiled, and with his smile he pulled them in. It was a smile not of a con-man, but of a man who believed in what he did, believed he had a gift and wanted nothing more than to share this gift with the world. To help the people here tonight.

"There is good energy in the room tonight," he continued in a near-whisper. The remaining flittering conversation stopped. "Many people in search of answers."

His gaze went from face to face, and the room fell deathly quiet.

Darcy stifled a laugh.

"My name is Nathaniel Mass," he said. He closed his eyes and spread his hands, as if about to embrace someone standing in front of him. Darcy noticed that the lights had been dimmed and now the only illumination was from the feeble candles on the table behind him and the little streetlight that managed to slip in through the grimy windows. "Shall we begin?"

She turned to Nena, to smile and share an eye-roll and a giggle but Nena was looking at the man as if hypnotized. She wasn't here just as a gag, Darcy realized.

"I hear something," Nathaniel said, a southern accent slipping in, making the word "hear" into two syllables. *Hee-ar.* Darcy looked around. An older woman on the other side of the room was holding a framed photo and a few rows behind her a woman held a comb firmly in her grasp, knuckles white. Goosebumps spread over Darcy's arms, and a coldness crept into the small of her back. Such desperation. She looked at Nathaniel. Such false hope.

"There is a man here," Nathaniel said, eyes closed. "He's wearing a shirt and he's… it's a blue shirt. Blue and white, checkered. He works in an office, I think or… he has glasses. Does anyone know who this is?"

The crowd was rapt, like a wound toy about to spring up. Darcy felt like a traitor, felt that at any moment the crowd might turn and point at her. "*She doesn't believe in this, she's ruining the energy.*"

Nathaniel continued, eyes still shut. "I'm getting a J in his name, James or John."

"I…" someone said. "My father? His name was Michael John."

Nathaniel looked at the woman. She sat in the second row, across the divide from Darcy. She already had tears forming in her eyes. "He's touching his wrist," Nathaniel said and tapped his watch. "He says something about time, does that mean anything to you?"

"He was always worried he'd be late to work," the woman said, smiling with relief, as if she was really being reunited with her father. "He was always telling me and my sister to hurry up." She was about forty, Darcy guessed, maybe forty-five.

"Yes," Nathaniel said. "I can feel that he wants to… he wants to tell you something." He laughed, eyes closed, as if sharing a joke with this man he claimed to see. "He wants *me* to hurry up."

A jitter of laughter from the crowd. Darcy wondered if she should laugh, if she should play a part. She was no stranger to putting on a play to fit in. Her whole life revolved around being "American" in one crowd and "Chinese" in another, as if either of those was shorthand for the way a person was, how they felt and what they thought. Like a test of a person, getting the simplest label to make those around you comfortable, while your own comfort was secondary, always. She couldn't shake the feeling that this was like an evening with a cult. She wanted to go home, felt unsafe somehow, even though she couldn't imagine how this could turn dangerous. She decided to relax, it was just a play and the people in attendance willing participants. He was giving them what they wanted to hear and they paid him for it.

Nathaniel took a step forward, smiling. "He says that there's a question you've had for a while, something about a school?" Somehow ending his statements with the inflection of a question.

"Yeah, I… I've been wondering if I should complete my degree," the woman said. "But I'd really rather—"

"What's your name?" Nathaniel asked before she could finish.

"Deliverance," she said.

"That's quite the name," Nathaniel said.

Deliverance smiled awkwardly, awaiting the message from her father.

"He is nodding, tapping his wrist again."

"So he thinks I should go back?"

"I think that's a fair interpretation," Nathaniel said. "Are you okay with that?"

"I…" she seemed to be expecting something more. "Yes, I suppose. But can I ask?"

"Yes?" Nathaniel said, grinning. Darcy thought she saw something move behind his teeth. Like his tongue was an actual snake, sliding around.

"My mother. Does he know what happened to my mother?"

Every head turned towards Deliverance and then at Nathaniel. This *was* interesting, Darcy had to admit.

"Your mother?"

"Yes, she went missing three years ago and all we ever found was some blood behind the sofa. Does he know? Is she… is she with him?"

Everyone was silent. All Darcy heard was the beating of her heart. Nena gripped her thigh and leaned over and whispered, "This is *so* great." Nena's uninhibited enjoyment made Darcy aware of her own, and made it feel tainted. A woman's grief turned into a mystery for their entertainment.

Nathaniel closed his eyes again and paced at the front of the room. "He is shaking his head. There's a tear in his eyes. He wants you to know he shares your pain, he feels it too, every day. He really wishes he could be with you and…"

"Harriet," Deliverance offered.

"Harriet. He wishes he was with you still."

He turned his attention away from Deliverance and closed his eyes again. The woman's question dealt with, he went back to the theatrics. The crowd seemed to eat it up.

"I'm getting a strong sense of… it's a smell. I'm in a kitchen now, or there's a person here who spent a lot of time in the kitchen."

Darcy thought of every grandmother in the world. What a crock of shit this was, but Nena was under his spell, still holding on to Darcy's thigh.

"There's… yes, there's a woman with an apron. A colored woman, or Asian and she's… I hear a bird."

Nathaniel turned and looked out at the crowd, looking to see if anyone liked the look of this particular bait. He could of course be describing Darcy's own grandmother, a woman who came to visit them once and spent most of her time giving Darcy's parents shit for not making her stick to every single Chinese custom there was. But she did also cook some great food while she was visiting, her father giddy before every meal. Each dinner a trip back to China, to a childhood completely alien to Darcy. But there was no bird.

Nathaniel kept playing the crowd. "The name she's giving me is… I'm getting an A. And an R."

No one in the crowd spoke.

The group's hypnosis was broken by a commotion at the back of the hall and then the door opened with a bang. Everyone turned to see what was going on. A man stood in the doorway, somewhat disheveled, like he hadn't bathed or changed his clothes in a week. No one said anything, but the first thing the man said was "Could you quiet down, please?"

Nena leaned even closer and whispered again, "Now what?"

"I need to speak to… are you Nathaniel? Are you in charge here?" The man didn't wait for Nathaniel to answer but charged in. He then stopped about halfway down the aisle, as if someone was in his way.

"What?" the man said to the air in front of him. "Yes, of course I can, but you are in my way." He moved sideways, pressing his back right up against the person sitting closest to the aisle, like he was walking past someone on an airplane. But the aisle was clear.

"Nathaniel," he said, charging right up to him. Nathaniel seemed unsure how to respond. Clearly this was not a common occurrence, though Darcy had little problem imagining that people who were mentally unstable were drawn to meetings such as this. "I need your help to, or well… Not me. There are spirits—"

Nathaniel Mass folded his hands together over his chest and gave the man a stern look. "Sir, you are interrupting this evening and ruining my connection to the spirit world." His voice, while full of understanding, was not free from annoyance.

"I'm… what? You can see ghosts, right?"

A look passed across Nathaniel's face that Darcy thought might indicate that he didn't like the directness of the question. As if the point of the evening was a shared secret, not to be spoken out loud. The rest of the people in the room seemed equally put off by the newcomer.

"I am attuned to energies and intentions from the other side, that is not the same. Now please, either take a seat and allow me to continue, or leave." It was clear from his voice which he preferred.

The man said, "No, wait, I'm not done," but not to Nathaniel. He spoke out into the air to his right, as if someone was standing there with him. "If you can talk to spirits then please take these off my hands, I don't have time to help ghosts with their problems." He then turned to his right again. "No, Troy, this man is a professional, he'll know how to help you."

Nathaniel looked taken aback, left without a way to reply, now that the man had turned his back and was walking out of the room again. His eyes darted around as he walked, and he looked somewhat embarrassed now, as if just realizing that the room was full of people at an event. If he hadn't been so unkempt – it looked like he hadn't showered in days – Darcy would have found him handsome. Now she was just annoyed with him, the opposite of attraction. He stopped, and looked as if he were thinking about something.

He turned and spoke to the air next to Nathaniel. "Troy, trust me, he is a much better—" he stopped mid-sentence, as if interrupted. "Yes he can, he just said…" he turned his attention to Nathaniel. "Mister, would you please tell the spirit standing next to you that you will help him, he doesn't seem to think that you see him."

"I'm not… sir, if you want me to converse with someone in particular you will simply have to pay the entrance fee and wait and hope that I am able to establish a connection. It's not a simple matter of—"

"You don't see him," the man said then. "You can't..." he looked around the room. "What about the old man standing there, against the wall?"

Darcy looked and saw no one at the spot the man was pointing to. What was this, a duel of spirit talkers? A meeting of men, both claiming to be able to speak to the deceased, neither seeing what the other saw. Darcy felt silly, exposed somehow. Then the man turned to her.

"And here, this old Chinese woman, do you see her?"

Old? I'm not old, Darcy thought.

"Sir," Nathaniel said, voice now moving into pure anger. "Please leave. You are ruining this evening for everyone."

"Calm down, calm down, I don't understand Chinese, lady."

He then looked at Darcy. "You look Chinese, can you tell the old lady to calm down, I don't understand her."

Darcy felt butterflies in her stomach, made of ice. Everyone was looking at *her* now. "What... what old lady?" Darcy asked. She wished she hadn't come.

"Isn't she with you?" he asked and then. "Oh. Oh I'm sorry, I didn't realize." The man spoke to a point behind her, hands out with open palms. "Sorry, I don't speak Chinese."

"What is she saying?" Darcy asked.

The man seemed to concentrate. Nathaniel was saying something but this man had the room's attention. He certainly had Darcy's. "She's saying, hang on..." The man seemed to be concentrating. Then he spoke in a slow rhythm. "*Shu wu hei lon den shis Daiyu fon*... and then something I don't know."

Darcy felt like her heart was collapsing, like she was falling into herself, into a blackness within. Imploding, falling into a hole made by her heart. Her cheek felt cold and she realized she was crying.

"What does she look like?" Darcy asked.

The whole room was quiet. Even Nathaniel had stopped objecting. All eyes on the strange man.

"She looks like an old Chinese woman. There's a birthmark on the side of her nose."

Darcy gasped, hands numb but feeling like rocks on her thighs. Her grandmother was right here, with her. "Please," Darcy managed to say. "Please, what is she saying? Just... just repeat it."

He spoke. Awkward, stunted syllables, clearly repeating something, or at least not speaking words he was familiar with.

"What does it mean?" the man asked as he finished, a tenderness in his voice having replaced the gruff impatience that had been there.

Darcy felt light as a feather but also as if she were a stone at the bottom of a cold, deep lake. Nena touched her shoulder.

"What does it mean?" she asked and Darcy turned to face her.

She felt safe, as if Nena were not just a friend but that she was a safe place and a warm meal, a comfort.

"She... she said she was proud of me. She's happy to see me embrace my new country and hopes I do well here. She's sorry for—" she couldn't finish, racked with sobs. She took a deep breath, composing herself. "She's sorry for trying to push Chinese customs on me, she was just worried I wouldn't love her. That she'd lose me. But I love her, can you tell her that? I love her."

"I don't... Chinese," the man said and gestured into the air.

"*Wo... wo ay nee*," Darcy said through the sobs. "*Woo annie*."

"*Wo ay nee*?"

"Yes," Darcy said and felt something crack inside, like a layer of early-morning frost on a lake, broken with a carelessly thrown pebble.

"*Wo ay nee*," he said to the air. Then he stared, wide-eyed, questioning. "She's gone," he said.

What struck Darcy was that he looked amazed by this fact as he spoke it, and it was this she would wonder about in the days to come. Was it part of the act? Did this man interrupt every meeting, pretending to see spirits that the medium didn't? No, he knew her name, her real name.

"You all right, Darcy?" Nena asked. She had taken hold of Darcy's hand without her feeling it.

"Yes, I think so." Darcy closed her eyes and tried to catch hold of a feeling, any feeling. Everything inside her was tumbling, as if her identity and emotions were toys falling down a flight of stairs. If she could just grab onto something.

"You look pale, you sure you're alright? Darcy?"

"Daiyu," Darcy said.

"What?"

"My name. That's my real name. Daiyu. He... he said it and he couldn't have known. He couldn't have known."

They stood up together. The room was still silent, all eyes on them. It was like everyone was waiting for her permission to speak. She looked at Nathaniel Mass, who stood at the front of the room. His mouth was open but snapped shut as she looked at him. The look in his eyes was defeat, but as Daiyu felt she was about to say something to him, to apologize, feeling suddenly that the disturbance had been *her* fault, his eyes, his whole composure went from defeat to defiance. Tensing up, he went from merely looking towards her to a look of loathing. His mouth turned down as he spoke.

"Get out of here. You planned this together, didn't you? You planned this."

"No," Daiyu said. "I…" She didn't know what to say, how to defend herself from what had just happened, not sure she even should.

"Come on Darcy," Nena said, pulling on her hand, "Let's go."

They left, Daiyu's mind still reeling with emotion and confusion. They left the seance hall, and Daiyu left Darcy behind. After that evening, she would linger at her parent's house after dinner invitations, asking about life in China, about her grandmother and what life had been like in China in the middle of the last century. She proudly said "China" when people asked her where she was from and then added "Well, not me exactly, but my parents. My grandmother."

Chapter Nineteen

The interrogation room at the station felt smaller and colder than it had when they talked to Stillwater. This was the second time John and Monique were interrogating a suspect in just a few days, when there would often be weeks between interrogations. Maybe the renewed familiarity made it smaller. The way your hometown never seems as big as it was when you were a kid, even if more people live there.

John had figured the world out early. Grown-ups told lies to protect you from the truth that the world was a horrible place, and John had decided at an early age to see for himself just how bad it really was. He resented his parents for maintaining the lie about Santa Claus. The tooth fairy. Resented himself and felt foolish for believing in them. And this just about the time he turned seven.

He got interested in war, became a quiet and reserved child. Excelled in reading and mathematics. By the time they started teaching history he had already read everything he could get his hands on. Told the other children stories of Eichmann and Mengele. Mai Lai and what the Belgians did in Africa. How the slaves had gotten to America. It did not earn him popularity among classmates and teachers.

At nine he would debate his priests and soon he was not welcome at their local church. Religion, to him, was just another thing grown-ups lied to children about, without proof. They had him tested on the autism spectrum but he had no problem reading into the looks on people's faces, had no issues *feeling* anything.

"He's gifted, there's no doubt about that," his principal said to his parents once. John sat outside the office, but the hall was quiet and the walls were thin. "I just wish you'd encourage him to pursue more lighthearted endeavors. His obsession, at this age, with atheism and the history of war is, frankly, a bit unsettling. Not that this is an overly religious school, it's just that we're getting complaints. Perhaps you could just ask him not to proselytize his godlessness during school hours."

"Why? The school certainly has no problem trying to convince *him* of the truth in Catholicism and I'm sure a healthy debate is good for the kids." It was his mother speaking. She admonished him at home for talking to the kids and John had argued with his parents on numerous occasions but now, here, hearing her defending him, John felt a pang of love for her.

"I will not have the child equating Catholicism with Santa Claus, Mrs. Dark, not during my… whatever the disagreement we may have on theological grounds, your son, while gifted, needs to conform better to school activities and refrain from subverting the other children's religion."

Gifted. That was the label they stuck to him. The box they put him in to make themselves feel better. It would exclude John from more things than it ever granted him, despite it supposedly being a positive thing. It gave him permission to be academically lazy, always sure he could get better grades if he wished.

Meanwhile, opportunities passed him by. Being told at an early age that he could excel at anything he wished to had the opposite effect; him applying himself at nothing. Becoming a cop somehow by default, entering the academy with a buddy who later dropped out, leaving John with something new but unchallenging enough for him to actually complete.

A cop, and then a detective, through gifted inaction.

-

The chair squeaked against the floor of the interview room as John moved it. The man sitting across from him, Ruiz Ortega, jumped at the noise. John paused, holding the chair, poised to sit.

"Sorry," he offered and thought about the irony. The image of Ortega's wife flashed across John's mind. The body, face-down with hands spread out. Feathers, hastily arranged to make her look like a bird, the illusion ruined by the blood sticking to them.

Monique sat down next to John.

Ruiz Ortega's skin was oddly pale, with dark circles around sunken eyes as if he was just recovering from a pair of black eyes. His hair was cut close, shaved at the sides and combed sideways. An odd haircut for a man of his age. His face was broad, and the slight second chin gave him the look of a boxer, though his body was too slim for it.

"Do you know what happened? Did you find something?" he asked them. As if he weren't under arrest, but here just to hear how the investigation was going.

"Mr. Ortega," Monique said. "We are talking to your neighbors and people who knew your wife. Friends you have in common. But you have to see things from our side. Your wife was killed when there were just the two of you in the apartment."

"Tell us again, Mr. Ortega. What happened last night?" John said.

"You… you're not looking for a killer? You just *assume* I did this?"

"We are not assuming anything," John said. "We will investigate any and all possibilities. We just want to hear your side of the story."

"Should I get a lawyer?" he asked, not in the arrogant way powerful men tended to, but in what sounded to John like a man truly seeking his advice.

"Do you want one? Do you have one?"

"Yes, but for the business. For the money. Not for… not for this."

"We're just looking to find out what happened, Mr. Ortega."

"Yeah, well, let's catch whatever *culo* set me up. I'll tell you whatever you need." His emphasis on the Latino slang was a bit off, the accent staying American, not Mexican. Not a man that often swore, John thought, or maybe he was putting on a show.

"Mister Ortega," Monique said. "If you want to have a lawyer present, you need to say so, otherwise we'll continue."

"Will you have to wait for him?" he asked, again more concerned than anything else. "I don't want to slow this down."

"Yeah, we'd have to wait," John said.

"Then no, I don't want my lawyer here."

"Okay, let's start. This conversation is being recorded, both sound and video. Do you object to this?"

"No."

Monique took a sip of her coffee, grimaced, and then placed the paper cup on the table. "Mr. Ortega, why did you kill your wife?"

"Me? I didn't..." he said, sounding like he was trying to convince them as much as himself. "You have to believe me, please. You need to be looking for the guy, whoever did this."

"We are, Mr. Ortega."

"Just tell us what you remember," John said.

"We'd just gotten home. Maria could get moody and we'd been fighting in the car so she went to bed and I went into the living room."

"You'd been arguing?" John asked.

"Yes, she wanted to go to my sister's next month and I didn't. I don't have the time to go and, well, my sister and I don't always get along."

"But *they* do?" Monique asked and then corrected herself. "Did?"

"Yes," Ruiz Ortega said. "It's like they're cousins or something, annoys the hell out of me." And then, as if realizing what he'd just said. "But I didn't kill her! I just, all couples argue, it was just an argument."

Ortega covered his face with his hands, as if playing peekaboo with a child. He took a deep breath and then his shoulders shook. When he removed his hands from his face his cheeks were wet. Eyes sinking in a red-rimmed lake of tears.

"Was there anyone else in the apartment?" Monique asked. "A maid or a butler or something?"

"No, we have a maid, just for cleaning but she had gone home by then. Why, you think she had something to do with this?"

"No," John said. "We're just trying to establish the whereabouts of people with access to your apartment."

"There's a guard in the lobby. Security footage," Ortega said.

"We are looking into that now, along with security from inside your apartment."

"Yeah, yeah," Ortega said and seemed to light up. "That'll show what happened. Of course! You'll see who killed my wife on there."

"Do we have your permission to view the footage recorded inside the apartment last night, Mr. Ortega?"

He paused. Seemed to be evaluating this.

"What is it?" John asked.

"I didn't…" Ortega looked genuinely afraid, like a boy caught doing something he wasn't supposed to. John thought it a good act, but still just that, an act. "I mean, yeah, we came home and we argued and then she went to bed and I went into…"

"Into what, Mr. Ortega?" Monique said. He looked confused.

"I don't remember. Did I go to the kitchen?"

"To get the knife?" John asked.

"What, no I…"

"Have you had these episodes before?"

"Episodes?"

"Well, I'm no psychiatrist, Mr. Ortega, but it sounds like you had a bit of an episode. Amnesia while killing your wife, that's a heck of a defense."

"I didn't kill my wife! Oh God, she's dead, she's dead."

"So we can view the footage?" Monique asked. "The sooner you consent the better. Saves us a lot of time and paperwork, Mr. Ortega. It will let us see what happened and catch whoever did this."

"Why the feathers?" John asked. "Why go to all that trouble?"

They were throwing it all at him. Any and all questions but really, their hearts weren't in it. They had him. Security footage of the lobby that evening, acquired with unusual speed and viewed already, had shown no unusual movement around the time the Ortegas got home.

"I didn't – you don't believe me."

"I believe what the crime scene tells me, Mr. Ortega. And a locked door in a private-access penthouse apartment tells me a lot."

"I didn't—"

"Your handprint on the knife, her blood on your clothes. The 911 calls."

John felt a pang of regret. Did he push too hard? Was the Reid Technique creeping into his words? There had been times when he'd affected the outcomes of interviews. Pushed too hard. It wasn't exactly a fine line, confessions mostly came when lawyers convinced their clients to plead guilty for a reduced sentence. Others gave him nothing until the evidence couldn't be ignored.

"Yes," Ortega said. Meek. Defeated was the way John would come to think of it. "Yes, you can look at the recording."

John took a look at the mirror on the wall, and then turned back to Ortega.

For now, permission to view the security footage from inside the apartment was enough of a win for them. A camera covered the living room, so this time they knew they would see the crime itself, not just glimpses of before and after.

"Who else called 911?" he asked.

"What?"

"You said 911 calls. As if someone else had called."

"You called twice, Mr. Ortega," John said. "You called them twice. What do you remember about the first call?"

"The first? I… maybe I called twice. I just remember seeing the blood and Maria."

John couldn't shake the familiarities with the Stillwater case. There was too much in common for this to be a coincidence, thematic similarities. Happenstance didn't apply here. He cleared his throat. A moment passed as he prepared to ask his next question. "Mr. Ortega, do you know a Michael Stillwater?" The question hung in the air for a while. John felt weightless and cold in the silence between question and reply.

"Michael Stillw… Still Mike?"

"Still Mike?" John said.

"Yeah, I know Michael Stillwater. We went to school together."

Monique stole a glance at John and then leaned forward. "What school was this? When?"

"Whitesands. It's a prep school. We were there together back in the late Eighties. I mean, just kids. Teenagers."

"When was the last time you spoke to him?"

"A couple of years ago, I think. We met at a gallery opening."

"Just you or you and your wife?" Monique asked.

"It was… it was… Maria was with me. We had drinks after with him and Ellen. Why, does he have something to do with this?"

"No, Mr. Ortega. I can assure you that Michael Stillwater was nowhere near your apartment last night," John said.

"What, Ellen then?" he asked. Grasping at anything.

A moment passed in silence, and John felt like something dragged across his scalp. He was reminded of the bloody feathers on the floor of Ortega's apartment and wiped the back of his neck with his palm, expecting to see crimson.

"Why 'Still Mike'?" Monique asked.

"What?" Ortega replied.

"You called him 'Still Mike'. Why?"

"He was the calmest person I knew. Like, things could be on fire and he'd just sit and read. Sitting still. Still Mike."

"So you were good friends," John asked. "The sort of friends who do anything for one another?"

John never got an answer to the question. As Ortega looked at them his face fell completely slack and then his whole body went limp. He slid off the chair and banged his head on the corner of the table.

"Mr. Ortega?" John said and stood up. "Mr. Ortega?" He motioned to the one-way mirror for them to send someone in and walked over to Ortega's side. The body spasmed once. Then slowly, Ortega sat up. Something about the way he moved gave John chills.

A tear ran down his cheek and his eyes were wide open as if in shock. Slowly, the pupils expanded and spilled over the brown of the iris and the whites until the eyes were completely black. John had the sensation of falling as he looked on. Ortega's eyes held John whole.

"Mr. Ortega?" John said.

Then Ortega spoke, in a voice that sounded double, like they were also hearing the echo.

"He deserved it," he said. The emphasis and accent was different, though the voice was the same. The door burst open and an officer came in holding a defibrillator. John held out a hand to stay the officer, not taking his eyes off Ortega for a second.

"They all—" he started. Empty shock in the all-black eyes and half a grin on the lips, as if the face wasn't completely under control.

"The police never helped," he said. "They hardly even looked into it."

"Mr. Ortega?" John asked, still standing. "Are you all right?"

"Ortega was one of them. Stillwater too. They did it together."

A flower of ice was spreading from John's gut out into his limbs.

Ortega stood up in a single sharp twitch. He stood with shoulders high but his head hanging loose, as if he was being held up by hooks. The body twitched and Ortega bent over like a hinge and banged his head against the table. And then he did it again and again, the bang-bang-bang echoing in the small room as his forehead slapped against the cold metal.

John grabbed a hold of his torso to try to stop him but it was like gripping a train, his hands just went along, back and forth, down and up, bang-bang-bang.

"I can make my puppets play," Ortega said as he slammed his head against the table. "I can make them play and kill and play and kill."

Finally something gave and John managed to push Ortega against the wall and down to the floor to keep him from hurting himself.

"Goodbye Officers," Ortega said. "See you again soon." His body went completely limp in John's arms. There was a gash in his forehead and blood on the table.

Monique was looking at John, hands over her mouth.

"Did... did you see his eyes?" she asked.

Chapter Twenty

John had been demoted after the scene at the theme park. He had been running wild with department resources, calling in favors from the FBI in O'Reilley's name, sending officers to knock on the doors of all known sex offenders, guys whose doors the police were often knocking on. He begged search warrants for men he thought particularly suspicious, with little or nothing to back it up. He pushed against the very limits of O'Reilley's patience until, after a meeting with a medium, he pushed that bit too far.

Dreamcatchers, frazzled and sun-bleached, hung from the front porch of the house the navigation told them to stop in front of. "You have arrived at your destination," the voice said. Something about the inflection of the voice was wrong to John, like there was more it wanted to say.

It was a nondescript pale blue house, a welcoming pale blue. The street was one of those that appear in television shows and seem to go on forever, an endless suburbia of mediocrity and normality. The kind of street boys in horror novels rode their bikes down before encountering clowns in the gutter, or finding a body by the train tracks.

Lonei took his hand as they stood on the sidewalk in front of the house. She hadn't taken a hold of his hand for a long time. It felt good. She was wearing a yellow sweater, and was clutching an enlarged photograph of Emily. A recent yearbook picture. She had been missing for five weeks and John and Lonei's rush to find her had soured into a desperate grabbing at straws.

As they got closer they noticed that the house was in slight disrepair, nothing too serious. John felt as if he'd been here before. A subtle déjà vu as they walked towards it.

The porch steps creaked under their weight. The dried-up carcass of a frog lay belly-up to the side, by a porch swing. It almost felt like a stage to John, somehow unreal. As if the dreamcatchers and the dried-up frog were props. The swing just a set-piece. They might walk through the doors onto an actual stage with people cheering.

"This the right place?" John asked.

There was a sign on the front door. A laminated poster advertising Kiernan Strange's services. "Tarot readings, futures unveiled and communication with the other side. Appointments at strangekiernan@hotmail.com."

John grinned and looked at Lonei. She was not in on the joke and John's smile fell dead at their feet. She was still holding his hand and holding Emily's photo with the other so John knocked. The door was flimsy and loose in its frame, making John's knock seem hollow.

A bird landed on the porch railing and pecked at nothing.

Through the thin curtains covering the windows in the door, John saw someone approach to answer the door.

"Hello," the man said as he opened the door. He was a thin man, short, with a pleasant look to his eyes. "Welcome. You must be the Darks."

"Yes," Lonei said, her voice already at breaking point.

"Come in, come in."

The house smelled of incense and dust. It was tidy, and a sort of disquieting normality hung over everything. Wooden floors with carpets, worn and faded. Framed photos on the walls of castles and a country with a cragged coastline.

"Dark, that's an unusual last name," the man said. John wasn't sure if it was supposed to be a question or a statement. He didn't answer.

"You have a lovely home," Lonei said to deflect. Or maybe she hadn't heard him.

He led them into the kitchen. It was a small room, with a kitchen table under a small window and an affixed bench on the wall next to it. He invited them to sit down on the bench.

"Tea?" he asked.

"Yes, please," Lonei answered.

John shook his head when Kiernan turned to see why he hadn't answered. Keirnan rummaged through several little bowls looking for tea bags. John's attention was momentarily focused on a framed photograph. It was a faded black-and-white photo, blacks closer to greens. A soldier stood in a field of leafless trees. There was a rifle by his side on which he was supporting himself. John thought he saw something in the distance, almost hiding in the trees. The man's face was without expression. He resembled Keirnan very closely, almost to the point that John might think it was him, but the photo must be really old for it to be that faded.

"Hard candy?" Keirnan offered, holding out a dish with small mud-colored crystals.

John shook his head again. Lonei had taken a seat on a bench at the small kitchen table, head brushing up against a bookshelf. John sat down next to her. Kiernan sat down across from them. Lonei put her hands on the table, fingers locked together as if she were about to pray. They were shaking. John put a reassuring hand on top of hers and she took a deep breath.

"Why do you come to me?" Keirnan asked.

John thought it an odd question. Not "How can I help you?" or "Why are you here today?"

"Our daughter—" Lonei said but her voice cracked and she couldn't finish the sentence. She trembled.

"Our daughter is missing," John said. "Lonei thinks, hopes, that you might help us find her."

"And you?"

"Me?"

"Do you not think I can help you?"

"Does that matter?" John asked.

"It helps me if all our expectations and emotions are in tune. We are on a boat here, Mr. Dark, and we all need to be rowing in the same direction."

There were things he could do for Lonei; holding her as she cried into his chest, allowing her to scream at him for not finding Emily, taking the blame. He did it all. John hadn't known the sort of stable love Lonei gave existed, the example set by his mother of what love was had been hard to shake off. Hard to let himself believe that there was another kind. Right now, to repay his love for her, he could play along here.

"I believe you can help us, Mr. Strange," John said.

He thought back to the man's comment about his last name earlier. That Dark was somehow an odd last name. This from a man named Kiernan Strange.

"I see, and I sense that you are in great pain," Strange said. "Before we begin, I just wanted to acknowledge that.

I also want you to know that this is a safe place, and that you are welcome here."

He patted their joined hands on the tabletop. It made John feel like a little boy being patted on the cheek for being good. Behind Strange, the water for the tea started boiling loudly and then the kettle clicked.

"Ah, just in time," he said and stood up. He pulled down two mugs with an old, faded orange-and-brown checkered pattern. He placed leaves into strainers, put them into the mugs with a little clink, and then poured the water.

"I speak with the spirits," he said. "They are chaotic and noisy." Outside, through the window behind him, the light was changing. Stretching out as the day drew to a close. "The spirits do not always cooperate. But let's start with the tea," he said as he placed one of the mugs in front of Lonei.

"Tell me about Emily," he asked them.

"Have you ever helped anyone before?" John asked. "I don't mean to be rude, but has information from you ever lead to—"

"Lead to what, Mr. Dark?"

"John," Lonei said.

"I'm—"

"Drink your tea," Strange said to Lonei.

The fridge, a mustard-yellow vintage thing, clicked to life and whirred. A moment passed where John sensed that Lonei and Keirnan were waiting for some of the awkwardness to fade.

"Maybe this would go smoother if you waited in the hall," the medium said. John gave him a look that stated, simply, that there was no way he was leaving his wife's side. Lonei took a sip of tea.

"No," John said. "No, I'm here for this. I'm here."

"All right," Strange said. "Well, once Mrs. Dark finishes her tea I'll take a look at the leaves, see what they tell us."

The words sounded like they should come from a middle-aged, former hippie woman with dreads, not this receptionist-looking mole of a man. John disliked him, had disliked him from the moment Lonei mentioned him. "A friend," had mentioned him, Lonei said. Apparently, Kiernan Strange had helped this friend get over the loss of her father by allowing her to speak to him in some way. It had helped her get closure.

John had not come here for closure, and neither had Lonei, but her friend had said that in addition to helping this friend find closure, Kiernan Strange had helped another friend find a husband. The story, as John remembered it, was that this person had talked to Keirnan Strange who had told her both the time and the place where they would meet and given a detailed description of this man of her dreams.

John didn't buy any of that shit.

His grandmother had been a voodoo priestess. She had a little space in the basement. John remembered her decapitating chickens and writing on his forehead with the blood. "To keep tha spirits out," she would say and chant. John had a fear-laced respect for his grandmother's powers until she was hospitalized with a brain tumor from which she never recovered. It had all been bullshit, all her talk of magic, and his recollections of his grandmother were all tainted with the question; was it her voodoo, or was it the tumor pressing against her thoughts? It wasn't as if the voodoo had helped much anyway.

Lonei finished off the rest of tea and handed the cup to Keirnan. The show was about to start and John was too aware of the fact that he was a mark in it. But then there was always that little grain of doubt.

Strange raised the cup and looked into it. Moved it around so it would catch the fading daylight better. Lonei's hand found John's and they locked fingers. He felt her heartbeat through her palm.

"There is no death in this cup," Strange said. "I see pain, but no death. Your daughter is alive."

Lonei was crying, tears streaming down her face and she squinted and tilted her head. John was betrayed by his own thoughts, as he felt that he allowed himself to believe Strange. As much as his common sense wanted to write this off as nonsense he hung on to those two words together. *No death. Pain, but no death. Your daughter is alive.*

The world contracted. Nothing outside the cramped kitchen existed anymore. All cars were parked, all birds silent, all children still. John inched closer to his wife's side and allowed, for a moment, the walls built around his view of the world to come down.

"There is loss here, a great loss. And a space, see." He turned the cup towards them and pointed to a place the tea leaves, fragmented and moist, had left clear. "There, that's maybe where your Emily is supposed to be."

Her name and John's defenses fell completely. The pain of her loss needed to go somewhere, and he had pushed his fellow officers as much as he could. Maybe this was another line of inquiry for him. Maybe Emily really was somewhere, alive, defying the statistics.

"I also see love. There is a lot of love in the leaves. There is—" He stopped and looked up into the air. Like he had just remembered something. "You have seen difficulty before this," he said and turned the cup in his hands. He blew into it to dry the leaves off. "You will endure this, as you have endured before."

The smell of tea filled the air, mingled with the smell of old incense and food burnt in days past. He was about to show them something on the inside of the cup, but just before he spoke he closed his eyes. The cup fell from his fingers and clanged on the table.

"There's someone here," he said.

Goosebumps came crawling over John's skin, from his forehead downwards. Heard his grandmother's voice, "*There's someone here.*" He saw himself standing in that basement, with a smudge of blood threatening to drip into his eyes. It had never been fully free of chicken feathers, and to this day John would not eat chicken. "*There's someone here*," his grandmother would say to them in that basement. "*Da spirits are come, children*," and they would shake and try to laugh off the fear of their grandmother and her spirits. "*Don't let them inside you, children, or you won't get them out again.*"

And now here, again, in the kitchen of some strange man claiming to be a medium he heard the words, but this time he *wanted* to hear them. Wanted anything to hold on to as his own logic has failed him. What kind of detective can't find his own daughter?

"They are telling me something," Strange said. "Whispering. There's… there's something about a photograph. And a comb. Did Emily have a comb she really liked?"

"Yes," Lonei said and leaned forward. She let go of John's hand and dried her eyes with her sleeves. "Yes, a blue comb. She'd run it through her hair for hours, trying to get out the knots."

"I see it!" Strange said. "I see the blue comb but… it's on the ground. The spirits are showing me that there's a blue comb on a road of yellow bricks."

John wanted to take hold of the table and flip it over and punch the man in his face. Hope restrained him. A feather of hope against a hurricane.

"She's there, she's close to the comb! She's alive. Emily," he said, addressing her directly. "Emily, come home."

For a while he said nothing. The fridge stopped whirring and the silence in the room made it hard to even move. They were encased in cotton, having silver poured into their ears.

"Is she all right?" Lonei asked. "Is she hurt?"

"There's pain," Strange said. "There are leaves on the yellow bricks and the comb is becoming harder to see but it's there. Someone dropped it. I hear sounds. There are… there are. Happiness. This is a happy place, or it was. It's closed now."

His eyelids fluttered as he spoke, eyes unfocused and rolling backwards in their sockets. His lower lip glistened and John hoped a halo might appear as a sign that he was speaking the truth. Or a forked tongue appear to show that he wasn't.

Lonei was enraptured by his words. Finally, after all this time someone was saying things that they could work with. Something for her to hold on to. A few meager morsels of hope to feed a starved heart.

John noticed movement on the floor. A rat had crawled out of a hole in the floor and was sniffing the air. He grabbed the empty tea cup off the table and threw it at the rat. He hit it right in the head and it squeaked in a rain of porcelain shards and it ran back into the wall.

"John!" Lonei exclaimed. Strange had been startled out of his reverie and had stopped talking. "No!" Lonei grabbed a hold of Strange with shaking hands. "What else did you see? Where is she?"

Strange was clearly startled. He looked pale and looked between the two of them without blinking, and then at the rat. "I…"

"Where!" Lonei shouted at him, almost accusingly.

"There was a playground, a park. She was there. I… a white house!"

"She's at the theme park, John," Lonei said.

John had no reply. His thoughts were on the way Strange had looked at the rat, and he had the smell of his grandmother's basement in his nostrils, her voice in his ears. "*There's someone here.*"

"Call them, John! Call them!"

"I can't, Lonei. I can't."

"Don't you…" he saw her breaking, the last straw she was holding onto was slipping and she needed him to pull her up. She had been given a sliver of hope and she wasn't letting go. She was stronger than he was, more tenacious.

He tried to think of someone who owed him a favor. Anyone. He had to have a favor remaining. Or be able to ask for one.

He stood up and walked out into the hallway as he dialed a number. Keirnan Strange was gathering the shards up and putting them in the trash.

There was an answer on the second ring.

"Hello?"

"I need a favor," John said.

-

The Wizard of Oz theme park had once been a place of happiness and unbridled joy. Families would come from out of state to enjoy a day of frivolous, guiltless fun walking down the yellow brick road, making their way through a maze and talking to the Lion and the Tin Man. The smell of cotton candy would mix with the sound of laughter, making grown-up ears feel sticky after the day.

But such popularity is nothing if not fleeting, and in the early Nineties the park closed. A new movie ignited some investor interest but not enough to reopen the park, just enough to prolong the inevitable paving-over and the strip-mall that somehow never came. So the park was left to slowly rot and decay.

A patrol car was there before John Dark arrived, parked outside the entrance gates as if responding to the murder of the Wicked Witch of the West. John parked and he and Lonei got out. It was raining, a cold drizzle.

Two officers exited the patrol car as John and Lonei arrived. The four of them walked to the entrance gate without saying a word. There was a lock and a chain on the gates, high walls surrounding the park. The walls had been a bright and cheery green but the years had pulled the green down to reveal a dull and ragged brown.

"Detective Dark," one of the officers said as he approached. A stout and broad-shouldered man. His badge said Okinimo. John didn't remember seeing him before. "They are bringing the owner over. He'll open up and let us in, Detective."

John looked at the lock and imagined Emily being held on the other side. "I'll buy him another lock," he said as he pulled his gun and shot the chain. The impulsiveness of the act surprised John no less than the noise. The chain rattled as it slid and coiled on the ground like a snake.

Lonei was covering her mouth with her hands. Something burned in John and he kicked the gates open and walked inside.

There was another gate just inside, a small one to direct people to the ticket booths on either side of the path. Weeds and bushes had grown wild in the park. Somewhere a large bird took off, flapping its wings in the night-time drizzle. Otherwise the park was silent.

There was an ominous quality to the park, the faded signs and the faux-happiness plastered on everything. A sign hung tilted over an arch above them. "Welcome to Oz".

"Detective," Okinimo said. He stood beside him, unfazed by John's urgency and recklessness. Good man. He handed John a flashlight and turned another one on. Together they walked on into Oz.

John had to push against his instincts in every step. His gut told him Emily wasn't here. Turning it over in his head, it didn't make sense. But he so longed to see her again, to hold her and tell her that he missed her, and it was her face he saw any time his mind wanted to examine the logic in being here. The flimsy reasoning.

He took another step forward, the beam of his light finding a twisted face staring back from the bushes. It was a winged monkey on roller-skates, a grotesque on rails that ran along the path. A row of them stretched out, waiting for something.

"I went to this park once, as a kid," Okinimo said. "The monkeys would slide along the rail with you and talk at each stop. A sort of guide. But they were always a little too fast or slow."

"Yeah," John said. "I remember."

"What was the tip, Detective?" Okinimo asked. "Why are we here?"

John hadn't thought this through. In effect, he was trespassing, breaking and entering. He would get a chewing out from O'Reilley but any reprimand paled in comparison to finding Emily. He knew he was standing on a rope bridge leading into darkness. The police force was waiting behind him, watching him walk off into an unknown. He felt them judging him, wondering what happened to make such a promising detective go off the rails.

They didn't know. They hadn't lost a child.

"Eyewitnesses place a missing child here recently," John answered. He felt the lie as it came out, and he couldn't take it back.

"Reliable?" Okinimo asked.

"Reliable enough," John said and picked up the pace.

The beams played over a path of yellow bricks littered with leaves and twigs, made dark in the rain. The pattern made it look like they were walking on the back of a yellow python.

Something fell with a crash ahead of them. They raised their flashlights but the beams were no match for the misty rain. John ran.

"Emily?" he called out into the dark and it echoed back to him through the rain. "Emil…" out of breath, almost out of hope. Desperation pushing at his back, with hopelessness and defeat waiting their turn.

John ran along the road, turned and stopped. He was standing in front of a house. Originally a recreation of Dorothy's house in the book, crooked and tilting after the tornado dropped it in Oz, it now looked haunted. In the park's brighter days, groups of people would walk through the house, decorated in the style of a Fifties

Kansas farmhouse. Now, the windows were broken and the front door hung open on a single hinge. Leaves and dirt covered the roof and weeds pulled at the porch, as if trying to drag the house down into the ground. The Wicked Witch's feet stood out from under the porch, pointed toes pointing skyward. John thought he saw them twitch as he moved the flashlight beam away from them and quickly moved the beam back. This time the feet remained still.

Okinimo caught up to him and his radio screeched with static and then a voice. "The owner is here. He's not happy we shot up his chain but he's going to turn the power on for us. Detective Dark's wife is walking in ahead of me to find you guys, where are you?"

"We're at Dorothy's house," Okinimo replied. "About to go in."

John stepped onto the porch. It creaked loudly under his weight and he wasn't sure it would hold. Another step and another step. Leaving the yellow brick road to enter a house from a story. The house fell on a witch in the book and then was abandoned, the girl going off on adventures with new friends, only returning home through some magic. The debris on the porch seemed somewhat sparser in front of the door. Maybe someone had been in and out recently. Emily had been missing for three weeks. John didn't want to think about her state if she had been in this house all that time.

John bent down and played his flashlight beam back and forth, examining the space in front of the door. Broken twigs, weeds kicked aside, faint coloring from berries crushed. Someone had been here, going in and out of the house regularly. He took a step inside.

His flashlight beam seemed constricted inside the house, as if the air here were thicker. Little motes of dust, and a darkness that seemed to dislike the light. A bulb popped in a lamp socket and startled John to within an inch of his life, with his gun out and pointing it at a small lamp in a corner of what must be a living room. Outside, a few lights were lit, none really reaching into the darkness here though.

Okinimo's radio hissed.

"We got the power back on."

"No lights in the house," Okinimo called back.

John was breathing quickly.

What was that smell?

He walked briskly into a hallway. The floor was wood, with wide gaps in between boards. A musty red carpet on the floor running the length of the hallway. Mushrooms grew in the far corner. Two doors on either side and a large window at the end. No light outside the window, just the dark looking in.

He opened the first door on the right. It was a bathroom. Tub full of stagnant yellow water which rippled as the air in the room moved around. John covered his nose and mouth with the crook of his elbow. Syringes and needles on the sink. Brown stains and bent spoons.

He stepped back into the hallway. Opened the door on his left. Okinimo stood beside him. They exchanged a glance but no words. John pushed the door open with his flashlight, which lit up a kitchen of sorts. Clearly meant to imitate a Fifties-style kitchen, it just managed to look creepy. The grime of years of neglect crawled up the walls and tiles. A dark mess in the sink that was spreading out onto the counter. Curtains pulled to the side, rotting.

Roaches fled from the beam.

John let the door close and stepped further down the hall. The wood creaked under his step but he didn't hear. Nothing registered now except a growing lump in his throat and a cold emptiness in his stomach. Had Emily been here? Had she died in this horrible place. Forced to— John stopped his train of thought. There were too many possibilities if she *had* been here, and none of them were good. Thinking of them brought nothing good.

He thought instead of the repercussions if the medium was wrong. He'd called the force. Two patrol cars were here, he'd shot up a lock and broken in, trespassing. All on the word of a man who claimed to speak to spirits. Goosebumps, slithering and sliding along his skin as he was suddenly gripped by a million what-ifs.

His step was less sure as he approached the next door and pushed at it. Something was blocking it. He looked at Okinimo. He pushed harder and felt a little give. He was able to open a sliver and was rewarded with the strong smell of decay. A mass of ants tumbled about and roaches scurried.

"Body," John said as he realized what the dark mass on the floor was. Decomposed and half-eaten by insects, but unmistakable, even through just the little sliver in the doorway. It was up against the door so it was hard to open without disturbing it. "It's a body!" John said again to Okinimo. "Call it in!"

Okinimo was still. A statue of a police officer standing in Dorothy's house in an abandoned park. It was an image John often thought back to, the adrenaline making everything clear and slow; Officer Okinimo, to whom he had for some reason not spoken after this, no interaction apart from a gentle nod of the head if they passed each other at the station, standing there with his mouth slightly open, his head illuminated only from the odd angle of a flashlight beam.

Darkness still pressed against the hallway window, witnessing all this.

"Emily?" John said weakly. "Oh no no no no." He pushed hard against the door and squeezed in but the body, still pressing against it, closed it again, leaving Okinimo in the hallway alone.

The floor was literally crawling with roaches and insects. The window had been boarded up, so even the meager light outside didn't get in. It was only the flashlight beam which, as John moved it over the room, showed him the horror. There were two bodies, badly decomposed and crawling with maggots and beetles, what John had thought were roaches. The stench of decomposition forced its long fingers into John's nose and felt about his throat and lungs. Syringes on the floor, a mass of mold that might have been food at one point, slivers of black moisture seeping down along the walls, flies buzzing, happy that there was now more flesh in the room to feast on.

"Emily?" he said weakly, crying. Flashlight went back and forth between the bodies but there was no way to tell anything about the people they had been. John covered his mouth and nose and went to the door, bugs crackling under his feet. He pulled at the door, forcing the body aside and stirring up the mass crawling over it. He pulled harder, opening the door half-way and forcing his way out.

"It's not her," he said. "It's not her." Not knowing how he knew. He just knew. Emily was still missing, and for once, John was glad of it. Better missing than dead like this.

O'Reilley, enraged but understanding, had suspended John for two weeks without pay. Destroying private property, trespassing, and all on the flimsiest of leads. The bodies were of two men; nineteen and twenty-five. Both had most likely overdosed on heroin in the house. The fact that there had indeed been bodies in the house was, according to O'Reilley, the only reason John was not suspended indefinitely.

The park owner was fined for a number of infractions with regards to health and safety. He was currently counter-suing the police department for destruction of property, seeking millions.

John and Lonei didn't talk much for weeks. She blamed him for disturbing Kiernan Strange just as he was about to give them the location of their daughter. She went to him twice after that, John knew that, but she never said anything to him about what transpired.

Returning to duty, the former looks of reassurance from his fellow officers had turned to looks of pity. They all felt sorry for the once-promising Detective Dark, now an empty shell of a man.

John's dislike of mediums and psychics became a ball of hate at the center of his being. He'd argue fiercely with anyone about religion and spirituality, putting it all under the same hat of "utter fucking bullshit, believed only by morons." It didn't help.

Weeks turned to months, and the leads dried up. Emily Dark once missing, was now simply gone. Another cold case, buried under the next missing girl's files, and the next and the next.

Only Monique's attitude towards him remained unchanged. Monique alone seemed to accept this new John, unfazed by rumors or accusations of misusing his position or the police itself. She was the rock John hung to for his life as the current threatened to pull him under.

Once, in his darkest moment, John sat on the end of his bed with his gun in his hands. Lonei was away, Orlando staying with a friend. The gun felt heavy. Final. A way to move on somehow, not a way to end things. He didn't raise it with any intent but the thought was there, and a tingling in his fingers. As he cried, hoping for the courage to make a choice instead of continuing this nothing of an existence, it was Monique's voice in his head that held him.

"No John. She's still out there. Let's find her. Let's find her."

Chapter Twenty-One

The sun stretched a few fingers through the wind-tossed clouds, touching the ground for a moment and then receding, relinquishing rule of the earth to the storm. Daniel stood on a narrow sidewalk and shivered. Behind him lay the cemetery, a peaceful and quiet place during the day but now, in the late afternoon light of grey clouds and rain it felt uninviting. He drew his thin coat closer and looked over at the man who had appeared in his apartment.

The medium hadn't seen him, hadn't been able to take him off Daniel's hands. Instead, the spirits had followed him from that room, pleading with him to talk to their loved ones, to avenge their deaths. A few had stranger requests. Daniel Hope ignored them all, but felt compelled to help this man, Troy. At least he might get his apartment to himself again. Or maybe prove to himself that, schizophrenia or not, there was something to be gained here.

To Daniel, despite the setting sun and dim daylight of deep gray clouds, the world seemed brighter somehow. The thin slivers of sunlight that managed to break through here and there were like a god of some kind was stabbing swords of light through the clouds and into the ground.

"This is your house?" Daniel asked.

"Yes," Troy answered. He appeared, to Daniel at least, like any normal person might. Nothing about him hinted that he wasn't real, nothing to make Daniel think he wasn't actually there, apart from the man's own pleas. And the fact that nobody but Daniel paid him any attention. Though, in the world as it was now, that wasn't saying much. Everyone just trying their best to get through the day, head down.

They stood in front of what Troy said was his house. The street was normal enough, apart from the fact that the other side of the street was a cemetery with high walls. Daniel heard things on the other side of the wall that he tried to ignore. He looked instead at the tree that took up most of the yard in front of the house. A tangle of branches, like a wooden artery rising from the ground and breaking up into smaller and smaller veins reaching into the sky. It reminded him of images of streams from above, gathering into a river. What was it pumping into the air?

A car drove along the street and turned into the driveway.

"That's her," Troy said. He had been growing faint. There were moments when he faded, became insubstantial.

The woman exited the car and went to the trunk. She opened it and pulled out paper bags of groceries and then awkwardly closed the trunk with two bags in her hands. She looked at Daniel as he approached but didn't pay them any mind.

"Talk to her," Troy said to Daniel, worried that they might lose their chance.

"I'm doing it," Daniel said.

The woman looked at him again, a brief look of worry crossing her brow. She took faster steps toward the house.

"Excuse me," Daniel said.

"Clarissa," Troy said to Daniel. "Her name's Clarissa."

"Clarissa," Daniel added. She turned and looked at him. She was standing by the hood of the car, still holding both bags, her hair, long and brown, whipped and snapped in the wind. She wore a bright red sports jacket that looked expensive, black jeans and leather boots.

"I'm sorry," she said. "Do I know you?"

Daniel looked at Troy inquisitively.

"She can't see me," he said. "Really, she can't. I'm dead."

Daniel turned to her. "I, uhhm, I know Troy."

"Oh?" The mention of the name made her stand a little straighter. Took a bit of the worry out of her stance. The sadness that flickered in her eyes stood out to Daniel, a quick dimming behind the eyes that she recovered from almost immediately. But there it was. Unmistakable.

Daniel shielded his eyes from the laser-bright rays of sun sneaking their way through the clouds as a storm ripped them apart like cotton. The few birds singing in the trees in the yard sounded really close, as if he were sitting alongside them on the branches.

"I have a message from him," Daniel said. "Like a request."

"A request?"

"Yes. He asked me to..." Daniel didn't know how to continue. This sounded crazy. "He told me before he... he told me..."

"I'm sorry," Clarissa said. "How did you know Troy?"

"I don't, not really. I mean, I just met him. No," Daniel didn't want to do this. He heard how ridiculous he sounded. He thought of Stacy, and the look she got when he tried to explain how *they* would listen in on their phone calls. That same look was now on Clarissa's face. Daniel wondered what Stacy was doing. Wondered why he wondered.

"Tell her I want to see Olivia," Troy said, his voice now on the verge of breaking.

"He says he wants to see Olivia."

"Says?" Clarissa asked.

"Yes, he..." Daniel worried at a fingernail with his thumb. He looked at Troy, whose gaze was on Clarissa. There was so much emotion in the way he was looking at this woman that Daniel's heart nearly broke, cracked and strange like his head. He saw the mild madness in Troy, the little, innocent madness called love. It was clear in the way Troy stood, the way his fingers reached out for Clarissa. He could almost hear the heartbeat, feel the tension between them.

"This will sound strange, I know, but Troy is here."

Clarissa had nothing but fury for Daniel. "You fucking... who the hell do you think—" but she didn't finish, just turned away from them, still holding the groceries in each hand and thundered toward her house.

"Tell her she cut her finger in the hotel in Paris, it wouldn't stop bleeding," Troy said.

"You cut your finger in the hotel in Paris. Troy said... Troy told me to say that to you. He's here. He said it didn't stop bleeding."

Troy walked towards her and now stood between Clarissa and Daniel. He looked at her as he spoke.

"Tell her we had to skip going to dinner, to the Michelin-star restaurant."

"You couldn't go to dinner, because the finger, the bleeding. It was a Michelin-star place."

Clarissa stood deathly still in front of the door to her house.

"How do you know that?" she asked without turning, she was angry, not surprised. An accusatory note in her voice. "What is it you want? Is this some sort of scam?"

"No," Daniel said. "Troy is really here. I don't want to be here, I was going to the—"

Daniel spoke as Troy spoke, hearing himself as an echo of sorts.

"You're afraid of spiders, he says. You eat a spoonful of peanut butter in front of the TV most nights, but only one spoon. It's to keep you from eating chocolate."

Clarissa turned and faced Daniel. Her face was a storm of rage and deep sorrow.

"He says he's sorry. He says you were fighting that night, the night he… you were fighting and he rushed out and he says he's sorry, he's so sorry about what he said to you."

"Who *are* you?" she asked.

"He says he didn't mean it, of course he didn't mean it."

Clarissa dropped the groceries but didn't seem to notice. Oranges and a carton of milk fell onto the porch. Something broke but Clarissa didn't take her eyes off Daniel as he continued speaking Troy's words.

"He wants to see Olivia. You know, Clarissa wanted to name her Toni, like the writer."

Clarissa looked confused at that.

"Oh, he says that was just for me."

"How is he?" Clarissa asked. "I mean, oh I don't know what I mean, I'm not sure what's going on."

"He wants to see Olivia. Where is she?"

"At a friend's house. I don't, can you tell him I'm sorry?"

"He's here," Daniel said and pointed at Troy. "He can see you and hear you."

Clarissa looked where Daniel pointed. She looked near Troy, not directly at him but not far off. "I'm sorry I was so mean. I'm sorry about how everything—" but she couldn't continue.

"He says he was jumped," Daniel said. "He was walking back from the store when two guys tried to mug him. He was still so angry that he told them to fuck off, that they had picked on the wrong guy. But they shot him. There was a bit of darkness at first, and then just light for a while. It was… like he had a rubber band tied to his soul and he just was suddenly standing here, in front of the house.

"He can't go far away from the spot or he gets the same rubber-band feeling and has to come back. He watches you and Olivia. He says he's tried to talk to you many times but has accepted his fate. Maybe it's his punishment."

She was visibly crying now, heavy sobs.

Daniel wondered if this was *his* punishment for something.

"How are you doing this? *Why?*"

"Please. He says he can't go into the house but if you would. Please, just ask Olivia to play by the tree sometimes. If the two of you would… sit by the tree together."

Clarissa, guarded against Daniel but clearly unable to contain her grief, nodded.

"I'll do that. Tell him I'll do that."

"He hears you," Daniel said.

He looked at Troy and Troy, crying, just nodded with muted gratitude and looked at Clarissa.

Daniel watched them and felt a closure of sorts. Feeling content, he walked away and left them to their grief, both the living and the dead. He walked along the other side of the street and, thoughtlessly, wandered into the graveyard.

Chapter Twenty-Two

The quickest way for them to view the security footage from the Ortega apartment was on the system itself at the building. The room they offered Monique contained a sleek desk with a computer screen, a mouse and sharp corners. It was a small room off to the side of the reception hall and had a pile of boxes in a corner and little else. If she were to lay down her feet would touch one wall and her head the opposite one.

The security guard on duty wasn't the one who had told them the ghost story in the elevator.

"Just you?" he replied. He didn't look like he could chase anyone down but had a stern look to him. Monique liked him but couldn't tell why.

"*Si*," she replied, taking a chance after seeing his name tag. It said Francisco Hernandez Lopez and she didn't feel like it was a stretch.

"*Bien*," he said. "*Déjame saber si necesitas algo.*"

"*Gracias*," she said and closed the door. She sat down and for a moment indulged herself by getting down on the floor on her hands and knees, placing her ear against the ground and listening for shouts from the ghosts of any trapped bootleggers. She heard nothing.

The chair was set a little high for her but she couldn't figure out how to lower it so she was forced to sit hunched forward. Asking the guard for help with lowering a chair would be embarrassing.

John had gone to meet with the bartender who claimed to have some information about Emily to offer. Monique couldn't fault John for still following up on leads into Emily's case. She had done some questionable things for Valeria herself.

She dreaded this, felt a heaviness breathing and the small room seemed to be contracting. She wished it had a window. Monique was about to view a murder. A woman killed in her own home, by her own husband.

The job hardens you. Life prepares you for some things and the world itself makes you expect a certain amount of unfairness. But this was a known; at some point on the tape she was about to view, Maria Ortega would be stabbed to death and the only justice Monique could offer her was to not shy away as it happened. To witness it and record it and prepare it as evidence to put Ruiz Ortega in prison for the rest of his life.

Of course she shouldn't decide that he was guilty, of course she should wait for a jury to decide, but goddamnit if she didn't just burn that little bit inside. A fire of dread and despair for all the women killed in their homes and on the streets, every day.

The tape rolled. It was clearer than the Stillwater tape and had audio, though the first minutes had no sounds since no one was home. The Ortegas arrived home at 8:22 p.m. and it was as Ruiz Ortega had described; they came home and though little was said there was a tension in them that told Monique they had indeed probably been arguing in the car. Maria went off to the side and out of view of the camera. The screen was split, showing four views of the apartment. The living room, a dining room off the living room, the kitchen and a roomy office and workspace. No cameras showing the bedroom or bathroom.

Ruiz walked over to the grand piano and looked out over the city. He then went over to the kitchen and poured himself a drink. He appeared calm, if a little stiff. He turned as if responding to a sound and then he just fell down. Ruiz Ortega stood in the living room with a drink in his hand and then he crumpled backwards into a heap. A few seconds passed and Ortega stood back up, his movements now stilted and awkward and Monique wondered if he was having a heart attack or a stroke.

The glass had broken loudly on the marble tiles and crunched under his feet as he walked. He seemed to ignore it and walked into the kitchen.

"Maria," he called out and a coldness pressed down on Monique's stomach. It was as if there were two voices, a distortion on the audio. Ruiz walked into the kitchen and got a knife, pulled it awkwardly from a magnetic strip, like Wabash had said. He walked back into the living room.

Maria called out from the living room, "What, Ruiz?" Her voice was clear. There was nothing wrong with the audio.

"What?" she called again when he didn't reply.

Ruiz Ortega was standing by the piano again. The broken glass must have been cutting into the soles of his feet but he seemed not to notice or care. "Maariaaaa…" he called, almost sing-song.

She walked towards him, cursing in Portuguese and then as she came nearer he turned on the spot and stabbed her in the stomach. He screamed at her and stabbed her again. She staggered backwards and Monique watched as he raised the knife and stabbed down, and then a clean straight cut into the heart and Maria Ortega fell to the floor.

But Ruiz was not done, no. He hacked at her and screamed, the scream like two people shouting at once. Monique was stifling her feelings, pushing down the revulsion, but she was sure that there was a woman shouting along with Ruiz.

There was no gun to his head, no phone call prior, nothing but his intent to kill his wife.

He stopped and was unnaturally still for a long time. The only thing that told Monique that the recording hadn't stopped was the slow trickle of blood from Maria's body. Then with a twitch Ruiz's arm shot out and slammed the knife onto a small table.

He got up and looked around, his gaze settling on a pillow. He cut it open and roughly expelled the feathers, yanking out handfuls and tossing them at the floor by Maria's body. He took the knife back and cut her clothes, a straight line from the—

And then Monique's phone rang.

-

Monique paused the video and picked up her phone. She didn't recognize the number but answered anyway; anything was better than what she was watching.

"Hello?"

Silence on the line.

"Hello?"

Then a voice she knew. It was hoarse and vulnerable but so strong at the same time.

"Hi, Mama."

Valeria was eleven when she decided that Spanish was something that belonged to her mother and she would only talk to her in English. She had been twelve the first time she had smoked marijuana and it had gone downhill quickly from there. Monique was single and worked a lot and Valeria had been a strong independent kid but somehow fell in with a wrong crowd and into a pit of drugs so deep that when Monique noticed she was too far down to save.

Monique had never loved her more than right now, alone in a cramped room, watching a man kill his wife. She was vulnerable and afraid and Valeria always, always spoke right to her heart.

It took all Monique had to keep it together.

"*Ola* Valeria. How are you?"

"I'm... I'm gonna go to that place. The clinic. Mama, I'm gonna go. I just..."

"*Sí?*" Monique had fallen for it before. Valeria, now twenty, had said she wanted to get clean and promised to go to a clinic, first at fifteen and again at seventeen. So Monique had booked her in and paid a deposit but Valeria hadn't shown up, and had instead gone home and stolen a lot of money while her mother waited for her at the clinic.

Monique bought the safe after that.

"Yeah, Mama, I'm going to do it. There's some strange stuff going on and I just want out."

"What strange stuff?" Monique asked.

Monique stood up and walked out of the room. She nodded to the guard as she walked past the small reception and out into the night. She couldn't talk to her daughter with Maria and Ruiz on the screen in front of her. Outside, cars sped past on the busy street. It felt like a different world.

Valeria didn't answer so Monique thought maybe she hadn't heard her.

"Valeria, are you all right?"

"Yeah, I'm just. I'll go, you know. I have to, I just need you to—"

"I'm not paying another deposit, Valeria. Not after last time, and not after what you did on my rug."

"That wasn't me, Mama, I swear, it was Navajo. He thought it was funny."

"I don't care who did it, it was your doing."

"Mama, listen." There was a tone in Valeria's voice she hadn't heard in a while. She called every now and then, asking for money, but this was new. "Mama, I have to get clean. There's… can you pick me up?"

"I can't now, Valeria, I really can't. I can send a car for you."

"No police, they'll kill me."

"Taxi then. I'll send a taxi and you can go home." Then she remembered that she had changed the locks. "Go home, but you can't go inside. Maybe just wait for me in the backyard?"

"When will you be home?" That tone again. It was like she was five, saying she couldn't fall asleep because she was afraid of burglars. Maybe this was just a new trick.

"I don't know baby, I have to…" *I have to watch a man stick feathers on the body of the wife he just stabbed to death.* "I have to work. I'll call a taxi and pay in advance. Where are you?"

Valeria gave her the address and Monique called a taxi. She wondered what sort of shit her daughter had gotten into this time. It had to be bad if she was willing to admit to Monique that she was scared. And she had sounded it.

Monique looked up at the sky. It was a smog-tinged blue but a blue nonetheless. Sunshine reflected off the building across the street and people walked by, couples and young women and families. She envied every one of them and would, if asked, trade her life with any of them. The feeling passed and Monique turned and walked back into a haunted building to return to her lot in life, return to a duty that had only the darkest, grimmest of realities.

Her phone rang again as she was about to enter the room. It was John.

"Monique!" John sounded like he was running. "It was good, the bartender came through."

"What did he have?"

"I'll tell you when we meet. What's on the tape?"

"Ortega did it. But it's strange. Remember the way Stillwater walked down the stairs?"

"Yeah?"

"It's the same. He had a drink just before and fainted and then when he stood up he – maybe it's something in the drink." Just realizing it as she said it.

"What about the feathers?"

"I'm just getting to that. I had to… I had to take a break."

"I'm coming," John said. "Wait for me with the rest, okay?"

Monique had never been so happy to wait for someone in her life.

-

It took John almost an hour to get across the short distance to the building the Ortegas lived in. When he arrived, Monique was outside, and it seemed to John like she was pacing. If she were a smoker, John thought, there would be a dozen butts scattered around the sidewalk.

"John," she said. "Finally."

They walked inside. John greeted the security guy who hardly looked up at them as they walked past him into the small room.

"What?" John asked. Monique was usually very professional in everything she did but she seemed very much on edge. "Was it that bad?"

"Yeah. Yeah but, it's not that John. It's Valeria. She just called and she wants to come home."

Valeria. The daughter that Monique lost. John knew she was the reason that Monique was so willing to look past everything John did after Emily disappeared. She had a missing girl of her own. Missing in a different way.

"That's good, right?"

"I guess. But she was scared, John. Something has her scared. I ordered her a taxi and told her to wait for me at home."

"So what then?"

"I don't know. I've fallen for it before."

"You're there for her. That's all you can do."

They sat in silence for a while in the small room, Monique on the chair that was too high and John on a foldable metal one. They thought of their children, and of their failures as parents. The room, sterile and still, offered no respite from their thoughts. Nothing for the eye or the mind to rest on except the screen.

"Let's take a look at the rest," John said.

Monique pressed play on the video and they watched as Ruiz Ortega turned his wife over and cut her clothes off. His mannerisms had changed; no longer angry and stiff, his movements had become smoother and there was a gentleness to how he touched Maria. Once he had removed all her clothes he fetched a wet towel and scrubbed her back and hands clean.

He then got more pillows and cut them open and made a mound of feathers on the floor next to her body. In the course of opening the pillows and getting the feathers out, tearing and ripping, feathers were lifted into the air and floated down onto the floor around the body. It was almost as if they were not in an apartment but in a field, open to a winter evening's gentle snowfall.

"What is he doing?" Monique said.

"And *why*?" John added.

He took a single feather from the mound and dabbed a finger in blood and then on her arm. He placed the feather onto the smudge of crimson on her arm and then did it again. Gently, slowly.

"What is that… is he singing?"

"I'll turn up the audio," Monique said. She had turned it down when he stabbed Maria. Silencing the screams.

And unmistakably, Ruiz Ortega sang as he daubed his finger in her blood and, feather by feather, turned her arms into the outstretched wings of a swan in flight. If not for the brutality, it was almost beautiful.

John strained to recognize what he was singing "What is that, some sort of nursery rhyme?"

"It's not English."

"Spanish?"

"No, not Spanish either."

They watched on in silence as he covered her arms in feathers and then took a rose and tied her legs with the long stems.

"How are these so similar?" Monique said. "Did they plan this in advance? Did they make a pact in that school?"

They watched on, their spirits again hammered by the ugliness of the world. These two detectives who once had the spirit and drive to change an ugly world now just wished it didn't have to be so bad so often. It was hard to remember that there was goodness and beauty when confronted with such darkness.

After Ruiz Ortega had completed his decorating of the body, he sat down on a sofa and seemed to be admiring his work. He kept signing the song. It was short, just two verses, so he sang it over and over as he worked and he sang it still as he sat down. He seemed to be falling asleep.

They were both startled as Ruiz Ortega suddenly shook and looked around the apartment as if seeing it for the first time. He leaned over his wife's body and turned it over.

"Maria? Maria?!"

He put his hand in the blood and touched the cuts and ran to the phone. He came back to her, holding the phone, repeating her name.

"Yes, my wife, she's been killed. She's… there's blood, please help me. Help me!"

He was no longer singing.

Chapter Twenty-Three

John Dark sat in the passenger side of their car as the city thinned out into strip-malls and McDonald's. There was a pool of cars at the station, cars meant to be low-key, to blend in. Nothing flashy but nothing trash either. On paper you were free to take any car anytime you needed one for police business, but the unspoken convention was that you picked one once and stuck to it. Theirs was an older model, an American sedan. Fast, and comfortable enough, but turned like a hippo on skates.

A drizzle of rain settled on the windshield and was wiped off with a squeak from the wipers.

"This is bullshit," John said.

"What?"

John was trying to find something about the Vestigial Flock on his phone as they drove.

"This Vestigial Flock, it's what the bartender led me on to, it's bullshit. Emily didn't run off to join a religious cult. We don't even… it's…"

"It's the ultimate teenage rebellion thing, when your father is John Dark?" Monique said.

She tightened the grip on the steering wheel. Bracing for what would come.

John didn't say anything. Anger swelled within but there was a modicum of self-awareness that held it in check. Was she right? Could this be an act of rebellion against a father that didn't tolerate religion in his house, lectured his kids if they spoke of alternative medicine or psychics?

"Emily wouldn't—"

"I know, I'm sorry."

Would she? They hadn't had the best of father-daughter relationships, but did anyone really have that with his teenage daughter?

According to his research, The Vestigial Flock used to be a thing, back around the Great Depression. Traveling preachers who would take on anyone who would listen to the word of God and live according to a few set rules. People were attracted to the food mostly though, as they had a farm where things actually still grew.

"It's all starting to look the same, you know?" Monique said. Maybe she felt she had to change the subject. Avoid an awkward silence, even though John felt they were above that.

"What?"

"The U.S. – it's all starting to look the same. Rural flat motels and strip-malls smeared thin between cities of shiny high-rises and urban sprawl. Is there anything unique anymore? Anything that's actually new and American?"

"It's not so bad," John said as they passed a small Home Depot next to a boarded-up storefront. Parking lots in front of brand-name stores mixed in with more boarded-up retail outlets. He wasn't sure that he could see America from here. "Niagara falls? Savannah Georgia?"

"You're not taking me seriously," Monique said.

"I don't like it when you philosophize," John said.

A stream of water ran along the side of the road, the light of the setting sun reflected in it, but in too many colors. *Water should just reflect the one*, John thought. *That water ain't right.*

"I don't think America exists anymore," Monique said.

John put his phone away. The internet had very little for him on the Vestigial Flock. He sighed.

"What do you mean?"

"The concept died with, I don't know, Kennedy."

"'America died when John F. Kennedy was gunned down' claims the female Latino immigrant who is also a detective with a police force in the United States," John said, faking incredulity.

"I'm not an immigrant, John," she said. "And I'm half French. Not a lot of Mexicans called Monique, you know."

"Fair enough, but you see my point?"

"I just mean that the ideals we held on to so hard once, they've all been abandoned for never-ending war and tax cuts for the rich and a constant reduction in welfare."

"I know what you mean," John said. "I know. But the people vote for that shit over and over, because they want to be on *that* side once."

"What side is that, John?"

"The rich white-guy side. If they vote for the sleaze-bag they themselves might one day become *that* sleaze-bag. Just once, you know. I think that's why all these people vote Republican. If you vote Democrat it's like admitting that you *need* the safety net, that you need access to welfare and Medicaid and affirmative action and—"

"Or maybe you're just white," Monique added.

"Yeah, or that, but it's not that simple. Plenty of white people are black too. They just don't want to admit it, so they vote—"

Monique pulled the steering wheel sharply to the left, into the other lane and then back just as quickly. John just managed to put his hand on the door to avoid slamming his head against the window.

"What the hell?" he asked.

"Sorry, there was something on the road."

They were now driving along a narrow street with trees on either side. Deep country.

"My main point is, John, the point I wanted to make, is that you can no longer 'become whatever you want' in the U.S. The American Dream is dead."

"That is such a bad cliché," John said.

He liked these conversations with Monique. Apart from his wife, she was the smartest person he knew. Her brand of smart came with an edge of real-world sharpness. The daughter of immigrants, she saw the world differently than most. Clearer. But she was fatalistic, John thought, not allowing for much wiggle room for the human spirit.

"Tell me I'm wrong, John. A kid born to heroin addicts in the Heights, how much of a chance at the American Dream does he really have? A Cubano girl born to illegal immigrants picking oranges in Florida? You think they're going to find a book on engineering among the orange trees and become astronauts?"

"Their chances are certainly better than if they lived in Bangladesh," John said.

"That's not what I mean. Or wait. That's exactly what I mean, where you are born and who your parents are is like 95% of what you can achieve in life. We hold the outliers up as heroes but disregard the fact that almost everyone else gets stuck in a trap unwittingly set by their parents."

John didn't have anything for that. His dad had been a cop. Damn, was Monique right? Trump's dad had also been a useless, racist millionaire.

"Obama," John said, as if he had just made a real discovery.

"Oh, give me a break, John."

"He's an example of—"

John didn't finish. The trees opened up as they drove under an iron arch marked with the words "Whitesands." John shivered and images of blood on walls flashed in his mind, along with the all-too-well-known metal arch over the entrance to Auschwitz.

"Well that looks nice," Monique said.

Whitesands came into view. It was a gray-brown building of impressive size. A large central building with a clocktower and to either side stretched two wings of cement and small windows. Something about the proportion of the windows made John think of teeth in a grimace.

Only a few cars were parked in front, one of them an impressive Range Rover, the latest model, in a space marked "Headmaster."

"I bet that thing gets keyed a lot." Monique said as they parked next to it. They got out of their standard-issue Chevy which looked like, well, a police department's Chevy next to a Range Rover.

A creek snaked its way past one side of the building, and tall trees threw long shadows outwards from the streetlights dotted near the school.

–

Whitesands clearly had a history. It was a history that was thrust upon you as you entered, with large portraits of successful alumni on the walls. Grim white faces stared down at you, the portraits placed unusually high on the walls.

The foyer was two stories high, with a block of a staircase in front as you entered. To the left and right, double doors were open into what John assumed were dorms on either side. Glass cabinets showcasing trophies stood against the walls under the portraits and John walked up to one to examine. Chess and archery seemed to be the school's pride and joy.

"I didn't know archery was such a big thing," Monique said over John's shoulder.

"Archery is the sport of the gods."

They turned swiftly, an element to the voice making John feel as if he had just been caught doing something he shouldn't have been doing.

"My name is Richard Keyes, headmaster of Whitesands," the man said. He was thin and had a complexion like an earthworm pinned into a black suit.

"Richard Keyes?" John asked.

"Yes. How can I help you?"

John held out his hand. "Detective Dark. This is Detective Moreno. We are here to speak to you regarding—"

"Ah, the detectives from the city. Follow me please, I'll answer any questions you have, though I don't see what this has to do with Whitesands."

"No, of course. Thank you. We're trying to keep some facts of the case out of the press, for now."

The few students that walked past them were all well-dressed, Whitesands clearly not a place where students wore pajama pants and clever T-shirts. They followed Keyes up the stairs, sharp mahogany worn down and waxed through the ages so that now it was wavy and smooth.

"Whitesands is an old school, a proud school."

"I read that this was one of the last schools to desegregate in the entire country," John said. Prodding, always prodding.

"Yes. Not all of our history is something to be proud of, any more than any country. Everyone has something about them that, in a certain light, can be misconstrued."

Keyes led them to the right at the top of the stairs. "The school was built in 1738, as a hospital at first, but was closed down and sold in 1902. It has been a school since 1905, proudly preparing many of our country's greatest for leadership and business."

Keyes slipped on a step and almost fell but John caught him with an outstretched arm. Keyes looked back at John, at the hand holding him up. There was a moment when John thought he saw anger in his eyes, as if John had caused him to take a false step, but it softened quickly and was replaced by what felt like an insincere gratitude.

"Thank you, Officer Dark. These stairs can be a bit slippery."

"Detective," John said as he let him go.

"Yes, indeed. Now, my office is just here to the left."

They walked on, Monique turning towards John and mouthing the words "What the fuck?"

-

Richard Keyes's office was as John had expected. The windows faced out towards the woods at the back of the school, with more of the tall, bare trees visible, along with tennis courts in the distance. He sat behind an overly large desk and picked up a letter-opener.

"This was a gift to me from the previous Headmaster. Orville Masterson-Oates was a great man, and he kept a certain discipline here at Whitesands that might seem, by modern standards, to be a bit draconic."

He picked up an envelope from a small pile of incoming mail, stabbed the letter-opener into it and rather roughly opened it, tearing more than cutting. He then placed the envelope, without removing the contents, on the other side of the desk. He looked at them while he did this, but said nothing.

John was expecting to hear more about the previous headmaster when Monique cut in.

"Mr. Keyes, are you familiar with the names Michael Stillwater and Ruiz Ortega?"

Keyes picked up another letter. He inserted the small blade into the top of the envelope and slowly dragged it across, the sound of paper being cut filling the office. As if he were trying to remember something.

"Yes. As it happens, I am. They were students here, oh, about thirty years ago. Graduated in '89 I should think."

"That's some memory, Mr. Keyes," John said.

"Well, Detective, I graduated a year later. I remember them well though they were, unremarkable, in terms of the students we graduate here."

A bookshelf behind the headmaster was filled with books on leadership and history, along with framed certificates of some sort and a picture of the headmaster himself shaking hands with George W. Bush. It felt a little over the top and still somehow expected. Cliché.

"Were they friends?" Monique asked.

"Is that what this visit is about? What happened – there was a rather unfortunate incident where a pupil went missing and Stillwater, Ortega, and three others were said to have had something to do with it."

"Wait. Three others?"

"Yes, I think they were Chastain and... no, sorry I can't recall the names of the others. It was in the papers at the time, made quite a splash. Unfortunately."

John and Monique looked at each other.

"Were they found?" John asked. "The missing pupil?"

"No, she never was. Ran away is what happened. She'd done it before. Not everyone is Whitesands material."

"But why question those five then?"

"Well, as I recall, witnesses said they saw the girl go with them out into the woods here," he said and pointed out the window with the letter opener. "There was an inquiry and a bit of a media frenzy. Of course, they were cleared of all wrongdoing. This is not an inner-city school, detectives." Somehow managing to make that sound dirty and beneath him, while also looking directly at them as he spoke. There was an implication there that John decided to let slide. It wasn't the worst that had been implied about him.

"What happened?" Monique asked.

"Why, the press dragged the Whitesands name into a sordid courtroom drama. Needlessly, as it turns out; the poor students had nothing to do with the runaway girl," Keyes said. He took up another envelope and opened it. He was not removing the contents, just opening the envelopes.

"I meant the missing girl," Monique said.

"She was never found. Like I said, a runaway."

"Wait, she was *never* found? As in still missing?"

"Yes. Very sad. Her parents made quite a bit of fuss about it but there was nothing to be done. The girl had run away. Packed a suitcase and left."

"What was her name, Mr. Keyes?"

"I think it was," he paused. "Alice... Alice Whitacre."

"Thank you. Perhaps you've heard that Michael Stillwater and Ruiz Ortega were recently arrested," John said. "For rather violent crimes."

"Arrested?" Keyes said.

"Yes," Monique said. "Domestic disputes, apparently, but they had certain unusually violent aspects and—"

"The only thing connecting the men appears to be Whitesands," John interrupted. He had stood up and looked out a window. It had started to rain, puddles already forming on the distant tennis courts. No one was visible outside.

"There are no stores or bars or anything here," John said. "What do the kids do for entertainment?"

"A connection to Whitesands?" Keyes asked. "I hope it won't be in the press."

"I noticed that the dorms are separated, Keyes, girls and boys. Why is that?"

"We find that it aids in concentration. These are, after all, young adults and they are not completely in control of their desires, if you take my meaning."

"So you have a problem with boys and girls being... boys and girls?" John asked, still looking out the window. A drop slid down the glass, running into other drops, falling down faster as it grew and blurring the distant dark forest. "Is campus rape an issue?"

"I beg your pardon?" Keyes asked.

John turned. Both Monique and Keyes were looking at him, Monique wide-eyed but clearly frustrated. Keyes had the same look as when John had caught him on the stairs.

"There have been incidents that required some discipline, yes. As there are on any campus of any real size. But I would not say that rape is a word that I've had to use in recent conversation, no."

"Did they have many classes together?"

"Who? Oh yes. A few, yes. They were the same age and so their schedules will have intersected in at least a few mandatory classes." Tearing open another letter as he spoke. "And did the press mention Whitesands?"

"Do you have photographs of them together?" John asked.

Keyes had stood up.

"There will be a class photo, at least. I can have a copy of that made for you, Officers."

"Detectives," John corrected again.

"*Detectives*," Keyes said and smiled.

"That's some car you have in the driveway," John said. "Not bad for an administrative man."

Keyes said nothing to this.

"Ask Clara for a copy of the photo on your way out, she'll supply you with one. Thank you for your time."

"Thank you, Headmaster," Monique said as she stood.

"Was there anything else I can help you with?"

"No, not unless something comes to mind. If you remember the names of the others that were with the girl that night."

John handed Keyes his card.

"Dark," Keyes said, almost inaudibly.

"Sorry?" John said.

"Unusual last name. Dark." Keyes was looking at John's card.

"My grandfather took it up. We had been 'Simmons' for generations, though I believe it had a possessive apostrophe at first. Said it was a slave name. The property of Simmons. But apparently grandpa Dark wasn't havin' none of that, he didn't want just any name. Didn't want to just let go of all *that* history. Still, the story says that he didn't exactly want our last name to be 'Nigger' either, so he went with Dark. Blackness as armor, not a target."

Keyes' mouth was open in a sort of shock, face drained of color. Monique was looking down and gently shaking her head. Something in John burned, he didn't know if it was the confines of Keyes's office, the institutionalized racism in every stick and nail in the building, or in the white faces staring back from all paintings and photographs. Not a black person entered here but felt the white stares wanting them out.

"Where did you say Clara was?" he then added, slipping back into his detective-self. Relief filled Keyes, propped him back up. As much as John liked being the 'uppity negro' sometimes, as much as he liked the rage pumping in his blood, he hated that it was a role he had to put on so white people would just *listen*. That *this* was how he felt empowered.

"Right… right where you came in, door marked Administration. Was it… a single incident?"

"Sorry?" Monique said.

"Were they together at the time of the crimes you are investigating?"

"No. The incidents are a few days apart. Different people. Different homes."

"Then I still don't see how this is not just a coincidence. Or why Whitesands needs to be dragged into this."

John took hold of the door. Keyes was holding on to the doorknob and John stood in the doorway itself, but stepped back into the office, pushing the door closed again. Keyes reluctantly letting go of the knob. Keyes seemed smaller, up close. John looked him straight in the face.

"They killed their wives, Headmaster. They stabbed their wives and then dressed the bodies up to resemble animals. Branches and feathers to make a deer and a bird. They then called the police and claimed that someone else did it. You can imagine our surprise that the same men were investigated and charged in a missing person's case here as teenagers. *That* is the connection to this hallowed institution."

Keyes seemed not just surprised and taken aback, but all blood drained from his face. He seemed unsteady on his feet and John was about to catch a hold of him again, worried he was about to faint.

"This is classified, of course," John added as he saw Keyes regain his composure.

"Of course," Keyes said.

-

"What the hell, John?" Monique said as they were walking down the stairs, Keyes safely shut out of earshot in his office. "What the actual—"

"He knows something. Did you see his face when I mentioned the bodies."

"John! Not everyone deals with murder on a weekly basis. Most normal people are shocked to hear details of crimes, much less when they learn that people they went to school with murdered their wives."

John said nothing.

"He went deathly pale, I mean—"

"John! Get a fucking grip. The man's an asshole, but you… that was seriously unprofessional, what the fuck got into you?"

"You didn't get that vibe in there?"

"Sure, like we're kids in a place we don't belong. Sure John, I get it all the time, probably twice as much as you. Don't give me that shit. You don't always need to pick up every racist insinuation, you'll go nuts."

Monique stormed ahead of him to the Administrative office. It carried the same air of self-importance as most everything else within Whitesands. Framed letters of recognition, along with a small corner booth selling books, scarves and ties with the Whitesands insignia on them. The room smelled strongly of coffee.

Clara was a black woman. Smartly dressed with straight hair and an air of competence.

"May I assist you? Parents of a Whitesands pupil?"

"No," John said as he showed her his badge. He disliked the formality, of feeling like he was putting the woman in her place instead of just presenting his professional identification. "We're from the police department."

"Oh," she said. "Well, in that case let me get you some coffee."

Monique raised her eyebrows at John as Clara went to get coffee, and grinned.

"Someone investigated the case of the missing girl," he said to Monique. "We'll have to find out who and get their take on this," John said.

Clara returned with paper cups bearing the Whitesands insignia on them. "Now, what can I do for you, Officers?"

John wasn't used to this comfort from people he spoke to officially, usually people went distant and nervous, always wondering if the police were there for them. He didn't correct her getting their rank wrong.

"We'd like to get copies of the transcripts of Michael Stillwater and Ruiz Ortega, please. They graduated in '89. We'd also like a copy of that year's graduation photo and a list of the people in that photo."

"Hm, part of that I can get, no problem, but the transcripts I can't give to you."

"Okay, just get us the photo then."

"I'd like to give them to you, the records, I mean. I'm just not allowed to. They're confidential. You'd need a warrant, but I assume you know that."

Monique's phone rang. She excused herself out into the hall. She would excuse herself away from John when it had to do with her daughter, most other calls, even from jackass boyfriends she had no problem taking in the same room as John, but never when it was her daughter. To spare him or to spare her, he wasn't sure.

She never mentioned it, not once, even to him. Any time he tried bringing it up she shut him down. But defiance isn't that big, and cops talk. What John knew of Monique gave him no cause to think that she had neglected her daughter in any way, she wasn't the type. Sometimes there just really is nothing you can do.

"Here's that photo," Clara said as she handed him a photocopy across the high desk. "The names are there at the bottom, starting from the bottom row left."

White faces stared back from a black-and-white photo. Even Ruiz, the only person of color in the class of '89, seemed drained. Camouflaged to fit in. John knew that feeling, that mask you put on to make the people around you feel comfortable with your "otherness." It became easier with time but it didn't make him feel any less himself when he did it. A demand of a society that, no matter the progress made, always felt white.

Ortega and Stillwater were in the same row, with a few people between them. Some of the names John recognized. These were people just a few years older than him but the names were institutions. Politicians for life, trust-fund kids now turned business owners.

"Why black and white?" he asked.

"Sorry?"

"Why take the photo in black and white? I mean, it's not like 1989 was a hundred years ago. Why not take class photos in color now?"

"It's a tradition. It has to fit in with the rest of them."

"Sure. Thanks for this."

"What is this about, Officer?" Clara asked as he was about to leave.

"It's nothing really," he said. "Some former students were involved in a case we're working on, that's all. The school is not in any trouble."

"Well, you have yourself a nice day," she said, a little song in her voice.

"Thank you ma'am."

John walked out into the hall. Monique was standing by the door talking on her phone and, upon seeing John, headed out towards the car. John followed, out into the evening rain, feeling like he had accomplished nothing.

Chapter Twenty-Four

The man who had been in charge of the search for Alice Whitacre in '89, Horace Jensen, approached John and Monique as they stood eating tacos out of a truck in a strip-mall parking lot. John had watched with interest as he parked a large black SUV in a handicapped space nearby and then, slowly, lowered an electric scooter from the back, awkwardly strapped himself in, and rode towards them.

After Monique called to find out who had been lead on the Alice Whitacre case, John had called him from the parking lot at Whitesands and he had agreed to meet them. Had seemed eager, even.

"You buyin'?" Jensen asked as he approached. He smiled. "I assume you're John Dark."

"I'm buying," John said.

"And that makes you Detective Moreno," he said.

"Detective," Moreno said.

"We've spoken before," the man said. "You don't remember me?"

John looked at the man and thought how even with his memory getting a little rusty with age he'd remember meeting Jensen. "No, sorry. Have we met?"

"No. But we spoke on the phone a few times. About two years ago. I remembered when you called. I knew the voice."

The lingering taste of the taco soured in his mouth and his fingertips went cold.

"You… you helped with Emily. You're *that* Jensen."

Jensen smiled but said nothing.

"I'm sorry," Moreno said. "You know each other?"

"No," Jensen said. "I talked to him a little about his daughter. Offered what help I could. I have contacts with NaMUS and was able to get his case some attention."

"NaMUS?" Monique said.

"The National Missing and Unidentified Persons System," Jensen said. "A friend of mine works there and I made some calls for Dark when his daughter was missing."

"Is," John said.

Monique stood still in the silence that followed. Each of them contemplating Emily, wondering where she might be, how they had each individually failed her. In the distance a car honked and they heard the bleating of a fire truck's sirens. It was getting colder. John finally broke the silence.

"We were just up at Whitesands. You had worked a case there in '89."

"The runaway," Jensen said. "Alice Woodacre, right?"

"Whitacre," John corrected.

"Yes, I worked that case. Not much of a case though. There really wasn't anything to it except the trial and an odd push to have it all go away as soon as possible. Those kids had some powerful parents."

"It's a whole school of kids with powerful parents, is how I got the vibe," Monique said. "Kids with powerful parents that turn into powerful people with kids of their own."

"Anyway," Jensen said and drove his chair closer to them. He stood up and slid himself awkwardly over to the bench John was sitting on. The taco truck was playing mariachi music and the smell of fried meat lingered. They were the only people there, and the parking lot behind them was mostly empty. Slow taco day, John thought.

"So," Jensen said. "The girl that went missing from Whitesands in '89, Alice Whitacre. I interviewed some people, took a look at the woods behind the school, and went around the motels, YMCA, and bus and train offices. No one had seen her. If she ran away she stayed away after that."

"You think she ran?" John asked.

"I think," Jensen said, "that something about that case was off, but I could never figure out what. The trial was certainly a bit much and the judge rightly threw it out. Hard to prosecute without a body."

"What were they charged with?" Monique asked.

"The murder of Alice Whitacre," Jensen said.

"On what grounds?" John said. "There was no body, right?"

"So, as the story goes, they… hey you guys buying the tacos or what?"

John walked over to the truck. It was painted a cheery yellow with blue and black Mexican death masks on. Like a kindergarten class had selected the colors and then teenagers had picked the theme. The girl making the tacos had tattoos up the length of both arms and a bandana holding back her hair. She smiled at John as he approached, showing a gap in an otherwise perfect row of teeth. Somehow this made her endearing.

"Back for more?" she said.

"I'll have three of the pork and pickle," John said.

When he sat back down, Jensen had a folder out.

"I pulled the file for you, such as it is. Hard to build a search for a girl that so little is known about. Her parents, like all parents at the school, had money. Father was in shipping, some import-export deal. Mother killed herself not too long after."

"This doesn't sound like a happy story," Monique said.

"You get a lot of cases that have happy endings?" Jensen asked her.

"Some," Monique said. "Some."

"Anyway, yeah. There were five kids that they charged with her abduction and murder, all based on witnesses seeing them walk out of the school into the woods with Alice and then later returning without her."

"That's not bad," John said, "as far as evidence goes."

"She was going willingly with them. In broad daylight."

"So?" Monique asked.

"The kids returned to the school. Confronted, they had a story and all of them stuck to it. They had brought Alice out into the woods to play a prank on her. A hazing. They tied her to a tree and left her, but when they came back for her an hour later she was gone. The ropes they used were on the ground so they figured she wiggled free or had been helped."

"And what, they just went on with their lives?"

"They searched the woods for a while, they say. Called her name and got students to help look for her. Many students interviewed said the same thing."

"Three pork and pickle!"

John went over to the taco truck and picked up Jensen's food and brought it over.

"Drink?" he asked as he handed the tacos over to Jensen. Jensen's hair was neatly trimmed and combed to the side. He had shaved that morning. He looked at the food with admiration and smiled. He turned and looked at John, keeping the smile.

"Large cola," he said. John went and got that too.

"I have to tell you, Detectives," Jensen said, "coming here was mostly an excuse to get out of the office. I'm not sure anything in here is going to be of any help. With the attention the case got at the time and the trial, people have sniffed this up and down. The girl is gone, though the case officially remains open."

"What do *you* think happened?" Monique asked.

Jensen took a bite of a taco like he was being paid to in a commercial. Half a taco in a single bite, and then a smile.

"I think..." He chewed and swallowed. "I think the girl was so hurt by her friends hazing her that she ran away. Something happened to her somewhere out there, though. None of the ticket agents we spoke to remembered seeing her. She would have paid with cash so there's no credit card trail, but she would have had to use a kiosk. No automated ticket things back then. And people would remember her."

"How's that?" John asked. He had been there. Combing through Emily's credit card statements, looking for her in CCTV footage at bus stations and the trains. The same world that had swallowed Alice had swallowed Emily.

"She'd got a birthmark on her eyelid. See her blink once and you'd notice it. I'm sorry. You know the statistics. I'm sure they're burned into your mind. There's about half a million people that go missing in the country every single year, and thousands of bodies found but not identified."

He let it linger. Not wanting to say if he meant Emily or Alice. Knowing that John was thinking of his daughter, his mind ever bent towards finding her. Afraid that Emily and Alice were just statistics now.

"As it stands in my mind," Jensen said as he bit the end off his second taco, "Alice walked out on that school and her so-called friends and the world swallowed her whole."

Jensen fished a wet-wipe from a pocket and opened it. One of those packets you get at fast food places. He gently wiped his palms and fingers and then shook dry.

"Now, detectives, your turn. What are you working on now that has to do with a runaway that's been missing for thirty years?"

John was pacing in front of the table. Monique opened the file Jensen had brought.

"We have two men in custody," John said. "They stabbed their wives and then called 911 for assistance. Now, the cases get odd. They did this separately, in locked houses days apart. They both claim not to remember any of it and are mad at us for not chasing after a real killer, which one of them described as a black man in a hoodie. There's footage of them during the crimes, including full footage of the whole event for one of them."

"So?"

"The two men are Michael Stillwater and Ruiz Ortega, two of the men charged as kids with the murder of Alice Whitacre."

Jensen looked at Monique and then at John. His mouth opened and then closed again. He blinked rapidly. "What?"

"So you understand our interest in the Alice Whitacre case?"

"They can't possibly be connected," Jensen said. "It's… a girl runs away from a boarding school and what, bam! Thirty years later two men kill their wives?"

"We don't know if there really is a connection," John said. "But we were surprised that the men knew each other, more so when we discovered that they had been implicated in a crime together thirty years earlier. We went to Whitesands, talked to some people. Then we called you."

"They were cleared, like you know. The girl, she ran away."

"How do you know that?"

"Her suitcase. There was a suitcase missing from her room and clothes gone."

Jensen was still holding the last half of his third taco. Disbelief was smeared all over his face.

"So they, Stillwater and Ortega and the others, they really did the girl no harm?" John asked.

"Well. We don't really know what happened, of course. But I don't think they did, no. They did push her into running away, I don't doubt that. I mean, they tricked her out into the woods, tied her to a tree and left her, all under the guise of friendship. I think it broke something in that girl and compelled her to leave the school as fast as she could. Not a criminal offense, sure but—"

"What is this?" Monique said, softly.

"Wait, how did she pack a suitcase and leave without anyone seeing her?" John asked.

"My guess was that everyone was out—"

"What. Is. This?" Monique said louder, interrupting Jensen.

Jensen and John looked at Monique, who had been flipping through the report on Alice Whitacre Jensen had brought. Monique looked deathly pale and stepped back from the folder, which was open to some photographs. John walked over for a better look.

"What?" Jensen asked.

Monique said nothing. Her eyes were wide open, her hand over her mouth.

John looked. It was nothing, just photographs of the school and a dorm room, probably Alice's room at Whitesands. Then he saw it. He leaned in for a closer look and the parking lot tilted under his feet and John grabbed the edge of the table.

One of the photos showed a close up of shelves in Alice's room. Arranged in a neat row were some sort of natural sculptures. Animals made from twigs and stones and feathers. One of them was a deer and another a swan in flight. A deer followed by a swan and then a ram and something more but all John could see was Ellen Stillwater and Maria Ortega, dead and arranged to resemble not just animals, but to precisely resemble the animals he was looking at, in photos taken in a missing girls' room thirty years ago.

"What?" Jensen asked and swallowed the last bite of his taco. He looked from Dark's face to Moreno's. "What?"

Chapter Twenty-Five

Reykjavik, Iceland, 14 June 1952.

Jonelle Whitacre remembered her mother only as fleeting slips of memory now, all these years later, but remembered most clearly the last time she saw her. That evening, when Jonelle came home the police were waiting for her. They were taking photos of her mother's body, which was sprawled on the steps in front of their building. It was the clearest image Jonelle had of her mother, bloody and still in the cold autumn rain. Flash after flash lighting her up, burning the image into her mind.

"Hey, what about the kid?" one of the policemen said. It seemed an afterthought, as if Jonelle was not worthy of concern.

"What *about* the kid?" was the answer. None of them tried to shield her from the scene, no one comforted her. She was just an annoyance to them. Reykjavik just after the Second World War and everyone was just trying to get by. Compassion used up.

"It's a Situation-brat. Maybe somebody can track down the father. Won't *he* be thrilled, some American all cosy after the war and suddenly stuck with a kid he didn't know he had."

Jonelle knew nothing of her father, but had gathered from the words flung at them that her mother had gotten involved with an American soldier. Had been part of what became referred to as “the Situation” in wartime Reykjavik, when Icelandic women got involved with American soldiers. So handsome in a uniform, so worldly and brave.

Jonelle’s father had indeed been a soldier, who had conveniently been transferred somewhere else when the war ended. Her mother, oddly, would only speak of him when brushing Jonelle’s hair. She would tell her how handsome he was, and how kind he had been. All he had left Jonelle as he went back to the States after the war was his mother’s name.

They were shunned by most of Icelandic society. Jonelle had no grandparents in Iceland, just an idea of a father in a uniform and a grandmother who’s name she bore. They both lived in a place called Illinois, but to Jonelle they might as well live in the sky.

Now, her mother lay on the steps leading down to their front door, dead and bloody.

“Rape?” one of the officers asked.

“Not sure,” was the reply. “Why, you want a go?”

–

They placed her with a family out in the country. The nights were dark away from the city, a fuller darkness than Jonelle had ever experienced. The farmhouse was cold and damp, the sort of chill that settled in the bones and kept you up at night. The damp made deep breaths feel like she was trying to inhale a handful of earthworms. There was no indoor plumbing. No one bathed.

A letter arrived one day saying that they had located her father and that she was going to the United States. Five months after the letter arrived Jonelle went back to Reykjavik and from there to Illinois. The only thing

Jonelle took with her from Iceland was a nursery rhyme her mother sometimes sang to her in the evenings, when life still held the illusion of hope.

Jonelle was not welcome in Illinois.

They took away her last name, Johnsdottir, and gave her a new one. It was lucky that her mother had followed the Icelandic tradition of last names – simply the father's name followed by a "son" or "dottir" depending on the gender. Finding a John in Illinois who had been stationed in Iceland and had a mother named Jonelle hadn't been that hard.

So she became Jonelle Denning. The Dennings lived in an apartment in Chicago. Jonelle had never seen anything like it. A real city. Chicago was never really dark and never really quiet. She had two sisters that didn't know how to talk to her and a step-mother that didn't try.

It took a year for her to learn English, and another one to forget Icelandic. When she was grown, all she had left of Iceland was the nursery rhyme. There were parts of her childhood in Iceland that she remembered fondly. Not many, but they shined all the brighter for being rare.

Her life changed when she met Graham. She was eighteen and he was twenty-two. He invited her to the movies. It was the Sixties and they went to see *The Birds*. Jonelle didn't like it at all, but she liked Graham.

Graham was kind to her and smiled more than any man she had ever met. They were soon pregnant and when their little Alice was born Jonelle cried for days. Uncontrolled irrational sobs as she remembered her mother. Graham tried to console her, but he was clumsy. His manner around Jonelle was awkward, as he had expected her to be happy and didn't know how to deal with postpartum depression of a kind the doctors hadn't seen before. Unable to get out of bed for days. She never told Graham, but all she could see was her mother in the flash of a policeman's camera, with police officers snickering and joking about the poor dead promiscuous woman.

Then the depression broke, and Jonelle became sunlight after a storm. Jonelle held their baby and sang a nursery rhyme. It was all she had left of her youth in Iceland, and she sang it to hold on to something, hold on to who she had been.

Their daughter, Alice, became her world entire.

She was happy to be rid of the Dennings' name, feeling that Whitacre suited her better. She rarely spoke to her family, though she exchanged the odd letter with her sisters. She became obsessed with Alice, who began to resent her as she grew up. Hugs that Alice would push her way out of. Playing behind closed doors. Drawings with her father in the center and Jonelle to the side, not colored in.

The depression came back, and would ebb and flow for the rest of her life, in tune with her relationship with Alice.

It had been Graham's idea to send Alice to Whitesands. Jonelle suspected that Alice had put him up to it but neither of them would admit to that. It was only a two-hour drive away, and it was the best prep school in the state. Jonelle agreed, because though emotion often made one behave irrationally, she was able to see it for the opportunity it was for Alice. Graduation from Whitesands meant that she would be able to go on to a great career. She would be dependent on no one, something Jonelle had never known.

She was secretly happy to hear that Alice had been caught trying to run away. Apparently, Alice had simply left school and walked to the bus station and bought a ticket home. They caught up with her before she boarded the bus and brought her back to Whitesands. Jonelle consoled her, and it took a toll on her to convince Alice to stay at the school. All she wanted was to bask in the feeling that her daughter had wanted to come home. To her. She wished she had been able to take her and hold her and for them to just drive off somewhere.

As Graham's business grew he was away more, leaving Jonelle to wander the big house alone.

The call came on a September morning; Alice had run away again and they wanted to know if she had come home. Later, she learned the truth. Five of her fellow students at Whitesands had taken her behind the school, tied her to a tree and no one had seen her since. Jonelle was furious, she knew the kids had killed her Alice and she told anyone who would listen, screamed and howled. The five kids were charged but Alice's body was never found and eventually the judge threw the case out. The girl was a known runaway, after all, and the kids all professed their innocence. The fools believed them, but Jonelle knew better.

The hate she had for them burned in her bones.

After a few weeks Graham turned back to his business. This time Jonelle wandered the house alone with her rage. She would flinch and see her mother's body any time she saw a staircase. They said that Alice must still be out there somewhere and that a letter or a postcard would arrive. But the world had twisted and broken Jonelle's heart beyond repair and one day, finding herself alone on the roof somehow, Jonelle sought relief from the pain of the world as she stepped off and fell.

Graham found her body days later, bloody, sprawled at the base of the steps.

–

There was a flashing brightness. There was a blur of days and Jonelle found herself in Alice's room at Whitesands for a moment. As soon as she realized where she was she wasn't there anymore. She stood in her living room and watched as the sun raced across the floor.

Were the days always this short?

The days slowed down and she walked through the empty house again. Jonelle thought she was being punished. She felt confused. Time would pass in fits and starts, whole days lost in stillness. She would find herself roaming around her home but not able to affect anything. Watching Graham sit alone in the living room with a drink

did I die?

as together they had mourned Alice. Alice had gone and now she was gone. For a while Jonelle wallowed in her grief and misfortune, screamed at guests who came to the house. They seemed uneasy as she screamed at them, though they did not seem to hear her. They looked around with the words "Did you hear that?" unspoken on their lips.

She was dead, gone from the world but still in it.

Everything changed for her when she realized that she could enter the bodies of the living. She discovered this when Graham's sister was staying in their house, with her husband and son. Graham was away somewhere.

Where did he go for so long?

They were staying in the house. Her house. As if they owned it. As if the tragedy of Jonelle's life had been a boon for them. She was furious and shouted at them and tried to throw things but she was made of nothing but anger and anger didn't grip. Her hand passed through anything she tried to touch.

Graham's sister entered Alice's room and was looking at the sculptures she made at school and sent home, the pretty animals, and then she touched one and Jonelle just could. Not. Have. That.

Jonelle, knowing she was dead, knowing she had no power left, tried to push her away with all her might but instead she *merged* into her and they collapsed onto the floor, Jonelle mixed with Graham's sister in a single body. Twitching and crying, Jonelle was able to move the mouth to make a sound as the husband looked on in a confused shock. Jonelle raised an arm, forced the body to do as she willed and she examined fingers that weren't hers.

"Eh-ish" she croaked, forcing air out of the lungs and she heard her own voice for the first time in years, mixed in with Graham's sister.

-

Jonelle, alone again. The incident with Graham's sister had brought with it an epiphany to stoke her anger. An idea formed.

The five that killed her daughter and got away with it because the judge was a fool. They would suffer as she had suffered.

-

It took time just to be able to leave the house. She would walk down the road but if she paused and closed her eyes for too long she found herself back in Alice's bedroom or standing on the roof. It was as if something pulled her back to the house, a coil wound up that snapped her back if she let it.

It became easier.

With time she was free from the pull of the past. She would spend days away from the house, away from the memories of Graham and Alice.

Her beautiful Alice, they killed her beautiful Alice.

Years passed as Jonelle wandered the world, time passed around her. She was no longer bothered by it. Time was a flowing river and she a rock in the depths, unmoved by the current. She found herself attracted to tragedy. She would emerge from the depth of time and stand by the side of car accidents, a lonely suicide, shotgun murders in damp cellars. She wondered why that was, as she found she savored the pain of others. She grew to forget love, delicate frail love, and came to recall only the scratch of hard pain.

She missed her daughter, she knew that, but that feeling was now muddled with a lust for revenge. Jonelle stood next to a body by the side of a road and remembered the ones who killed her Alice and how they got away. She remembered anger and hate.

And then, Jonelle Whitacre found herself standing next to two men huddling by a barrel fire. They were under a bridge, the three of them, though they didn't notice her. The men argued. They wore layers of clothes in shades of dirty brown and they argued over a bottle. One of them pulled a knife and Jonelle smiled. A glimmer of a thought sliced her head in two and she moved and *fell* into the man holding the knife.

They were together in a muddled swamp of his consciousness and she pushed him down, down, down into the below as she took over his body and head. She tried moving the knife and the legs. It was hard work, like walking fully clothed in deep water. She *was* the man now, his mind and soul tucked away somewhere.

"Eric, put the knife away," the other man said. "Eric, your eyes…"

And Jonelle, in control of the man's body, pushed it forward, knife-first, and they tumbled down to the ground. She stabbed the man, and stabbed again. It was not easy, the ribs protected too much, but she made the man whose flesh she wore stab the soft parts. The belly, the legs. The eyes.

Jonelle Whitacre, twisted and different now, left the body of the man called Eric and watched as he saw what happened.

"Stan? What happened?"

He looked at his hands and at the body of his friend, coughing through bubbles of blood. He grieved, confused. Alone and afraid in a world he no longer understood.

Jonelle savored it, revelled in it. The man's confusion and fear and remorse *tasted* delicious and an idea that was a mere sliver of malice bloomed into a plan for revenge as she saw Eric standing over the body of his friend, distraught and confused with blood on his hands.

Chapter Twenty-Six

Any case that made the news was inevitably followed by a number of crank calls, confessions, phony leads, and unhelpful advice from the public. They took up time and paperwork and a great many hours were swallowed as officers tried to separate the junk from actual, useful leads.

"My neighbor has been going out about the time of the murders," is a surprisingly popular one.

"My ex-husband is who did those murders," is another.

"It's the Zodiac, they never caught him."

The rise in popularity of true crime and the nation's obsession with serial killers had increased the number of these pseudo-helpful calls, ironically making the work take longer as more fluff needed to be sorted through. More man-hours wasted. People would also show up at the station, offering information. Clogging the veins.

And so it was that John Dark didn't recognize what Daniel Hope had to offer for what it really was – a break in the case.

Daniel didn't want to be here. Police stations were strange places, full of strange people who has done strange things. At first he had paced around the little waiting hall, trying to ignore his own thoughts. He then sat down and rocked in the chair. He was sure this was all being recorded and filed but he had to tell them what he knew. It was the surest way to be free of his burden.

He had seen something about it in the paper, that was about the people she spoke of in the graveyard.

They can't track you if you read a paper you found, can they?

He needed tell them about what he knew.

-

John was sitting at his desk in the bullpen, trying to make sense of the pictures of Alice Whitacre's nature sculptures. He couldn't find how she was connected to the case. Closest he got was a thought that didn't make much sense; that Alice was alive and seeking revenge against her schoolmates for a prank from thirty years earlier, and that she was doing it by somehow, without a trace, breaking into her former classmates' homes and forcing them to kill their wives.

An officer called across the bullpen. "Dark, there's someone here for you."

Why wait thirty years?

"Dark!"

"What?"

"There's someone here. Wants a word."

"Reporter?" John called back.

"Could be, the way he looks, but no. Some rando walk-in. Says he knows something about the case in the paper. Will only talk to you directly."

He closed the file on Alice Whitacre, a teenage girl assumed to have run away. Lost and taken by the world. John stood up and shook off the cold clammy feeling he was being observed.

He invited the man into a small meeting room and immediately regretted it. He looked disheveled and John's nose filled with the familiar funk of sweat and dirty clothes. The man had a nice enough look to his eyes and while he looked tense it was a harmless tension.

"Sit," John said and gestured at a chair.

The man sat down. It was a much nicer room than the interrogation rooms below. Windows facing the hallway, a water cooler that gurgled occasionally and a warm yellow paint job. The cushion in the chair gave softly as John sat down. He took out a pen and straightened a page of yellow legal paper with the flat of his palm. The paper felt good. John felt tired.

He was about to ask the man's name when he spoke.

"She knows you're looking for her."

John blinked twice.

"What?" he asked. "Who?"

A drumbeat in his chest, the loud empty thud of his heart. *Was this something about Emily?*

Please be about Emily.

"She doesn't want you to stop her."

"Who?"

"I don't know her name. She… I spoke to her in the graveyard. Is this being recorded?"

"No," John said as he tried to attach meaning to the man's words. "This is just a conversation. Do you want me to record anything?"

"No!" he said and looked up into the corner to John's right. The eye of a security camera was directed at the table.

"That thing is not recording anything. Your name?"

The man rubbed his hands together as if cold.

"Daniel Hope," he said.

John wrote the name down.

"And what is it you wanted to tell me?"

John played at calmness. Every nerve taut, every synapse coiled and ready to spring and burst at the sound of Emily's name.

"I think I know who's doing the killing. Committing the murders, I mean."

"Murders?" John still trying to hear something about Emily.

"The men in the houses, they didn't do it," Daniel said.

John felt a swipe of vertigo. A schism as his mind shifted from Emily to Stillwater and Ortega.

"You mean the… the case in the paper? Michael Stillwater?"

Murders didn't tend to make headlines anymore, but Stillwater was apparently more of a name than John thought. The media had chewed over it and talked to several of his clients. Singers and rap stars that quickly distanced themselves from him, but didn't shy away from having their picture taken first.

"Yes. She said that *she* did it and that she—"

"Who is this?" John interrupted. The first indication they had that someone else had been in their homes. Corroboration of Stillwater's account.

"I don't know her name. She was turning black, swirling and strange. Like, like, thick smoke under water."

"Black?"

"Yeah. I mean, not like you black, she's a white woman but something is corrupting her or changing her. Like she had been dipped in tar. Black."

John scratched behind his ear and took a deep breath.

"A woman you met in the graveyard is turning black and made Michael Stillwater kill his wife?"

"She said there would be more, that she wasn't done and wasn't going to let anyone stop her. She is dead but I could talk to her. But she was different than the other ghosts. Mean and angry."

"You… You talk to ghosts?" John asked. He doodled a small box underneath Daniel Hope's name. He was thirsty.

"Yes. Or well, they talk to me. I don't want it. They say I'm the only one that sees them and hears them. They want me to help them. Even *they* are afraid of her, though."

"Mr. Hope," John said and stood up. "Thank you for your time."

"You didn't write any of this down," the man sitting across from John said. He seemed hurt by John indifference to his nonsense.

"I don't have time for this. Sorry. I do appreciate you coming down though."

He opened the door.

Daniel Hope stood up and looked at John. John held his gaze and felt pity for the man, who broke the gaze first and looked down at the floor. He shuffled towards the door and then out of the room.

"Can I… if I can help more? She isn't going to stop."

John handed him his card and told him to have a nice day.

Chapter Twenty-Seven

John put a mug of lukewarm coffee down on his desk and grimaced. He remembered a time when the station coffee hadn't tasted sour, when he could drink a cup and not have to trick grease off the back of his teeth with his tongue for hours. Or maybe his palate was changing. He looked at the cup and tried to remember the last really good cup of coffee he had. The last really great meal. Some time before Emily disappeared. When things had taste and the world had color.

The cup, like most of the ones around the station, was a leftover from someone else. A reject from some officer's home. This one had a picture of a lighthouse on it and said "Shine for our sailors. Come home safe." There was no boat on it but John had the feeling it was from Maine. How the hell did it end up in a police station here?

His desk was a mess – unfinished paperwork, newspapers, and food wrappers. He sighed, licked his teeth and stood up. Threw some of the wrappers away. He was about to call it a night when the phone rang.

"Detective Dark," he said as he answered.

He was hoping Steph would call again, that he would remember another something that might lead to Emily. He had become jumpy around phones, always, always hoping, expecting a message from her. Never a moment when she wasn't in his thoughts.

He now had a deeper, more sincere understanding of people who came into the station. A spouse or a friend reported missing. A child. The accusations that the police didn't care. The problem was explaining the statistics; in all likelihood the missing person would show up within hours. But then there were the real missing cases, where the person stayed missing and their family showed up day after day after day, demanding the police find them. John understood them now.

"Detective Dark, there's someone on the line that wants to speak to you." John was startled, had managed to lose focus in the single second between answering a phone and hearing the other person speak. It was a dispatcher, sounded like Grace. John liked Grace. "They sounded a little, well…"

"What?" John asked.

"A little intense. Said they had information about Ortega and Stillwater. Knew their names."

Something in the way the last sentence was spoken broke through and focused his thoughts.

"Put them through."

A click and then silence.

"Hello?" John said. The system must have dropped the connection. Then John heard a sound like dry leaves rustling on a tree.

"Hello?" He said again.

"Detective Dark," the person said. The voice was hollow, as if speaking to him from the end of a tunnel. There was a strange quality to it as well, like two people were speaking at once. He had heard it before, not the voice but that way of speaking.

John shot up straight. His teeth went cold and his heart slowed down.

"Are you recording this?" the person asked. Every word spoken slow and enunciated. John banged on the top of his desk with an open palm to get Monique's attention. He motioned her over. She picked up a different receiver, one that allowed her to hear but not to speak.

"Yes. All calls into the station are recorded," John said.

"And are they admissible as evidence?" The voice was a raw nerve touched, ice cracking, stone-on-stone, biting aluminum foil, tearing cotton, metal scraping metal.

"Yes," John answered.

"Good," the person said, dragging the word along. Savoring it.

"Who is this?" John asked.

Monique gave him a look. *What the hell is this?*

"My name is Wendy Bartlett. I live on 233 Hillcrest. And I just killed my husband."

"Ma'am?" John asked. It was out before he had time to think. The most automatic of replies. He felt light-headed.

"I took a knife. One of those nice ones from the kitchen that seem to always be sharp. Hungry almost. I took that knife and I surprised him. Stabbed him until he stopped fighting. Is there anything you'd like to ask me, John?"

"Is your husband all right? We're dispatching an ambulance."

"Hearse, John. Let's get the car right. Maybe a photographer as well, I think I really outdid myself this time."

A pause. John didn't know what to say. He wasn't prepared for this. The room spun. John's knuckles white as he tightened his grip on the phone.

"Now, I have to go but… stay on the line. The real performance is about to begin."

"Wait, why are you doing this?"

"What did you find at Whitesands, John?"

Goosebumps slid across his skin, as if he were standing naked in a snowstorm.

The line was quiet for a heartbeat. John heard it somewhere inside himself, a heavy *thump-thump.* She dropped the phone, John heard as it fell to the floor, could almost envision its slow descent. Then a larger thump, like a person falling to the floor.

Someone coughed.

Monique was talking into another phone, pacing. Frantic. "Send officers and an Ambulance to 233 Hillcrest, now! Possible homicide. Suspect still at scene, possibly armed with a knife."

John couldn't move. Phone against his ear, he listened intently, afraid that if he put the receiver down he would make it real. He then heard something. Movement. Coughing again.

"Hello?" It was the person he had just been speaking to. The phone was on the floor, close to her, but she wasn't talking to John, he was hearing what was going on in the house.

"Hello, Henry are you here?"

The phone was picked back up.

"Hello?"

"Ma'am, are you all right?" John says.

"Who… who is this?"

"Detective John Dark, ma'am."

"Detective? Why, what did… oh my god. Oh my god. There's blood…"

"Ma'am?"

"Henry!"

The line went dead. John slammed the phone down and in moments he and Monique were rushing to their car.

-

Monique drove. Sirens on, lights flashing, regular drivers not getting out of the way fast enough. The buildings seemed dark and deserted as they passed them by. John was cold, his world coming undone somehow around him, a truth collapsing – a brightness in the collapse he didn't dare look at directly. Not yet.

"I was right," he said. He had known it from the moment he saw Michael Stillwater in the interrogation room. The whole case was wrong. Like trying to solve a Rubik's cube when you could only see one side. Stillwater really was innocent, in a sense.

And then he wondered again. *How good a detective can you be if you can't even find your own daughter?*

"Stillwater, Ortega, and now probably Bartlett. They're not doing the killing. Something's driving them on."

"What do you mean?" Monique asked.

"Hang on," John said.

He called O'Reilley. As soon as she picked up he started talking.

"Chief. It's not a coincidence. Someone is deliberately targeting a group of people who went to that school, Whitesands. There were five of them charged in a missing person's case; a student."

"Dark?"

"Listen! You need to find them and get them to safety," Dark said. "They're being targeted."

"What are saying John, someone made Stillwater and Ortega kill their wives?" O'Reilley not missing a beat. Almost as if she had been expecting his call.

"Something like that, yes, I haven't connected all the dots yet. We're on our way to a third one. Wendy Bartlett just killed her husband and called it in herself. She confessed in the phone call."

"Confessed?"

"Yes, made sure we were recording the call first. Look, Chief, I don't have time to explain, but I think there are two more people in great danger. Dora Elizabeth Chastain and Peter H. Howard. They and their families need to be found and placed under protection."

"Hold on, Dark," O'Reilley said. "What are you basing this on?"

"They went to that school together, Whitesands. The five of them were charged in a missing person's case about thirty years ago. The charges were dropped and the records sealed, but it's in the newspapers from the time. The girl was never found. Now someone is making them kill their spouses, some kind of revenge thing."

A moment's hesitation on the other end.

"John," O'Reilley said. "What are you doing?"

John knew that tone.

"Goddamnit Chief, it has nothing to do with Emily. These people are in real danger. Find them, get them protected and above all else Chief, separate Chastain and Howard from their families as soon as you can."

"I'll see what I can do John, but this… this is not looking good for you right now."

John hung up.

When he was a kid, John used to go to church with his parents. Church was always a place he liked, though the disillusionment that came with his atheism leeched the colors from those days. There was singing, a strong sense of community that John didn't remember feeling anywhere else, even on the force in the beginning.

They would go for food at a diner afterwards and talk about the sermon or gossip about the people in their church. Sundays became his favorite days of the week because there was no pressure on him to perform. If anything, all church required was that you not consider anything. Sit with your community and listen. Be yourself.

It was during a Sunday school thing when he was ten that his mind took over for him. The pastor spoke of other religions, in a somewhat well-meaning but condescending manner. In India they were Hindi because that's what they were taught, and in the Arab countries they were Muslim because their parents taught them that. The discussion was meant to infer that if only these people were exposed to a little Christianity they might see the light, but the effect it had on John was quite the opposite; if our religion is based only on what we are taught by our parents, does that mean that all religions are equal?

He gained a profound interest in the Bible, much to the liking of his parents and pastor but they missed the real reason. John Dark read the Bible cover to cover and lost all religion somewhere between the pages.

Just a book, written by men, taught as truth.

He still enjoyed going to church, but the food in the diner never tasted as good after his loss of belief. The sermons that once seemed drawn from a well of truth were now just clanging on the truth, but tainted with John's newfound clarity. It seemed silly, even to one as young as him, that no one else seemed to have realized the simple truth. It made him feel intellectually isolated, and this he would carry with him throughout life – a sense that he should keep things to himself to not disturb the self-delusion that gave other people a sense of purpose and direction in life. A reticence born of guilt, as if he himself had bitten of the forbidden fruit and, out of courtesy, was not to offer it to others.

-

The Bartlett house was two stories and rather intensely white, a white accented by large windows. There was a long, winding gravel driveway leading up to it, with a well-kept lawn, and ancient oak trees up against a tall fence surrounding the house. High windows that John envisioned someone standing in, drink in hand, looking out and down at the less fortunate. The windows looked like eyes peering out. Right now, however, the house was lit up in alternating red and blue from the lights on police cruisers and an ambulance. John had seen too much of this lately, it wasn't something he wanted to get used to.

He dreaded entering the house, knowing he would find a body decorated to resemble an animal and a spouse that would claim they hadn't done it. He knew it was coming and wasn't sure he could take it.

The woman who had called him at the station, Wendy Bartlett, was already in custody. An officer on patrol nearby had arrived mere moments after they called it in. Her statement would be taken, her clothes removed for forensics. John and Monique would then question her, later.

They walked past uniformed officers, nodding a greeting to them in the flash of lights. Grim faces all.

Inside the house, white-clad forensics officers were milling about, industrious as ants. Taking photos, tagging possible evidence. Genderless in body-covering zip-up gowns that crinkled as they moved. John half expected to see a boy in pajamas and a small alien that just wanted to call home. John and Monique put blue plastic on their shoes and walked in.

"Detectives," one of the forensics team said as they spotted them. John nodded. "The body is upstairs. No sign of forced entry, nothing taken as far as we know, and very little sign of struggle."

"What is it, some sort of grisly assisted suicide cult?" Monique asked. They both felt how off it seemed, the taint of weirdness connecting the cases. Murder. Amnesia. The way the bodies were arranged.

John's phone dinged. Text message.

"Chastain family located. Separated and placed under police protection. Howard family being contacted."

He read it and then showed the text to Monique.

"That was fast."

They walked upstairs, dreading the sight.

John's mind was already spinning. You could always find similarities between cases, something that ties two seemingly unconnected cases together. The families owned a similar car, or the wives both had a framed photo of Björk on their wall. Something memorable but unimportant. It didn't always mean that the connection had weight, just that it was there. Stillwater and Ortega hadn't been in touch much since graduating, or so they said, apart from that single gallery thing.

They walked to the bedroom, John distancing himself by admiring the framed photography. A number of black-and-whites of what appeared to be the same farmhouse and an attached barn. No photos from inside the barn, just different angles of the barn from the outside. A study in rural life. He let his eyes jump from photo to photo as they walked, knowing that soon his attention would jump from quaint farmhouse to brutal murder. Stalling the inevitable. Hoping to be wrong, knowing he wasn't.

-

The scene that greeted them was more like the Stillwater case than the Ortega case. Already assuming the three belonged together. It looked to John like this had been done with more haste however, as if just done to make a point. Going through motions. John didn't see the same amount of care and time that had gone into arranging and decorating Ellen Stillwater or Maria Ortega.

The body of Arthur Bartlett was bent over an ottoman. He was a slight man, but tall, stretched out. A man some might describe as a "tall drink of water." He was clothed, hands tied together, fingers grasped as if in prayer. The room was clearly an at-home office, shelves against the walls to the side full of books that seemed meant to impress visitors, not actually for anyone to read or reference. Framed photographs and diplomas. The room seemed like a setup. Like what a child might imagine an important person's office should look like. A room that would seem large to a child, but felt claustrophobic and stifling to John. A boat of a desk in the middle of the floor, facing the door they had entered, as if to intimidate guests. A hurdle to overcome.

The focus of your eyes, however, went to the body of Arthur Bartlett, draped over and ottoman in front of the desk. Ram's horns were affixed to his head, which had been hastily shaved. Hair and blood littered the bone-white carpet on the floor.

John was startled as someone spoke. "Stab wounds are on the front of the body." John turned to see one of the sexless forensics officers. Voice a little shaky.

How could it not be?

"No defensive wounds," he added.

"Murder weapon?" Monique asked. At least she had both feet on the ground. John felt like he was caught in a long episode of déjà vu, that he could only say things he had said before. Acting out a script revealed one word at a time, not really in control of anything.

"Here," the forensics officer said and pointed to a plastic evidence bag against the wall. "It was on the ground next to the body. Kitchen knife."

"How many stab wounds?" John heard himself ask.

"Three," the officer said.

The forensic officer sidled up to John, as if about to confess something. "John," they then said in a near-whisper. "I have to ask. How are they doing this? Different people, killed in the same way I mean."

John looked into the clear plastic mask at the person inside. It was the same officer as in the first case, the guy whose name he really should remember. He seemed shaken by the crimes and John saw some real fear in his eyes.

But John didn't answer. Didn't know what the answer was.

"What did the wife say to the arresting officer?" John asked, not directing his question at either of them. He didn't get an answer.

"Where'd she get the ram's horns?" Monique asked.

John couldn't shake the feeling of being distant. Maybe he wasn't really here. The wife, Wendy, had been hysterical as they led her out into the police car. Shaking and screaming. In deep shock and denial. John would talk to her later, get to ask her about this but he knew how that would go.

He'd done this twice already now. She would be indignant in her grief. Tears of rage and fear as much as sorrow.

"She must have had them," John answered. Not really an answer though, just a reply. "Ram's horns aren't something you just go out and get. Those look ornamental. There's probably a shelf in the house missing a pair of ram's horns. One of them used to live on a farm."

The forensics officer seemed impressed. "You can tell that by just—" he said and gestured at the body.

"No," John said in response to the incomplete question. "Photos of a barn in the hallway and the rarity of owning horns. The simple answer is that one of them grew up on a sheep farm. Simple answers are usually the right ones."

He wished he could identify a simplicity in the motive though. No thought behind it, no reason. He could feel himself trying to tune out. Three murders. Three times someone killed their spouse, dressed up the body, and feigned surprise.

He had tried to tell them!

John thought of the sick man he threw out of the station. He really had known something.

"I think I'm losing it," he said.

"What?" Monique asked.

"There was a guy. A guy at the station, he said he knew how this was happening. He was odd and frantic, one of those, 'A voice in the sewers is telling me aliens want to kill the president' types. But… but he said something about this case. He *knew* things about *this* case."

"Wait," Monique shifted her posture. Dropped her hands to her side and she half-turned towards him. "Some guy off the street knew about this case? The details I mean?"

"Yeah. Mentioned Whitesands as well."

"John," Monique said. "Why didn't we hold him? Why didn't you *tell* me?"

John didn't answer. He took a few steps into the room, trying to think. Trying to get a grip on what was going on.

"John!"

John looked up at the forensics guy.

What was his name again?

He thought back to that afternoon, the discussion he had with the strange man who had come in. Reception would probably have gotten the guy's name and address. Daniel? Daniel Hope? He would have him picked up for questioning after this. He shouldn't have dismissed him so.

The body of Arthur Bartlett sprawled out before him seemed less sinister than the other two, John thought.

"He's clothed. Ortega and Stillwater both undressed their wives after, but he is clothed."

"So?" Monique asked.

"It feels rushed. There was so much patience and care with the other two, this seems rushed and imperfect. Is it because he's a man?"

"Could you kill someone? I mean, if a guy came to your house and had a gun pointed to your head and told you to kill Lonei, could you do it?"

John looked at Monique.

"You couldn't, right? We *can't.* You can't force someone to kill like this."

"What are you saying?" John asked.

They were circling the body as they spoke. Trying to make sense of it.

John had the feeling of being watched and just as he registered that feeling, the forensics officer, who had been standing so still and pensive by his side moments before, took a hesitant step backwards and then collapsed inelegantly into the corner of the room.

"Shit," John said as he moved over to him to see if he was all right.

Monique bent over and touched his shoulder. "Hey. Raymond. Raymond! You all right?"

"He's out," John said. The forensics officer, Raymond Miller, lay in the corner of the room like a human-shaped sack of grain. "Get one of the paramedics in here."

Monique walked to the door to the hallway. "Hey. Hey! We need someone in here, quick. Can we get an EMT in here!"

John zipped down the front of Raymond's coveralls and felt for a pulse at the throat. "He's all right," John called out to Monique. "Pulse is a little faint maybe, but all right." Raymond's head stooped over his chest and his limbs were completely slack.

"Did you see it, did you see him fall?" Monique asked John.

"I heard something and turned just as he took a step back and collapsed. I thought he was used to this."

"No one is used to this fucking shit, John," Monique said, gesturing at the body.

"I guess n—"

Raymond twitched and John pulled his hand back, startled. Not a seizure, just a single twitch.

"Is someone coming?" John asked Monique. He didn't take his eyes off Raymond.

Monique walked out of the room, into the hallway shouting for a medic.

"Is someone coming?" Raymond mimicked. There was something about his voice that John didn't like. His head still hung down, chin against his chest. He seemed unconscious. A discarded marionette in the corner of a crime scene.

"Raymond, what happened?" John asked. He leaned down to him. "You all right?"

"Is someone coming?" Raymond repeated and John's skin tingled cold and clammy. "Is someone coming, John?"

John stood up and took a step back. Raymond's head swung upright and he looked at John, the rest of his body not moving. His eyes were totally black, like the pupil had expanded and swallowed the iris and the white. He tipped his head in the direction of Arthur Bartlett's body on the floor.

"Poor Wendy's husband," he said. It was like on the phone with Wendy, two voices at once. "He was probably a nice man." Raymond stood up. Stiff and stilted, as if he was being pulled up by the shoulders. He grinned, teeth showing. A drop of spit on his lower lip.

"Wendy was really distraught when she realized what I had done. What *she* had done."

Raymond took a hasty, awkward step to the right along the wall and then seemed to be falling. Ungainly steps, as if he was a drunk trying to walk normally. He grabbed the doorknob and slammed the door shut, closing Monique outside. He locked the door and raised the evidence bag with the bloody knife.

"Just you and me, John." Two voices as one coming from the throat, pushed out. He slapped a closed fist against his chest. "And whoever this man is. He won't remember this. Any more than Wendy remembers *that*."

"Raymond?" John asked, hoping that this was just a crude and cruel joke. A practical gag that Monique had gotten him up to. Knowing full well it wasn't.

Monique knocked on the door. "John?"

"She'll just have to wait," Raymond said. "They'll never believe you, you know."

"What do you want?" John asked.

"What do I want? What do I want?" As he spoke he raised the knife in the evidence bag again. Unzipped the bag and removed the knife. The blood looked black. Still wet, it smeared onto the latex gloves. "I want them all dead, John, don't you see that? They need to die for what they did."

It was a woman's voice, the second one. Bile rose in John's throat as his nerves tingled cold, violin strings covered in rime and plucked. Was Raymond play-acting? Had Raymond done this? John's thoughts, which moments before had been like a school of fish moving in a single direction, were now all over the place. Disturbed by a shark. Dispersed and useless.

"John, what's going on?" Monique asked from behind the door.

Raymond's black eyes drew John's gaze, pulled in his attention. And the knife. Raymond raised it and put the tip up against his chin.

"Do you know this man, John? Will you be mad if I hurt him?"

"Who are you?" John asked.

"Now there's an interesting question, John. Who am I? I'm not this man. Oh, I can make him dance and talk and…" Raymond's head looked down towards his crotch, where a dark patch was forming. "Piss." He raised his head and pointed the knife at John. "Who I am doesn't matter. I just wanted to show you what I can do. To show you that you can't stop me, no one can stop me. And I won't stop until they're all dead!"

"All who?" John asked. He held up his left hand, palm out, towards Raymond. Unclasped his gun from its holster using the other. Hoping that he wouldn't have to shoot Raymond to keep him from killing himself. With the body of Arthur Bartlett between them on the floor he couldn't reach Raymond.

"What's your name?" John asked. "What did they do to you?"

"I don't *want* you to stop me, you see," Raymond said as he started to push the knife up. Blood trickled down the knife, Raymond's blood blending with Arthur Bartlett's. "I was just going to make Michael pay for what he did, that was all. But it felt so *good*. Oh Detective, you have no idea. He screamed and cried when he realized what I had made him do and then I just couldn't stop."

"What Michael did? You mean Michael Stillwater?" John asked and took a step closer.

"John?" Monique really banging on the door. "What the fuck, John?"

"Whitesands!" the thing in Raymond screamed, voice tearing at his throat. "Ask them… ask them about Whitesands. Ask them what they did to her and let the look in their eyes speak the truth to you."

"I'll ask them," John said and took a step closer. He worried that Raymond would not just taint the evidence but actually kill himself. "How do you know them, Raymond?"

Had Raymond gone to Whitesands?

Raymond tilted his head. He looked down at Arthur's body on the floor, as John sidestepped it to get closer. "Raymond is a little boy floating on a tiny raft on a big empty ocean right now. Raymond can't come to the phone at this moment. Raymond is about to kill himself, John."

Raymond eased the knife up into his chin. "Goodbye John," he said.

Raymond's shoulders tensed as he prepared to push the knife up into his skull. John raised his gun and fired, hitting him in the shoulder. Raymond spun and collapsed in the corner as the deafening roar of the gun echoed and died. The knife fell to the floor.

John's ears were ringing, heart racing, but he couldn't move.

Monique stood in the doorway, she must have kicked it in, John thought. She had her gun drawn. She was pointing her gun at him and John was pointing his at Raymond.

What had just happened? he thought.

"John, drop it."

John realized that he had his gun out. That he had fired. He had just shot another officer and he was suddenly very clearly aware that his career was over and he still had no idea where Emily was and for a second, just a tiny fragment of a second he thought of pointing it at himself.

"John," Monique said and the thought was gone and John was back. He put his gun into the holster and raised his hands.

What just happened? he thought again.

Chapter Twenty-Eight

After a detective uses his firearm, they have to face a Shooting Review Board. John faced his the day after. He had thoughts on how quickly they were able to convene the review board, but he kept them to himself.

"Thank you, Detective Dark," IA Officer Mukerjee said, as the interrogation drew to a close. She wrote something down and then looked at her watch. "Pending the decision of this review board you shall remain on leave from duty. You are not to work on this or any other case, and are not to come within 500 feet of Raymond Miller. I assume you have turned in your firearm, please turn your badge in as well."

And just like that, Detective John Dark's career in the police department seemed to be at an end.

Chapter Twenty-Nine

John Dark sat in his car outside a dirty apartment building. The building was four stories of small apartments. Litter on the front steps, grime on the windows and a disheveled black cat sitting on the sidewalk. He had driven here in a daze, the questions from the shooting board replaying in his mind. Should he have been more open? Should he have told them more? Above all else, the thought that he should have gone home.

He hadn't driven here consciously. It seemed the car had driven here on its own. John had known where the car was going, and hadn't fought it. The evening was settling in, crawling up on the city like a panther looking for something to eat. This night, like every night, it would have its victims. Messy murders, drug deals, homeless people beaten up for no other reason than being homeless and strange, cars stolen, women drugged and raped… the list was endless. Crimes came with the night, swam in her murky waters.

The hearing had been mostly as he had thought it would be, though if anything there had been even more pointless recounting of facts than he had anticipated. Each piece of the puzzle examined separately, no attempt made to try to put anything together. Like reading a paragraph letter by letter, not word by word. The whole picture never looked at.

He didn't want to think about the coming days. What Lonei would say when he got back home.

Even John would admit that as far as leads go, it wasn't much. A pamphlet of religious nonsense without a date or an address. The phrasing could have been taken off an advertisement for an astrology seminar or gimmicky self-help groups.

"Do you ever feel like there is unlocked potential within you that needs to be redirected for a renewed wellbeing? Do your thoughts and emotions seek better pathways?"

The only thing on the pamphlet that wasn't nonsense was the printer's watermark, barely legible on the inside fold. A watermark John knew. He had a case a few years back, before the world turned sour for him, which involved a person breaking into homes and stealing valuables and, of all things, underwear. It took a while to discover the part about the underwear, as most people don't know how many pairs they own, and the pamphlets he was leaving behind. Pamphlets he had had printed especially, advertising his family's dog-grooming business but with rather disturbing language. In the pamphlets he made it seem like the animals were being groomed in anticipation of, as it was put, "*the divine joy of human-animal intercourse*".

The pamphlets had a printer's watermark and John and Moreno had tracked him through that. Turns out, the idiot had given the printer his real name and address when he had the pamphlets done. It had simply been a case of going to his home and arresting him. He still had much of the underwear. He also had a dog in his apartment. John had seen a look in the poor animal's eyes and he had put it in his car and driven to a vet to have it put down. O'Reilly had given him some shit about that, how the force might now be sued by the guy, and rightly so. John hadn't replied to O'Reilly that time, but had just walked out of her office. She hadn't seen the look in the animal's eyes.

And now here he was, with another pamphlet in his hands, chasing another lead. Hoping the retired printer could give him a name or an address.

He got out of his car and rang the bell for Ames P. Abernathy. A few moments passed. John looked down at the street, back at his car, knowing that he should have gone home. A morbid thought passed through his head, like a brief wind stirring still water. The cat looked up at him, as if sensing a change in him. It licked a paw and walked off just as the intercom crackled. John had been about to give up.

"Yeah?" Spoken with impatience in a hoarse voice. Someone skeptical of the world, not used to people ringing his doorbell.

"Mr. Abernathy?" John leaned in towards the speaker. "My name is John Dark, I'm a detective. I have a pamphlet I want to ask you about."

"Pamphlet? I don't do those any—" a hacking cough and then silence. The intercom crackled again. "I closed my shop months ago," he said.

"I realize that, Mr. Abernathy," John said. "I need to ask about an older pamphlet, one you printed just before you closed. Please, sir. It concerns my daughter."

He heard the desperation in his voice. How close it was to breaking. How close *he* was.

"Your daughter? Who are you again?"

"John Dark. I'm a detective. You helped me solve a case a few years ago and I was hoping you might be able to help me again."

"The tall black one? That you?"

The world's lazy description of John Dark; the tall black one. A white man of his stature would just be referred to as a tall man. The default of whiteness.

"Yes," he replied. "Yes, Mr. Abernathy, that's me."

"Yeah, I remembered that name. But I'm... I'm sorry, the place ain't neat for guests," Abernathy said over the intercom. "Drop the pamphlet and your card in the mailbox. I'll call you if I know what it is."

"I truly do not care about how neat your apartment is, Mr. Abernathy. Please. You are the only person who can help me."

There was no reply from Abernathy. John turned and looked out at the street. It was a moment he would not remember fondly in the years to come. The silence from the intercom pushed at him and he resisted. And then the moment, a single fleeting moment where John Dark stood looking out at the world, resigned to the thought that another lead had just gone dead. He was back at square one.

The door buzzed behind him and John gripped the doorknob and stepped into the building.

–

Ames P. Abernathy had been correct in saying his apartment was "not neat for guests." John guessed Abernathy must have taken everything from the printing shop's storage when it closed. Boxes of pamphlets and posters were piled along the side of the hallways and rooms of the apartment, along with rolls of paper for large printers, racks of ink, and a few actual printers. Night had settled outside as John had walked the stairs up to the sixth floor, but Abernathy's apartment seemed to be in a darkness of a different kind. As if the ink was spreading from the debris of the print shop, staining the walls and the ceiling.

Abernathy walked ahead of John, taking slow steps. He used a walker that *just* fit the width of the box-choked hall. What little hair he had left was long and stringy, hung on his head like Spanish moss – as if it had not grown but settled for good. Trays of Meals on Wheels littered a kitchen and filled a sink. John saw something writhing in the corners, alive. The air smelled of mold and in places the debris was tinged with a pale green fuzz.

Abernathy's walker creaked as he led John into the living room. A single dim bulb fought vainly against the darkness; thick curtains kept any light from street lamps reaching in. A large flat-screen TV on a wall stuck out against the once-yellow wallpaper. It was the only thing in the room that seemed to be from this century. A glass-front cabinet stood against the opposite wall, thick with dust, and a small table that held a few trays of TV dinners and orange pill boxes. Somewhere in the room, something small was scratching at the wallpaper.

"Sit," he said as he parked the walker and sat down with a careful deliberateness. He gestured at the Meals on Wheels trays. "There was a time they would come inside and talk to people. Take the old trays back and maybe tidy up a little for people. My mother spoke well of them, I recall. Now the bastards don't check on you at all, they just leave the trays outside the door and knock and I gotta hurry to get it before my neighbors or the vermin get at them."

He looked from the trays up at John. "Sit," he repeated.

John looked and saw a folding chair that formed the base of a mountain of boxes. He estimated the effort involved and then told Abernathy he'd rather stand.

"Have it your way, Detective."

The TV was on, turned to one of those angry conservative news stations that served viewers fear and xenophobia. The ticker below the newscasters scrolled on, a sliding cocktail of lies, racism and fear that the just and the unjust swallowed alike. For a moment, John saw himself, standing in the living room of a man humbled by the way society viewed people; consumers who were told to expect less and less help from the government safety net, told to resent the poor and the sick for grabbing handouts, not realizing they themselves were poor and sick.

"I need your help with something," John said. The air was damp, and John wondered what the man's lungs looked like. Wondered what he was breathing in himself.

"Yeah?"

Abernathy coughed. It was a dredging slow cough, slick and rasping all at once. In the flickering light of the TV, Abernathy's skin had a sickly tinge, with dark patches John tried not to look at. "What can I help you with?"

John handed him the pamphlet. Abernathy looked as if he was melding with the chair, as if they were both infected with the same fungal growth and that over time they would merge, to be covered with the same mold, fed by the angry light blinked at them from the television.

"This pamphlet," John said. "What can you tell me about it?" Trying not to note the color of Abernathy's fingernails.

Abernathy looked at it. Turned it over to the back and then opened it.

"That's my mark in there," he said. "You see, I always mark my pamphlets. Never did buy any advertisements, I just always snuck my mark into the pamphlets somewhere and let them do the advertising for me."

"I know," John said. "You helped me solve a case a few years back."

"Ummm, what?"

His attention had turned, in those few seconds, away from the pamphlet in his hands over to the TV. Some question asked by the TV news anchor that was more pressing than his own.

"You helped me solve a case," John repeated, slower. Enunciating.

"Yes, yes, you said. What was the, ummm, what was the case?"

"There was a man breaking into houses," John said, speaking slowly. "He left these pamphlets behind with your mark on them. I visited your shop and you gave me a name and an address from a ledger. Helped crack the case. I was hoping you could do the same now. Look, Mr. Abernathy, can we turn the TV off?"

Had it been getting louder?

"What?"

"The TV. Can we turn it off, please?"

"Yes, yes." He grabbed the remote and clutched it for a few moments in thin, pallid hands. He stared at the screen intently, bathed in its glow. John was reminded of a piece of chicken under a heating lamp.

"Mr. Abernathy?" John said sternly and Ames Abernathy mustered the willpower to turn off the TV. A sense of relief descended, the same sense of auditory relief as when a heavy machine or a loud air conditioner turns off. The sense of a feather falling and reaching the ground.

"You want to see my ledgers?" he said.

"Yes, I'm hoping there's something in them I can use."

Abernathy turned his attention over to the pamphlet again. Looked at the front and then turned to the back.

"Have you ever been to the Catholic church over on Browery?" A cough after the question.

In the calm after Abernathy switched the TV off, the scurrying noises became louder. Scratching, almost as if he had insects in his ears. John scratched the back of his hand, expecting but not finding a roach.

"I don't think I have, Mr. Abernathy," John said. "Is that where the pamphlets are from?" John thought they were a little pseudo-religious to be from any established church. He knew the church, an ordinary enough building in an ordinary enough neighborhood.

"Not a religious man?" Abernathy asked.

"Can't say that I am."

"I don't blame you, with the world as it is today. I used to go there," Abernathy said. "The Catholic church on Browery. I was a priest there for a while."

"What has this got to…"

"They were doing things. After sermons, sometimes, with the boys."

John felt a coldness in his stomach. An anger rising up on a wave of bile.

"Abernathy?"

"The… I was a priest there for a while, like I said, but the things that went on, I went to the bishop when I found out and again when I had evidence. They said they would look into it, and then excommunicated me when I kept pressing them on the matter. 'Cause they didn't stop."

"Abernathy, are you admitting to your involvement in a crime?"

"I told the cops," he continued. "I told them. Gave them the rest of the tapes. They kept stalling. I couldn't understand it, and to this day I don't think I ever will. So, Mr. Dark, I don't give two farts from a diseased dog whether you are religious or not. I just wanted to be sure you didn't go to *that* church."

John sat, wanting this story to not be true.

"When was this?"

"Back in the Eighties. The thing is that I gave the bishop the evidence I had, photos and tapes, and then gave my copies to the police. I had nothing left and no one was doing anything. So, yes, Mr. Dark, I still have my ledgers. It was then that I stopped throwing things away."

"I… that was forty years ago," John said, as if excusing police incompetence. Realizing how it might sound, he said, "I mean, things were different then."

"Were they? Would the police go after the Catholic Church today?"

John wasn't sure he would like the answer. The Catholic Church still had deep pockets and many friends.

"Mr. Abernathy. I am no longer a police officer. I've been… excommunicated, if you will."

"I figured," Abernathy said.

"What?"

"Police. The Police always show the badge when they want things. Press it ahead of them like a bulldozer. You didn't show me the badge. What happened?"

"I… I shot another officer. He's fine, it was in the shoulder and I just did it to keep him from putting a knife up into his own skull." Saying it. Hearing it.

"What?" Abernathy asked. John wasn't sure whether he hadn't heard or didn't believe him.

"There… I was working an odd series of cases. And I'm looking for my daughter as well, it… I guess the pressure just got to me and I made a bad call."

"You shot another officer?"

"Yes. In the shoulder, just to keep him from hurting himself."

"I best not disappoint you then, Detective. Or is it just *Mr.* Dark?"

John didn't answer.

"The ledgers from my shop are probably over there," Abernathy said and pointed into a corner in the living room. "They are not in order, but I put the date I begin a new one in the inside flap. So you can sort of find your way around them."

"I don't assume you're going to let me take them with me?" John asked.

"No, Mr. Dark."

John walked to the corner. The air was thick and the little light from the corner lamp behind Abernathy wasn't really able to push its way across the living room. A stack of thick ledgers stood there, probably fifteen to twenty books in all. Black covers, bone-white pages. John picked one up. The inside flap put the date as the eleventh of January, 1997.

"They might be in a sort of top-down order, so the new ones will be at the bottom," Abernathy said.

It looked like he was sitting on a stage. Alone in a chair, a spotlight from the lamp on him and the rest of the room in a shadow that made it appear as if there were no walls. There was a sadness and finality to the scene John was looking at; a man living alone with his memories, unloved and uncared for. Trays of rotting food around him as he sank into a chair, pushed into place by a torrent of bullshit from the TV. John wondered if he would end up like that, still wondering where his daughter was.

"The ones you are looking for will be new. The style of the pamphlet, I didn't have the machines for that until 2005, and didn't really use them properly until about ten years later, if you believe that."

Something fell over in the kitchen, and John turned toward the sound. He looked down the hallway leading into the living room. A feeble light slid into the hallway from the kitchen but John couldn't see into it from where he was.

"Is there someone else in the apartment," he asked Abernathy.

"No, why?"

"It's… nothing," John said as he dug through the books.

"This pamphlet, it's recent. One of the last things I did. I think I remember the man who asked for them, he had a strange name. Sorta like you."

"What do you mean?" John didn't say what he thought Abernathy might be thinking.

"He was tall, like you. And his name was one of those you remembered. Like John Dark, it's a striking name. But his was odd in another way."

"November, 2011?" John asked, holding a ledger.

"No, more recent. 2014 maybe. And anything after that."

John pulled from the bottom and the stack fell over. Something fled from the falling pile and for a few seconds after there was more scratching from the wall.

"This says March 2015 on the front," John said.

"Give it," Abernathy said, extending a hand out from the chair. He seemed to be reaching out for help.

John walked to him and handed him the ledger. Abernathy flipped the pages. "What was his name… it was like a Smith or a James," Abernathy said, almost to himself.

"Not what I'd call unusual names, Mr. Abernathy."

John again thought about the flimsiness of the lead. About Lonei, waiting for him at home for news of the hearing. He thought about what his life would become now that he was probably not going to work as a detective again. Looked at the sad lonely man in the lounger in front of him and wondered if that was where he was headed. A slow death by solitary rotting.

Abernathy stopped flipping pages and pointed into his ledger. "Jones! That's the one. Here he is, signing for his Vestigial Flock. *Brochure extolling the virtue of surrender and redemption* is what he called it. Here he is creating one in May of 2015. He came by the shop a few times, maybe every four months."

"How many did you print for him?"

"This says it's a batch of one thousand. Normal order, I suppose."

An idea crawled into John's head. "Do you have copies of everything you print as well?"

"No, not everything. I might have a copy of the pamphlet here. In the apartment." And then added, as if knowing what the answer actually meant, "…somewhere."

"What's his name? Jones isn't unusual and doesn't give me anything."

Abernathy looked back down at his finger, and the place it held in the book.

"Erebus," Abernathy said. "Erebus Jones. And it looks like I've got his address, too. *V.F., 1231 Fincher St.*, over in Timid Falls."

John took out his phone. He ignored the notifications, little electric blood drops over many of his apps and a row of tiny icons across the top, demanding his attention. He opened his note-taking app and wrote Jones' name and address.

"That has to just be the address of the church, right?" John asked. "What did he look like?"

"Jones? He was a tall fellow, like I said. Thick black hair combed back. He wore clothes that looked like they'd been washed a lot."

"Washed a lot?" John asked.

"Yeah, yeah." Abernathy coughed, a short fit that ended with him swallowing something and then having to catch his breath. John was struck by the sudden need to leave this infested hoarder's den of bronchitis. "It was like they were secondhand. Shirts had maybe once been white but looked grey now. Wore a suit like that pastor in the *Poltergeist* movies, you know the one?"

"Yeah, I know."

"He struck me as a younger version of that pastor. Like that's the man he was doomed to become. That slick, manipulative Christian type that nobody likes."

"Anything else, Mr. Abernathy? Any marks on his face?"

"No. Maybe I caught a glance at a tattoo peeking up from his collar. Maybe I didn't."

John had the feeling Abernathy was guessing now, trying to be helpful to the police but overreaching.

"How many times do you think he came by your shop to have something printed?"

"Oh, five, six times. No more."

The smell of something reached John's nose and he suppressed the longing to gag. He needed to leave, had to go home and tell his wife that he was no longer an active member of the police force, that the thing he had spent his life on so far was gone.

"Thank you Mr. Abernathy, you've been very helpful."

"He had a girl with him once."

Adrenaline surged. John felt dizzy and cold, as if he was suddenly outside in winter, naked. He felt like he was falling. It took everything he had just to maintain his calm.

"A girl?"

"Yeah. She seemed a little meek."

"Meek?" Odd choice of word, John thought.

"Yeah, small and meek. Well, most girls would appear small next to him, I guess. You ever meet a woman that's tall as you?"

John didn't remember that, no, but didn't answer Abernathy. Give people a silence and they tend to fill it.

"She was, Asian? Latino? Not white, at least. Seemed short. Didn't say anything. Just looked at the floor or at him. Dressed in all white. I remember her because there was something odd about how she acted around him. Like… like an obedient dog, maybe, waiting for its master to tell it everything was all right and give it a treat."

John had it, the last little piece of nudging he needed to fully convince himself that Erebus was the man he was looking for. His lead wasn't a waste of time. He was right to chase after it, right not to give up on Emily.

"Thank you, Mr. Abernathy, you've been a great help," John said.

He put his phone in his pocket and took a final look at Abernathy. He had turned the TV back on and John left him there, to a fate that he was sure awaited so many Americans in retirement; a slow marinating in pills and TV hate as their organs died one by one, waiting to rot as the price of insulin went up and the amount of government assistance went down.

Chapter Thirty

It was raining by the time John got out of Abernathy's apartment. He rushed over to his car and slammed the door shut after ducking in. He felt unclean after the visit, both body and mind, but wasn't sure there was a shower hot enough or a lake deep enough to ever get the stain off of him. He had seen a lot of these shut-ins but there was something about Abernathy that got to him. He had given up on the idea of having any sort of life himself after closing the printing shop. He was used-up. Fatalistic in his acceptance that society had no more use for him, and he had no use for anything apart from a few meager meals and whatever the TV shouted at him.

John took Emily's file out of the glove compartment.

"Erebus Jones," he said.

He took out his phone and did a quick Google search that didn't help. Lots of things named Erebus, including something about a failed arctic exploration in the 1800s and an endless list of people named Jones. No Erebus Jones though. So he dialed.

"John," Monique said as she picked up. Neither of them said anything for a few seconds.

"What did they ask?" John said.

"Everything. They… you're lucky this wasn't a normal trial, John, a jury would have convicted you."

"Raymond is fine," John said.

"You know what I mean. That reprimand two years ago, us on the regular beat, the thing with Ortega in the interrogation room, there's a way it looks like you slammed his head against the table. And then shooting Ray. It didn't sound good, the way they made it out."

That silence again, following Monique's laundry list of shit he'd done.

"How did O'Reilley look? What did she say?"

"She looked like a well-groomed stork. Where are you now? Home?"

"I… Monique I need a little assistance."

"John, let it go."

And so he became Caesar, stabbed in the back.

"Monique. I have a lead on a guy. Where are you?"

"John. I just got out of a three-hour hearing defending your ass to all sorts of suits. I didn't know they made so many varieties. Don't make me regret it."

"It's a single look-up. One guy. Either he has a record or he doesn't."

Monique sighed.

"I'm at the station."

Outside, the rain had let up a bit. People rushed by in the night, distorted by the rain sliding down the car windows. The people had a bit of a spring in their step, but their bodies were grossly deformed by the water. They seemed alien to John. Like his car was the last remaining safe place in the world. Like he was alone against everyone else. He needed to get home.

"One look-up, Monique."

"Call me in three minutes," she said. "I need to get to a computer." She hung up.

John flipped through Emily's file. So much minutiae. Time she left home that day. The girls she was with, information on past boyfriends, places investigated and ruled out, testimony from people who were with her that night. All painting a single picture; Emily Dark had been out on a night with friends, had had a single cocktail, the two friends had gone home with boys and Emily, left alone, had simply vanished.

He needed to get home. The weight of the realization hit him hard. Something had ended, and John had nowhere to go but home. But going home might make it real, would be a surrender on his part.

It dawned on John as he sat there that he really was no longer a police detective. He was just a man, looking for his daughter.

He called Monique again.

"Monique. What is it you need, John?"

"Erebus Jones. I need a file look-up."

"That a real name?"

"Yeah. I certainly hope so."

"Anything more on him?"

"He'll be relatively local, probably around twenty-five, thirty years old."

The sound of Monique hitting the keyboard. The sound your heart makes as it, too, stops and waits. The sort of expectant silence of someone holding their breath with their hands over their mouth after witnessing something shocking.

"Erebus Jones," Monique said. "John..."

"Yeah?"

"He has a sheet."

John let out a breath and felt the tension drain out of him.

"Yeah?"

"Erebus Jones, born 1990 in Daylight, Illinois. Busted there for stealing a car, spent a day in prison for it."

"A day?"

"Yeah, a bit odd, but there's more."

"Possession, there's a few notes here about the cops in Daylight paying him a visit for domestic disturbances but no charges made."

Domestic disturbance usually meant a heated argument with a girlfriend or a spouse and it was fast becoming one of the biggest of red flags. A guy who gets into a bar brawl is just that; a rowdy guy at a bar. A guy selling drugs is just a guy who grew up in a bad place. But a man who hurt women behind closed doors was a man who was capable of so much more. Most mass shooters had a history of domestic abuse.

It sounded like a guy John wanted very much to talk to.

"Most recently he's gotten notes for harassment, no charges just complaints but John…"

"Yeah?"

"Erebus Jones is dead."

John felt like he was falling. He was the last leaf on a tree in autumn, spiteful, holding on against all the odds, gripping and swaying in every storm but now, winter had come and he had to let go.

"Dead?"

"Heart attack, six months ago."

"Why wasn't this guy on our radar then, Moreno? What did we miss?"

"I don't know, where did you get the name?"

"It's a good lead. The last photo of Emily is behind a bar with a bartender in the nightclub the girls were in before going to the McDonald's. The bartender remembered her and said she was talking to this guy but he didn't know his name. He got me a pamphlet the guy was handing out and I talked to the printer who made them. He had the guy's name down."

"Okay. Not too bad. Not great, but not too bad. We've worked with worse. John. Hey."

"Yeah?"

"I fought for you. With the board. I really did."

"I know."

Chapter Thirty-One

John felt loose in the world, alone, like a child's tooth that had come out, bloody and raw. He sat down on the porch steps outside his house and looked out at the street.

He had to go in and tell Lonei how the hearing had gone, that he would never again work as a police officer, much less as a detective. The nature of the discharge meant that he would get no pension, no severance. Tossed out and left to fend for himself.

He didn't blame them. If Raymond decided to press charges he might be facing jail time and damages they would never be able to pay. A kid passed by on the sidewalk, riding a bike. The seat was far too low for him and he looked odd with his shoulders up to his ears so his hands could reach the handlebars. He seemed happy. Carefree.

John tried to remember what that was like.

He stood up, sighed and turned, trying to think how he would tell Lonei that he was out, that their chances of finding Emily now that he no longer had access to the resources of the police were almost none. He was about to open the door, only to be surprised by Lonei as she slipped out the front door and closed it behind her. She spoke before he could tell her what had happened.

"John," she said with a shiver in her voice. "I think there's someone in the house."

A coldness fell over John as the echo of Ellen Stillwater's words to her husband are spoken to him.

"What do you mean?" John said.

"It's… just a feeling. It was strange. I *felt* unwelcome, just out of the blue. Don't look at me like that John."

"Where's Orlando?"

"He's at Frisky's house, I think."

"Lonei." John spoke, wishing he still had his gun. "Go. Leave now. Don't go back inside, just walk down the street and – do you have your phone?"

"John, what's going on?"

"Do you have your phone?"

"Yeah," she said.

"Go. Walk down the street and call a cab. Get Orlando and go somewhere, some motel. Don't tell me where, no matter what."

"John, that's—"

"Do it now, Lonei, please." Desperation and love in his voice, mixed with fear.

"Okay John. Okay." She was crying. Maybe it was the way John looked, bone-tired and weary with the unkindness of the world. Something drove her to believe him.

"I'll call you when it's safe," he said and then, without really knowing what was about to happen, John Dark entered his house. No gun to hold out and yell "Police!", no backup to radio. He had to face this alone.

He opened the door and stepped inside.

–

The house was peaceful. It was warm and inviting, but John Dark knew better than to trust appearances now and tip-toed through the hall towards the kitchen. A picture of Emily sat on the table in the living room, in among the notes and the printouts of the meager evidence they had, Lonei's laptop open but asleep.

He stopped to listen and heard nothing but his own breathing. His heartbeat in his ears.

"Hello?" he called out. "Is there anyone here?"

Something moved to his left, towards the bedrooms, but John turned towards it and saw nothing. He walked down the hall, one slow step at a time, ready for a jump or an attack. Something. Anything. He almost invited it.

In Emily's bedroom, everything was as it should be. Still and calm. Waiting for a girl to come home. The curtains moved, billowed out towards him, someone was rushing him and John tensed up and raised his fists but it was just wind from an open window.

No, not wind. A draft.

Someone had just opened the front door.

"Hello? Detective?"

John rushed towards the door and saw a man standing there, letting himself in. "Detective?"

"You!" John said. He might have known. The man from the station, the crazy man, David or... Daniel! Daniel Hope.

"Is your wife home?" he asked. He didn't look at John. His eyes darted from corner to corner, his gaze flitting from furniture to doorway and...

"Is *she* here?"

"My wife is gone. I don't know where she is." And then it clicked. It had to be him. He knew about the details of the case. It had to be him.

He had killed Ellen Stillwater, stabbed Maria Ortega and Bartlett and he had made them—

"Good," he said, surprising John, breaking his train of thought. "She can't make you hurt her if she's gone. I need to tell you—"

"Get out!" John said. "Get out of my house."

He didn't move, his eyes fixed now on at a spot just behind John's shoulder. The sun had set and taken with it all warmth and comfort but what John felt from behind him outdid any lack of light and heat from the sun. Tendrils of cold and damp and hate leeched the life from the room, brought with it the stale smell of the grave.

"She's here," Daniel said, backing away, backing towards the front door again. "She's in your house."

John turned to look and thought he saw a shadow. Something touched him and *was* him and then he was falling and everything went black.

-

John felt like he was emerging from a barrel of freezing sludge. He gasped and inhaled and the brightness hurt his eyes. He was cold and damp, like his skin had been draped around rocks deep in the arctic seas. Empty, cold and alone, he regained consciousness on the floor in his kitchen.

Daniel was standing over him with a knife in his hand.

The floor was cold, or was he cold and the floor warm? John shook his head and regretted it, it felt full of marbles and sand. His vision doubled and his stomach felt bloated with oily crickets. He wanted to throw up.

"John?" It was Daniel talking to him, Daniel standing over him with a knife, saying his name but his voice was strange.

It was Wendy Bartlett on the phone and Ortega in the interrogation room and Miller holding the murder weapon. Two voices in one.

"John, you've been looking for me."

Daniel's face was expressionless and slack, like the face of a stroke victim. The arm not holding the knife hung limp and he seemed unsteady on his feet.

John crawled backwards and tried to stand up. The room tilted and swayed.

A weapon. I need a weapon. Keep him talking. A pot? A skillet? Why don't I have my gun?

He backed away from Daniel, who was gripping the sharpest of John's kitchen knives. No way out.

"What… what's going on? Daniel, don't… I can help you." Stupid words, but he had nothing else.

Daniel moved his head to look at John but overshot, as if the neck was a poorly oiled hinge. Turned it back slowly and lowered the hand holding the knife.

"It's not Daniel, John. I thought you knew," Daniel said in that double-voice.

John realized the pounding in his head was his heart, beating and shaking with the desperation of a rabbit trapped in a cage with a tiger.

"Who are you?" John asked. He staggered upright, opened a drawer and found not a gun or a knife but a meat-tenderizing mallet. It was something, at least, though it felt light and insubstantial in his hands. "What do you want, Daniel?"

"Detective Dark," Daniel said. "Still not seeing the answer though it is staring you in the face. Holding a knife."

"What do you mean?"

Keep him talking. Get to the phone, the phone is in my pocket, my pants pocket.

John reached into his pocket and pulled out his phone.

"Yes," Daniel said. "Call the police. Call for an ambulance. I'll be done by the time they get here and they'll have *this* dummy to arrest for your murder."

The two voices coming from Daniel stung his ears. An echo heard before anything was said.

"You hid them!" Daniel screamed at him. "The rest of the five who killed my daughter, you took them away from me. I need to finish this. For Alice. They have to die!"

Daniel took a step towards John but as he did so he dropped the knife, which clanged on the kitchen floor. Daniel swung his head to look down at it. He seemed confused. "How?"

Daniel bent to reach for the knife and John used the chance to dial 911. He then slid the phone behind him, out of Daniel's sight.

Daniel turned his head to John and spoke in a clear voice, just Daniel's voice. "Get out now or she'll kill us both."

A tinny voice from behind John. "*911, what's your emergency?*"

John spoke without taking his eyes off Daniel. "Detective John Dark, 1311 Lake Drive. Home invasion, attacker in the house, armed."

Daniel shot upright, knife in hand and John gripped the mallet, ready to swing. Daniel raised the knife, lowered it, raised it. It seemed like he was struggling with something.

"How are you doing this?" Daniel asked in that double voice.

Inside Daniel, a struggle was raging.

–

This one was different. Jonelle couldn't control all of him at once. She had no idea who the idiot was but he had appeared at the house at just the right moment. The cop's wife left just as he got home but then this man showed up at the perfect time. But something was wrong about him.

His mind was cracked and the body didn't obey. Jonelle looked at the cop, so afraid, so stupid and confused, standing in the kitchen holding a puny mallet. She didn't care. He had shot her in the shoulder, when she went into the policeman after she had made Wendy kill her husband. It had hardly even hurt. The puppets took the pain.

She raised the knife but lost control of the legs and the idiot used them to take a step backwards, and another one, away from Dark.

"How are you doing this?" she asked.

She tried to push his mind down like she had learned to do with the others, but this one's mind was different. Like trying to push a balloon into water. He managed to slip past her control somehow, into the head and she heard him use the mouth to warn Dark to run. She went for the knife again, raising the hand but the legs didn't move. Jonelle burned with rage and she felt for the idiot's mind and pushed it down, ripped at it with all her hate but it was like swatting a butterfly in the air; it just moved away, ignorant and content.

"Who are you?" she asked.

–

Daniel, frantic. His body was not his body; it was a foot and a hand and his voice and his head but not all of them together. She was inside him, filling out into the spaces, a meaty black slug inside him somehow. She brushed past Daniel's consciousness and in that moment they melded and Daniel *knew* her. For a moment he *was* her and her pain and her anger and her hate.

He was the step off a roof and he was the ground coming up to meet her and he was the sorrow and pain of a grieving mother, confused and alone and he was helplessness and rage and he was looking for the people who killed her beautiful daughter. In that moment, Daniel *was* Jonelle as she learned that the five kids who took her Alice from her were free because there was no body and they said that Alice just ran away again but she knew in her bones in her heart in her love that they took her and killed her and raped her and left her alone in the dark forest and they Needed. To. Pay.

Daniel was Jonelle Whitacre as she tried again to raise the knife to stab John Dark in the face but Daniel grabbed the hand, his hand, away from her and to end it all he turned the knife and stabbed himself in the heart and again he did it because he was her and she knew how to stab so well now

turn the knife between the ribs

and the pain bloomed into the body and they were in the same body the pain and Daniel and Jonelle and she was frantic and clawing and screaming and trying to get out but Daniel's mind was a maze and she was lost inside, a raging Minotaur wrapped and warped into Theseus and he stabbed again and again and fell and the pain was everywhere.

As they struggled for control, Daniel gripped Jonelle and held her. It was like holding a burlap sack full of tar. It was not a caress but a trap as they fell down and died together in his body. Daniel's heart, torn asunder by a knife and rage and sorrow, pumped out blood through open wounds and faltered and stopped.

They fell down, deep into darkness and died together.

Chapter Thirty-Two

John was breathing fast. Daniel Hope lay still on the floor in the kitchen, bleeding. John grabbed a kitchen towel and pressed it hard against his ribs. The police would be here soon, but now he needed an ambulance. The towel turned dark from blood flowing fast.

He reached for his phone and called 911 for the second time in what seemed like both a mere moment and a whole age. He wasn't sure he knew what had just happened.

A man had entered his home and tried to kill him but had had some sort of episode and killed himself. What was it he said about a woman?

"Stay with me," John said. He needed answers, and he would only get them if he managed to keep him alive. He drew in a deep breath and realized he was sobbing. Heaving bouts, and suddenly he couldn't breathe. He hoped the ambulance would get here soon.

John's world was full of sirens again, and the flashing blue lights in the night, only this time it was *his* home that the police were called to. John had directed the EMTs to the kitchen. They were fast, efficient. They spoke to one another and asked John questions and he answered them even though he still couldn't really breathe.

They brought him back. On the gurney, Daniel Hope thrashed and gasped and gulped in air as if he had been drowning. He let out a cry pulled from the core, a single star lighting up the night and hurtling his frail body back into the land of the living. He strained and cried, gasping for air as if it had been his lungs and not his heart that were split with a knife. He was back.

John still couldn't breathe.

As a courtesy to him, the police let John walk to the car and get in without handcuffs. As if he had just called for a taxi and the cops had arrived instead. Covered in blood, confused. He was Michael Stillwater, but now he had more pieces of the puzzle. Just missing one to make sense of the whole.

"Lonei?"

"John, what the hell was—"

"Lonei, I'm so sorry."

Lonei heard something in his voice.

"Where are you?"

"I'm in a police car, on my way to the station, or to a hospital, I'm not sure. Lonei, I can't breathe. I can't find her."

"We're okay. Orlando and me, we're at a motel, the—"

"Don't tell me," he interrupted. He knew then that if it took never seeing her again to keep her safe, it was a small price. The world was a far better place with Lonei in it.

Chapter Thirty-Three

Saint Mary's of the Light was a hospital so unremarkable you almost wouldn't see it unless someone pointed it out to you. Six floors stacked and painted bone-white. John drove down a street to the side of the hospital to a parking lot that seemed just as devoid of life and joy as the outside of the hospital.

Inside, there was the sterile smell of gauze and bureaucracy. People milling about impatiently in the entrance, arriving at the Emergency Room hoping against hope that they were somehow insured for whatever had happened, discovering more often than not that they had no insurance. Trying to find money to get through the door, fighting against copays and deductibles while also fighting for your life.

The system sicker than the people.

John entered the first door he saw that didn't say "Emergency".

"I'm looking for a patient," John said to a disinterested nurse at the desk. Her hair in a ponytail, white skin with freckles that made her look pale. Pupils small and hands moving fast. She looked like she hadn't slept in days, but she still had a smile for John.

"Name?"

"Daniel Hope. He came in two days ago. Knife to the chest, the police will be with him."

“Ah, him,” she said. “And you are?”

“Det… John Dark.” Just John Dark now. “They are expecting me.”

John waited all of five minutes. He sat in the arrivals hall, as if this were an airport and he was going somewhere, only there was no bar and no one dragging anything but their IV bags. He flipped through a magazine, not seeing anything on the pages but people smiling back, showing watches and coats. Glossy magazines selling glossy things to glossy people. John was not feeling particularly glossy at the moment. Instead, he looked around at the others waiting to see someone they knew in the hospital. All of them with a phone to their face, thumb poised over a feed, ready to scroll.

“Mr. Dark,” someone called. John turned to see a nurse, this one short and petite but with that same drained look on her face. She stood holding one side of a double doorway open, and did not look like she would be holding it open for long. John hurried over to her.

She started walking without greeting John. “Mr. Hope is out of critical condition and is recovering. He is, well you know about his schizophrenia I assume, Officer?”

“Yes,” John said without correcting her. He’d get more out of her if she thought he was still a cop.

“He’s improving but the medicine takes weeks to build up in the system so he’ll remain in supervised care for a while. Apparently he attacked someone and then stabbed himself in the chest, must have been quite traumatic, though I don’t think he hurt anyone else. It’s a myth, you know.”

“What is?” John asked.

“Schizophrenics. That they’re dangerous.”

"Is that so?" John asked. There was a quality to the way she spoke that cut through to him. A genuine concern. She seemed like the kind of woman who had doled out a bit of tough love in her time. John liked her.

"I'm sure you know this, Officer. Most crime is committed out of desperation or a drug- or alcohol-fueled stupidity, not out of mental illness. Anyway, here we are."

They were in a hallway like all hospital hallways, in a hospital like all hospitals. For a moment John wondered if the halls stretched on forever, if they turned and connected to corridors in other hospitals, and that if no one guided him back out he'd be stuck wondering these halls forever. Hearing Emily call to him from around the corner.

If you were a proper detective you would have found her by now.

That thought, even here.

"Officer," John said to the officer seated outside Hope's room. He looked at the name tag on the man's uniform and then added, "Officer Liguino."

John extended a hand which the officer didn't take.

"Sir?" he said. He was a short man with a broad face and a thin mustache. Short men sometimes took a dislike to John and it was clear from his demeanor that Officer Liguino didn't like John. In this case, he hoped it was his size and not his skin. He could understand the size thing.

"John Dark," he said, a ghost of the word "Detective" on his tongue. "I'm here to see Mr. Hope. Call O'Reilley down at three-five-seven for the go-ahead."

"You? You're Detective Dark?"

"Just John now. John Dark."

"ID?"

John handed the officer his driver's license.

"Can't be that many guys called John Dark, can there?" the officer said. "Go ahead," he said and winked. "Hey," he added. "I think it's just time for a little cigarette break. I'll be gone five minutes, if you take my meaning."

John hesitated a moment over the implication. The officer thought John was there to even a score. But he just wanted answers.

"I'm just here to talk to him. That's all this is," John said.

"Yeah, okay," Liguino said.

"Really," John said. "Just want to talk to the guy."

John walked into the room where Daniel Hope lay recovering. Self-inflicted stab wound to the abdomen is what the report would say. John had given a statement at the station. So often on the other side of the table. He hadn't held anything back but hadn't laid it on thick either. Just the facts, as someone once said. Just the facts.

John was relieved to see it was just the two of them in the room. Grayish curtains kept the daylight out and muted all color. John closed his eyes and took a deep breath. Walked slowly towards the bed where Hope lay.

The man in the hospital bed didn't seem like the same man that came to John's house, frightening his family and threatening him with a knife. Hospitals obfuscate the personality as they heal the body; everyone in identical gowns with identical looks on their faces. Just wanting to go home. But with Daniel Hope it was different. The other times John had seen Daniel Hope he had been in the swirl of schizophrenia. Facts were malleable, not to be trusted. Schizophrenics were known to latch on to otherworldly ideas and the problem was that the very thing we use to tell truth from lie, the pink lump of nerves and blood in our head used to navigate with logic and facts, was the one that was broken.

Daniel Hope seemed calm and in control now. He looked to John like a guy who had just had his appendix removed and was waiting for his family. Not a man who had invaded his home, threatened him and then stabbed himself.

"You died," John said. Fumbling for words like a teenager at prom, saying the first thing that came to mind.

"I'm sorry," Hope said. He pushed himself up and winced.

"You look good," John said.

"Better," Hope said.

John didn't know what to say next. But it was Hope who spoke.

"I'm sorry," Hope said. "That must have been frightening for you."

"It's not the best thing that happened this week," John said. He wasn't sure anything was his favorite thing in the last week. "In fact, it was just on par with everything else. It's been a very odd couple of days and I was hoping you could clear some of it up for me."

"I can try," Hope said.

John took a hesitant step further into the room. There was a chair by a sink that didn't look like it was used much. John took the chair and eased himself into it, eyes on Hope the whole time. As if he were talking to a tiger.

"There's a few things I need cleared up, Mr. Hope. Are you feeling well enough to answer a few questions?"

Daniel Hope looked down at his hands and then at the curtains. "It's… you ever been shopping in one of those big outlet places? The ones like warehouses with the clothes on those circular racks on the floor, in a store that seems to go on forever and the music is blaring?"

"I know the kind of place you mean, yes."

"Well, that's sort of what being me is like. That's what it's like being schizophrenic and trying to function is like, I mean, except when I'm at the outlet there's people following me, making notes of whatever I'm looking at and telling someone through a radio, and the music is even louder and if I get hold of anything it turns out to be something someone is wearing so now that person is angry at me and I just want to leave the store but there is no way out anymore. Someone is waiting for me to pick something to buy and I am no longer in there for me, but for that someone else, trying to remember what it was that they wanted me to buy and now everyone I went to school with is there, watching and whispering about me."

He had kept his gaze on his hands the whole time. As if confessing to something he was ashamed of.

"It... that sounds like my personal nightmare," John said.

"I know I need to buy something but I can't remember what. If I just buy that one thing I can leave the store so I ask the person standing closest to me 'What is it you want me to buy?' But they're not the person and they look horrified that I've spoken to them so I try to leave."

"Pills help?" John asked.

"The pills," Hope said. "The pills they have for schizophrenia aren't for the person who has it. They are for everyone else. On the pills I wander around the store, not caring and not trying to buy anything anymore but I don't bother anyone. All the clothes are grey and the music is gone but I don't talk to anyone and that's why they give me the pills."

"What do you remember about what happened?"

He raised his head slowly and looked at John. His eyes were rimmed with red, as if he were about to shed tears of blood. "I remember it all, Mr. Dark."

John pulled his chair closer.

"She… she was inside me. I think that was real. It's hard to tell, you know?"

John didn't know. He really didn't.

"I've been on meds since I got here and my thinking is clearing up. Or being clouded over."

"Clouded over?" John asked.

"Would you rather live in a world of color and complexity where your senses sometimes showed you things that weren't there, where you couldn't trust yourself to make the right choices and they are following you around all the time, writing down what you are doing… or in a world where everything is gray and slow but you trust that the things are what they appear to be?"

"I… I don't know."

"Neither do I, Mr. Dark. But I have no choice anymore."

"Mandatory medication?"

"For now, at least. Drugs take about two weeks to build up in my system, though, so maybe you're not really here."

"I'm here," John said.

"I know."

A moment passed.

"Why can't I hear any birds?" Hope asked.

"Birds? Well, I guess the hospital is in the middle of the city, there's no parks or anything around—"

"No, I mean in general. Where did the birds go?"

"Hope," John said to get his attention back. "What happened at my house? Why did you come to my house?"

"She was there."

"*She?* My wife?"

"No. Her. She was very angry at you, at everything. A feeling of a twisted motherly love."

For a while neither of them said anything. Daniel then broke the silence.

"She was inside me. She tried to control me."

John remembered his own blackout, as strange as that sounded. A few moments where he felt like he was at the bottom of a well. His body was moving, or being moved, but he had no control. Only lasted for a few seconds.

"But my mind is… it's broken. She couldn't hold on to anything for long. She was angry at you John."

"Angry?"

"You kept her from finishing her revenge. You hid some people from her. I didn't understand everything she was thinking or feeling but she was inside me, Mr. Dark. I *know* this person now."

This had been a mistake. Hope was in no state to tell him what had happened. His mind was a strobe light, each flash showing him something different.

"She was the girl's mother," Hope said.

"What girl?"

"The girl who went missing at Whitesands."

That feeling again, like stepping out into a cold wind. Like falling.

"She's… she's her *mother?*" John asked.

"Yes. She wanted to find her daughter, once, but what she wants now is to hurt the people that took her away."

John knew the feeling.

"I saw her memories, Mr. Dark. I felt her emotions and I felt the drive of her anger. She hated them. She hated them so much that she entered them and made them kill someone they loved."

"Hope," John said. "There's… I'm not sure I'm following you."

Daniel Hope looked up at John. He was crying and clearly pained.

"She was inside me, Mr. Dark. She *was* me. I know everything about her."

He hesitated. Looked at John as if he were deciding on something.

"They took her girl away from her and got away with it. She was so angry at everyone – her husband for not fighting along with her, the police for not trying hard enough to find her, herself for failing at everything she tried. But especially at the five who she thought took her. Those names will be burned into my mind for the rest of my life, Detective. Ortega, Stillwater, Chastain, Bartlett, and Howard."

"Why did she dress the bodies up like that, after?" John asked. He was sure Daniel was making it up. The names had maybe been in the papers or online, there had to be a way for him to know them.

"Her daughter used to make them. She'd pick up things on her walks. Twigs and feathers and all sorts of things. My daughter she…"

"Your daughter?" John asked. The room felt cold.

"She… the memories, sorry. They are in my head. Her emotions too. Sometimes they get mixed with my own. She's not *my* daughter, she is some woman's daughter but the memory is there, Detective. The emotions are there. In my head, she's *my* daughter."

"Okay," John said. "Go on."

"What?" Daniel said. He had forgotten his train of thought.

"The way she dressed up the bodies."

"Yes. The daughter did that. Used to do that. With the twigs and things she collected. Feathers and stones. Ever since she was a kid. She got pretty good at it too. She made birds and rabbits and little animals out of them. Kept them in her room. It was all the mother got back really, from Whitesands. Her clothes and her sculptures. She… the mother, the one that…"

"Yeah?"

"The one that did everything, she became obsessed with them. Thought there were clues in them. Like the daughter had left messages in them somewhere. I think that's what drove her mad."

It made a twisted kind of sense. If she really was a ghost, possessing people out of a rage and making them commit murder, that she would make the bodies into a tribute to her daughter.

John registered quite a few things in that moment. The sound of a cough just outside the door. The smell of boiled carrots from somewhere. The unexpected silence in the room, as if there wasn't a city outside the curtained windows. The nearly imperceptible buzz of the machines measuring Daniel Hope's vitals, keeping track. And the fact that Hope was certain the things he was saying were true.

"Do you know why she used them to kill?" John asked. "Why not just have them kill themselves?"

"She wanted to make them suffer. She wanted them to experience the pain and grief *she* felt when they killed her daughter. She was driven by revenge, and by hiding those people away from her you made her very angry at you. You took her whole purpose away from her."

John thought about this.

"So it's over then?" John asked. "It's really over? She's not coming back?"

"I… I don't think she will."

John leaned back in the chair and then leaned forward, sitting with his elbows on his knees and his face hidden in his hands. He wanted to sleep. He just wanted to…

"Daniel," he said as a thought formed in his mind. The most dangerous of thoughts. "Tell me this, then."

"Mr. Hope," someone behind John said. He hadn't heard anyone enter. It was a nurse, standing behind John. Short with a rather serious look on her face. She didn't approve of John being in there.

"Are you with the police?" she asked.

"Yes, I'm just asking Mr. Hope here a few follow-up questions."

"Well, you don't look like a police officer," she said.

It was the first time in a long while that John met someone who didn't immediately take him for a cop. He wasn't sure how he felt about that. Worried irrationally that it would impact his search for Emily.

"I'm—"

"Just make sure that you don't take up too much of Mr. Hope's time. What he needs now is—"

"Rest, I know," John said, annoyed at her presence and interruptions.

"No. He isn't really that badly hurt, as odd as that may sound. What I was going to say, before being quite rudely interrupted, was that he needs time so that the medication can build up in his body. Mr. Hope is not just here for what ails his body, you know."

John decided to be a model of composure. "Yes ma'am," he said. And then something occurred to him. If Daniel was right, the case was over. It would never officially be solved and, because the world was an unfair and unforgiving place, Stillwater, Bartlett and Ortega would lose their freedom. They would grieve and be made to go through a trial where they would all surely be convicted. It was impossible to prove spiritual possession in court. There just was no way.

John, having seen it for himself, wasn't sure he believed it.

The world was a far darker place than John even imagined. Vertigo as it hit him that some of that darkness may even have unknown and unknowable origins. That there really were things beyond our knowing.

That didn't mean that we shouldn't fight for the light.

"Excuse me, ma'am," he said. Each syllable drawn out as he really wondered if he was going down the path he saw before him. His heart raced. "How do the drugs work?"

"Well, Clozaril is an inhibitor, but it needs a certain volume in the blood before it really works."

"So he is still… unwell?"

"Yes. It's why we keep his room especially free from stimulus of any kind. Anything that might confuse him or bother him. It's also why we don't want him to have visitors for too long."

She checked his I.V. drip, gave John another disapproving look, and left the room.

John's mind was racing. He looked for a reason to not do what he was considering. He was off the force, this time probably for good. He had shot an officer at the scene of a crime, and was just lucky that Raymond had not decided to press charges. Yet. The only thing that made any of this better was that Monique would probably keep her job.

He shot up from the chair, propelled by anger and doubt. "Mr. Hope, excuse me," he said to Daniel, who looked a little startled by John's sudden movement.

John walked out into the hall and put on a cop face. Cop swagger. He needed Liguino to go along.

"Look, Liguino. I'm going to need those five minutes after all."

Instead of dismissing Dark's suggestion, as he should have, Liguino actually smiled. It was the grin of a man who had joined the police for the wrong reasons, and in it John saw so much he hated about the institution. About power in society. About white police officers, even after being an officer himself.

"Sure thing, Dark. I was starting to think you didn't have it in you. You said you'd cover for me when I went to the bathroom. You sat outside the whole time." And then he winked at John and strolled down the hall, as if he had just won something.

John swallowed his pride and the things he really wanted to say to Liguino. The only consolation was that if John managed to pull this off, Liguino was going to take a lot of shit. He went back into Hope's room.

John walked right up to Hope. "Mr. Hope. I hope you forgive me, but I am going to ask you blunt questions and then make a request that will seem absurd."

Daniel had been on the verge of drifting off. He blinked at John and looked around the room. A single tear was forming. "I just want to be well. Please. Please tell Stacy that I helped you?"

John was taken aback.

"Who… who is Stacy?"

"She's my… I had a chance at a normal life. She was it, but that's when I got sick."

John had read the file. An officer responded to a domestic abuse call at Hope's home over ten years ago. No charges filed, but Hope had been admitted to involuntary treatment. Medical records sealed, of course.

"Look, Hope. I don't have much time." *Emily is still out there somewhere*, he thought. "You see ghosts? Spirits? That's why you came to the police station?"

"Yes. But only when I'm off the medication. And maybe they aren't there, I… I'm sick, Detective."

"Yes. And the medication needs time to work, right?"

"Yes."

His next question delivered slowly. Make no mistake, he wanted Daniel Hope to hear and understand the implications. "How much time until they have built up sufficiently in your system?"

"I'm not… a day, two days maybe."

"Daniel," John said and looked at the door. He had maybe three minutes. "Do you feel well enough to travel?"

Chapter Thirty-Four

It was almost anticlimactic. John got Daniel into a wheelchair and they simply walked out. Liguino was good to his word and they never saw him. John's nerves were taut, raw, and twitching at every noise. Worried that at any moment someone would stop them and ask who they were. But no one did. John was just a man driving a sick friend through the hospital.

Hope had to lean on John as they walked to his car, John still worried that someone would stop them. But again, the world was indifferent. No one ever stopped anyone to ask what they were doing, or *how* they were doing. It wasn't until they were in the car that Hope asked.

"Where are we going?"

Daniel Hope seemed fragile. Like thin papier-mâché covering brittle bones housing a broken mind. John himself felt like he was breaking. He wanted to sleep for a year.

"When you were at my house," he said. His voice was breaking. It took real effort to string the words together. From outside they were just two men in a car in a hospital parking lot, having a conversation. Inside, both were waging wars the world knew nothing about and cared nothing about. "When you were in my house, did you see a girl?" He reached over to the glove compartment and took out Emily's file. He found a picture of Emily and handed it to Daniel. His hands were shaking. "Did you see *this* girl?"

He was ready to hear it. He just wanted it to end. It would be a moment he would be ashamed of for the rest of his life, a single moment that nearly broke him. Because in that moment, he was ready to hear that Emily was dead *just* so he would know.

"No. There was only the mother's ghost."

John sobbed. He gripped the steering wheel as the dam burst and he cried because she was still alive somewhere. She was still out there, alive. Waiting for her father to find her.

"This is your daughter?" Daniel asked. He was looking through the file.

"I need to be sure," John said. "If you can really see what you say you see. I need to be sure."

He turned the key and the car thrummed to life. He wiped his tears away and steeled his nerves. The street looked wide and clean and they had green lights all the way to John's house.

It looked like any other house. Since no real crime had taken place there had been no investigation. There was no police cordon. Just a normal house on a normal afternoon.

They walked in, with Hope leaning against John. To others they might appear as a man helping a neighbor home from the hospital after a fall.

Inside, the house was eerily silent. Lonei and Orlando were still at a motel somewhere. The house seemed full of ghosts. It seemed like someone else's house.

Daniel was looking around and then he turned to John and shook his head.

John pointed at a door. Emily's room.

They walked and John felt every step rattle through his stomach. He didn't remember the last time he ate or drank but as they walked towards Emily's room it felt full of greasy ice-water. He had to fight the urge to throw up. His skin burned and his bones were freezing, marrow brittle from frost.

He watched as he reached out to turn the doorknob, as if his hand was doing it on its own. John looked at Daniel, who nodded. John opened the door and Daniel walked in.

It took only a few seconds. Daniel took three steps into the room, looked at the bed, looked towards the window, looked at the desk. He then looked at John and shook his head.

"There's no one here. Nothing I can see, at least, Detective."

John dry-heaved and lost his footing. He worried that he was going too far and suddenly the foolishness of his actions dawned on him.

"What am I doing?" he asked. "What am I…"

He steeled himself and stood up. Daniel was still looking around the room, but he shook his head again to John's unasked question.

"There's no one in this house but us, Detective."

John took a few staggered steps into the living room and let himself fall into a sofa. He shook his head to clear it and then looked at Daniel.

"I'm sorry," he said. "I shouldn't have… I'm sorry."

Daniel Hope stood still. Beatific, almost, as he looked back at John. As if he held John's solace and redemption in his maze of a mind and all John had to do was ask for it. He looked, for a moment, like a ghost. The sky cleared up outside and a few rays of sunshine reached through the window, touching motes of dust and then shining their light upon Daniel.

It was at that moment John realized where they should *really* be.

-

The drive to Whitesands took just over an hour of awkward silence and some genuine soul-searching.

"Where this all began," John had answered when Daniel asked him where they were going.

Hope didn't object when he heard the answer and didn't ask any more questions. Just looked out the window. After a while he turned his head back into the car and looked down at his feet. John wondered if he saw something out there that he didn't like.

John fought his own convictions. What had he become? A twice-disgraced police detective, now on the run with a man who had come to his home and attacked him with a knife, a man who claimed not only that ghosts were real but that they made people commit murder. He wasn't sure which was worse—Hope being right or Hope being wrong.

If he was right, John's whole world was far more complicated than he ever imagined. If Daniel Hope was right and he really hadn't seen Emily in her room, that might mean she was still alive somewhere.

If Daniel Hope was wrong, however, it just made this world even more strange. That meant Stillwater, Ortega, and Bartlett must have conspired to kill their spouses. Some sort of pact made when they were at the school, maybe? The chance that this was coincidence was so far out there that it was beyond belief. Not that the existence of body-possessing ghosts was any easier to believe.

Would the truth be found at Whitesands? Would John like it any better?

-

Night descended on them like a sprung trap. John shot glances at Daniel as he drove towards Whitesands. He looked to be sleeping at times, only to occasionally stiffen and stare out the window at things John didn't find remarkable. Empty lots and husks of houses. Daniel would look at John with an expression of shock, as if about to ask him if he had seen something too. John saw nothing but a slowly decomposing America. Like a clock that needed to be wound.

"How do you…" John started but wasn't sure what he wanted to ask exactly.

"I think it started bleeding again," Daniel said and reached his hand into the collar of his clothes. He was wearing a tan and black flannel shirt that was clearly intended for a bigger man. It folded and bunched around him, almost like a blanket. He took his hand back out and stared intently at his fingertips. There was no blood.

"Do you see blood?" He asked John and showed him.

"No. There's no blood."

"Sometimes I can't be sure," he said, and let his hand fall down by his side. He took to staring out of the window again.

"You all right?" John asked. "You want something to eat or drink? We can stop at one of these places," John said and gestured out the window as they passed a truck stop.

"No. I'd really rather just finish this."

John fought the urge to just turn around. He would possibly face actual jail time for this, abducting a suspect in a homicide investigation, though he hoped that O'Reilley would make this disappear. She had her eye on a more comfortable chair than she was in now, maybe D.A. or maybe the mayor. She would want this to just go away.

"What is it you see? Out there?" John asked. There was just the thinnest sliver of daylight left on the horizon. Outside, they passed strip malls with bright parking lots and decaying storefronts, followed by patches of darkness.

"Just… the same as you."

John didn't push it. Daniel seemed to be falling into a lethargic funk. He must have quite the drug cocktail in his system. Schizophrenia medication blending with painkillers and antibiotics.

"There's…" Daniel said. Trying to find the words for something. "I can't know if what I'm seeing is real or not. I can't. I learned to just not talk about it."

Again, John had no reply.

"I'm sorry I came to your house, Detective. I know I shouldn't have."

"No, that's fine. My wife might be dead by my hand if you hadn't."

John turned and saw that Daniel was staring at him, wide-eyed and teary.

"Please don't kill me, Detective. I think I want to live."

"What? You think… no. Mr. Hope, I really just want you to help me. I'm not going to kill you, why would you—"

"I tried to kill *you*," Daniel said.

"Yeah, but that was… it wasn't you. No. I'm not going to… why would you even come with me if that's what you thought?"

"I didn't care," Daniel answered.

"No, look. I just need answers. We're going to the school, to Whitesands. I need you to tell me if you see her. The daughter. I need to know if the people who we arrested really did kill her. I just hope you can help me. If what you say you can see is real it's… I mean. I'm sorry, Daniel, you met me at a very strange time in my life."

"Or maybe I'm just sick," Daniel said, head turned out the passenger side window.

"I need to know," John said.

"It wasn't always like this," Daniel said.

"What?"

"Outside. The world. It wasn't like this when I was a kid, I mean." Daniel was wistful, looking out into the twilight as if he hadn't just been pleading for his life. "I've lived in three worlds, Detective. There's the one I lived in as a kid. A bright world. Free from worry. A child's eye seeing childish things. I was still a child when I got sick, I suppose. I mean, when do we become adults, really?"

"I'd say it's when you get your first bill for a utility," John said, in an attempt to regain control of the conversation. Still reeling from Daniel asking him to spare his life. "Childhood ends the moment you know you're going to spend the rest of your life paying for things you don't really understand."

"Then I got sick. The world turned against me. I was being followed and everyone was talking about me. Your own brain betrays you. Sights and sounds and smells and thoughts, no longer to be trusted. That was the second world for me. Totally different from the childhood one. Sorry, I'm talking too much."

"No, no, it's fine," John said. "Really. Usually it's me telling someone how shitty the world is. It's refreshing to hear it from someone else for once."

"Then on the medication. It's like walking in three feet of water, but with everything. Thinking too. Everything is just a different kind of gray."

"Well. That's not just you," John said, thinking of how things changed for him after Emily disappeared. Everything was just a different kind of gray now.

John saw the sign for Whitesands and turned.

-

Whitesands stood tall and seemed to lean forward. As if it had been waiting for them.

John got out of the car and grabbed his hat and two flashlights from the back seat. It looked like it was about to rain.

Daniel Hope got out and winced at the sight of the building. He accepted the flashlight John handed to him, but looked at it like seeing one for the first time.

"Are you all right?" John asked. Not sure what sort of an answer he expected.

"It's just… it's exactly like I remembered. Like, well, *she* remembered – in my head."

"You… are you okay with this?"

"I think so. But the memories are so real. It feels as if they are mine. It triggers the same emotions in me that it did in her. I hate this place," he said through gritted teeth. "Her feelings for the school are so strong because *I* have no feelings for the school. Just hers."

It was a mistake to bring him here, John thought.

"We're just going to walk in and straight out through the back."

"We're not staying in the building? I would very much like to see her room," Daniel said. There was an odd inflection to the word room.

"Would you? Or would she?" John asked.

"I… I don't know," Daniel answered.

"No," John said. "No, we'll just go to the woods. Through here."

John led Daniel through the building. Again there was that imposing feeling of white privilege, that feeling that he was in a place he wasn't welcome. Shame, for some reason, and a bit of anger at realizing they still had that power.

He picked up the pace through the hallway, strode past the stairs leading up to the second floor, out through a double door and into the forest and the dark night. Daniel followed him. He was pale, not that he had been an image of health before, but something he had seen had drained the color completely from his face. He looked like a ghost himself.

"All right?" John asked.

Daniel shook his head and kept walking. Tears were streaming down his face. John had to walk briskly to catch up to him.

"What did you see in there?" John asked.

"What sort of place is this?" Daniel said.

"It's… it's a school. A boarding school. I… I'm not sure what you're asking. What did you see?"

John felt cold rain run down his neck and chill his spine and his skin tingled. It wasn't raining.

"Daniel, what did you see?"

Daniel Hope shook his head and looked at John. Eyes bloodshot and cheeks wet, all sense of joy or desire drained from him. It was a look John had seen from people in front-rows at funerals. The truly bereaved, not just people paying their respects. Daniel looked *hurt*.

"Daniel, I'm sorry."

"They—" but he sniffled instead of finishing what he was about to say, sniffled and looked up at the windows on the second floor. "We shouldn't be here. I shouldn't be here."

"We'll just walk through the woods. I think I know the place."

According to the case files and the news reports, they tied Alice Woodacre to a tree about a mile straight west into the woods. Daniel turned to face away from the school building and took a deep breath.

"I'm sorry," he said to John.

"Sorry?"

"I can't do this," Daniel said. "I can't move. I can't move. I can't move."

"Easy, easy," John said. As if calming a horse.

"There's too much," Daniel said and gestured into the air.

"Okay. Listen. Close your eyes. Just breathe. Close your eyes and breathe." John couldn't turn back now. He'd be facing a shitstorm already and possible jail time and he knew he was being stupid. Just a few days ago he'd have laughed at the notion of ghosts, would have kicked anyone even hinting at the idea out of the station. Out of his life. Yet here he was, leading a schizophrenic man who had attacked him in his home through the woods in search of a dead girl.

"Just put your hand on my shoulder and follow me. You don't have to see anything."

John took Daniel's hand and placed it on his shoulder. Daniel's hand was cold and unsteady. He inhaled sharply and seemed to steady himself.

"Ready?" John asked.

Daniel didn't answer, so John just started walking. The night was thick in the woods. It squeezed into the spaces between the trees and didn't seem happy to give in to the flashlight beam. Daniel's flashlight was turned on but pointed at the ground. Something large was lurching through the woods in the distance, a moose maybe. John wasn't sure if there were moose in these woods, or bears. Suddenly felt exposed and silly, unarmed as he was.

Made a mental note to buy a gun.

They cut their way through the darkness. John almost felt it close in on them. Like the night was a series of curtains they were pushing through. Heavy and dark. This deep into the forest sound carried oddly. Cut-up by the trees and scratched on the rough bark. Again the sound of something big crashing in the distance.

They were getting close.

"All right, Daniel?" John asked.

"Cherry Hills," Daniel answered.

"What?"

Daniel was silent, as he looked at the leaves and the trees and, above them, the darkness of the clouded sky.

"It's like Cherry Hills. It's a small forest where I grew up. It's not there anymore. They trampled it all down, the whole forest, and then ripped the mountain apart. Coal or gold or something. They ruined the water and my parents got paid a bit to move so we did. To the city."

"When was this?" John asked. Relieved to see him out of his shell.

"In the Nineties. Ninety-four, ninety-five. I still remember the taste of the water and the way the air smelled. Stay out too long and it started to sting the eyes. We'd dare each other to stay out in Cherry Hills as long as we could. Of course, the trees were gone then, but the name remained. I wonder if there ever were cherry trees. Strange I never thought of it before."

"We don't question things in our youth," John said. "They just are."

"This forest smells nice. Nothing to sting the throat. No reason to leave."

They walked on and then John noticed a shift in Daniel's gait. He had let go of John's shoulder a while back and opened his eyes. They had been walking side-by-side.

"I hear something," Daniel said. "I hear..." and then he was running. Suddenly just took off, his flashlight beam jumping and skittering in front and John had to hustle to keep pace.

He didn't run long.

They were in a spot no different from any other. Leaves on the ground and ferns and all manner of flowers and weeds poking through the damp earth. Daniel was standing still with his back turned to John. The darkness seemed to want to get at them. As if it was waiting for the flashlights to fail so it could reclaim its territory.

"Hello?" Daniel said and John felt a cold snap of electricity in his scalp. And then he said "Hello," as if greeting someone.

It was an invitation.

"Yes," he said. John felt light. A feather on greasy water. He panned the flashlight around but saw nothing but darkness and tree trunks. Turned the flashlight back to Daniel, startled to see that Daniel was looking right at him.

"There's a girl here," Daniel said, and the whole forest seemed to hear him. A deathly calm quiet descended. Nothing rustled in the wind.

"Yes," he said again. "I see you."

John wondered if it was a show. If Daniel was putting on a performance for him. Showing him something he thought John might want to see.

"He is a police officer. We've been looking for you. We—" He had been interrupted, or so it seemed to John.

"No, I'm sorry. We didn't bring anything."

"What are you seeing, Daniel?" John asked.

Daniel turned to him. "There's a girl here," he repeated.

John had looked at photos of Alice Whitacre. She had brown eyes and a thin nose. A smattering of freckles in her school photo, the one that was used for the "Missing" posters but not in any other photographs. Brown shoulder-length hair. A single black birthmark on her eyelid. Not something John had seen himself, just read about.

"What does she look like, Daniel?"

"She's… dark hair. What do you call it…" He made a gesture with his hand on his forehead. "Bangs. Brown eyes and… she has a dark spot on one of her eyelids. I just see it when she blinks. She's wearing a dress with flowers on it and a sweater over."

John felt cold and hot. He felt like everyone he knew was watching him, frowning in disappointment. He felt silly and wanted to cry at the same time.

"Are you really seeing her, Daniel. This isn't a show for me?"

"Do you want me to ask her something?" Daniel said and then turned his head. His head tilted slightly downward, as if there really was someone in front of him. Someone *just* hidden by the trees and if John were to move slightly, take one step to the side, he would see them. He did, and saw nothing. Flashlight illuminating bark and fern and some small brown creature nosing its way through the forest floor in the peaceful darkness. No other forms were near.

Daniel spoke. "She says she's sorry."

"Tell her she doesn't have to be," John said. He felt, through Daniel, like he was conscious of a wayward and flickering existence.

A few light taps above them made John turn up as rain, softly falling, beat on large leaves.

"She's afraid. And lonely," Daniel said. "We should follow her."

Daniel started walking further into the woods. John followed.

Daniel stopped after just a few paces. "This one?" he asked the air. He turned to John and held a hand up to the flashlight beam. "She says this is the tree they tied her to."

John played the flashlight up and down the tree Daniel indicated. Just a tree in a forest. Unremarkable. The rain continued falling softly on the leaves and the ground. John wandered if it was falling too, wherever Emily might be.

"She says they tricked her into the woods and tied her to the tree. They laughed at her, touched her."

"Who?" John said. Regaining his senses. Daniel was making this up, it had to be. He should never have brought a schizophrenic man who stabbed himself in his home into a dark forest, alone. He waited for Daniel to try to remember the names from the press.

"Michael, she says. Wendy, Ruiz, Jo, and Ronald. They tricked her into coming here and then they tied her to the tree and laughed at her."

John felt pinned. As if he had taken root. Dipped in cold oil and hot wax. He wanted to throw up. "Say...

say that again." He had said Jo and Ronald. There was a chance Daniel had seen the first three names in the newspapers, but not the other two.

"She said Wendy, Still Mike, Ruiz and—"

John dropped the flashlight. It lit up a patch of weeds on the ground and a part of Daniel's feet. He focused on the light.

"Ask her how she died," John said.

"Detective, ghosts don't remember how they died, and if they do they don't like to—"

"Ask her!"

Startled, Daniel turned and tilted his head downwards again.

"What do you remember?" he asked. A gentler version of John's question. "What happened next?"

"They left her, she says. They tied her to the tree and left her. It was a warm evening, but she was cold. She thought it was just a silly prank."

"They left her? Are you sure that's what she's saying?"

"She was alone," Daniel continued. "She was alone for a long time she says. Then someone came."

Daniel stood deathly still as he spoke and stared intently at nothing, unnerving John.

"Someone came to help me, she says. They cut the ropes and took my hand to help me but… it was a boy. Not one of the others, another boy. He set me free."

"Ask her what he looks like, what he—"

Daniel continued, ignoring John. "He led me further into the woods and then he…"

Silence. Crickets and birds and silence. An eerie calm came upon the part of the woods they were standing in. The sound of the rain falling faintly through the air.

"Where?" Daniel asked into the air.

"Where what?" John asked. He was losing control of the situation. He was just a bystander now. Witness to a crime from thirty years ago.

Daniel turned to John and there was something in his look that John didn't like.

"He hurt her head. She fell to the ground and – what? Come, we have to follow her."

Daniel took off into the darkness and John followed, holding on to the flashlight as if he was his salvation. They didn't walk far, but it was through rough brambles and thick bushes. A place to hide a body if you were looking for that.

"Here," Daniel said. "This is the last place she remembers. This is the place she keeps coming back to. Detective, someone freed her and took her to this spot where they hit her on the head at least once, probably more. This is where you will find her body."

"They searched this area! Daniel, they… they searched this area. There is no girl and—"

"John, she's here!"

Daniel's words cut through the air and through John's daze.

"This is where she fell. This is where he…" Daniel Hope turned towards what John imagined was a girl standing in a dress with a wild rose print. Alone in the forest in the dark, forever.

"She says his name was Richard Keyes," Daniel said to John. "That's the name of the boy who came and she thought was freeing her. That's the last person to see her alive."

John almost swooned. He put his hand upon the rough bark of a tree and felt like the tree was swooning with him.

"How do you know that name, Daniel?"

"She just told me, Detective."

"No," John said. "It's… how do you know it? How did you know about that name and the birthmark, Daniel!"

"You don't believe me," Daniel said. "But you brought me here. This is your doing, Detective."

The night was still. John would remember this moment, later, with a feeling of a dam bursting. He was standing in a desert, knowing there was no water anywhere and then turning to see a dam bursting and a flood coming towards him. Nothing would ever be the same again. Because he finally found that he believed Daniel Hope and in realizing that he also realized that he was standing on broken ground. Up to this point in his life he had an incomplete picture of the world. He felt like a child having an epiphany, realizing that other countries existed, or realizing that one day they would die.

"It's too much."

Daniel was crying. "She says she's sorry, Detective."

John looked in the direction he imagined she was standing and wondered why he couldn't see her. She felt real to him now.

"Sorry?"

"She thinks she did something wrong," Daniel said.

"Tell her it's okay. Tell her she did nothing wrong."

"She hears you, John."

John spoke to the air. "It's all right. It's not your fault, Alice."

A silence.

"What now?" Daniel asked. "She wants to go home, John. She wants to go home."

"Tell her—" John said but Daniel interrupted him.

"She asks how her parents are. She hasn't seen them in so long. Why aren't they looking for her, she asks? What should I tell her?"

John's heart is a bird, its wings broken as it flaps alone on the cold ground.

"Did her mother ever sing nursery rhymes to her?"

Daniel looked at Alice. Where John imagined Alice stood.

"Yes," Daniel said after a while. "An old Icelandic one, from a play about forest animals. Why?"

"Ask her to sing it," John said. "Can you sing it, Alice?"

With a hesitant foreboding, John turned to Daniel "Can you hum what she's singing?"

John steeled himself. It was the last bit of confirmation he needed that Daniel was talking to her, that events had indeed transpired as Daniel claimed. That the world John thought he lived in was deeper and darker than he knew.

Daniel was silent for a while. Then he hummed a few notes.

"I don't understand the words," Daniel said. "It's not English." He kept humming.

It was the same. Daniel was humming the same nursery rhyme that Ruiz Ortega had hummed as he attached bloody feathers to his wife's body. As the spirit of Jonelle Whitacre, twisted and corrupted by grief and hate wrongly assumed that five kids had killed her daughter and hidden her body. So many lives ruined.

"Enough," John said. He vowed that he would release the hate he had for whoever took Emily, and remember only the love he had for her. He did not want his hate to corrupt him, as it had corrupted Jonelle Whitacre. He smiled and wiped his eyes.

"The truth. Tell her the truth," John said. He shook off the daze. In a moment, John Dark collected himself and made the decision to acknowledge the new reality and not fight it. "Tell her that her father is still looking for her but her mother died. Tell her that we'll find the man responsible and we'll make sure her father knows where she is. Daniel?"

"Yes?"

"Tell her she'll have peace now."

"She hears you."

"Now tell her—"

"She wants to know if it's true," Daniel said to John.

"If what's true?"

"About her mother."

John turned towards the spot he imagined she stood. Played the flashlight over the air as a way of stalling.

"She doesn't like the flashlight," Daniel said.

John pointed the beam to the ground and tried to choose his words.

"Alice. I'm afraid your mother is dead. But she never stopped looking for you, she never stopped fighting for you. Your father will be very happy to hear that we found you."

That last sentence played across the string of what he wanted someone to say to *him*.

If you were a real detective you would have found her by now.

"He'll be very happy to hear we found you," John said. "I'll tell him myself."

Chapter Thirty-Five

John and Daniel walked back in silence. At Daniel's request they went around and not through the main building. John called the police department and told them where he was and that, yes, Daniel Hope was with him. No, he was fine, they were both fine. But he now had reason to believe that the body of Alice Whitacre was buried in the woods behind Whitesands Preparatory School.

It took forty-five minutes for them to arrive, and another two hours for them to prepare the search and dig. The remains of Alice Whitacre were found, thirty years after she was reported missing, in a quiet part of the woods, between crooked fallen branches and spears of brambles. Wild roses grew to the side and the moonlight touched down on the site for a moment and disappeared behind a cloud and then rain, faintly falling, kept company with them as they disturbed the ground with their tools.

John called Alice's father himself from the parking lot outside Whitesands. Made the call he hoped never to get himself. There were groups of teenagers gathered around. Students were curious why all the police cars were there in the night, vans with forensic tools and people dressed head-to-toe in white.

A gruff man's voice growled a slow "Hello" into the phone at the other end.

"Mr. Whitacre?" John said.

"Yes. Who is this?"

"My name is John Dark. I'm a detective. I'm sorry to have to tell you this, but we have reason to think that a body discovered this evening is that of your daughter, Alice."

Silence. Then a crackle of static.

"You… what?"

"I'm sorry, sir. I really am." It was the first time John had said that and not only meant it but actually *felt* it.

"My Alice?"

"Will you be able to come speak to an officer about her?"

"I'm in Granada," he said.

"Sorry?"

"In Spain, I'm in Spain. My Alice, you said you've found my Alice?"

John was leaning against his car as he spoke. Still in the Whitesands car park. There were three police cruisers here. One for Alice, forensics officers, and detectives. They would be furious when they found out who John was talking to, but so be it. This far into it, John didn't see what one more infraction would do.

There was another car here to take Daniel Hope back to his supervised stay at the hospital. The third car was for John. It was only a final shred of professional courtesy that they allowed him a phone call before taking him in.

"Yes. Forensics still have to identify her with scientific certainty but I can tell you that I'm sure it's her, sir."

"Where has she been, what happened to her?" A certain relief in Whitacre's voice. The same relief John might feel if he could know where Emily was.

"As a police officer, I am not supposed to disclose anything at this point. As a father of a missing girl myself, however, I have the following information for you. Alice was tricked into the woods by her friends. A stupid prank, just teenagers being mean without meaning to. They tied her to a tree and left her."

"They," Whitacre said. "Those five? The ones they always said did it?"

"Yes," John answered. "But that's all they did. Their intention was not to hurt her. It was a warm evening and she wouldn't be harmed. They intended to haze her, I guess, leave her there for a few minutes, maybe an hour, and then come back for her."

John waited for Whitacre to say something, prod and ask, but he was silent. John continued. "However, someone intervened and ended the prank early. Came along before the five kids returned and were able to free her. Beat them to it, only..."

"What?" Whitacre asked.

"It appears your daughter was taken further into the woods by this individual."

"At Whitesands?"

"Yes," John said. "They took her further into the woods and they..."

"Tell me."

She's not Emily. You can say this. Emily will be fine.

"She was hit in the head with a rock or a branch."

"When?"

"Sorry?"

"How long has she been dead, Detective?"

"From the night she went missing." John had no comfort for Whitacre. Only truth.

"They said she ran away. They… how do you know this?"

"Like I said, Mr. Whitacre, we discovered her body this evening. I just wanted you to know."

"Wait," Whitacre said.

John looked up at the sky. Patches of clouds disturbed his view of the stars. Someone was smoking nearby. John was calmer than he had been in weeks. "Yes?"

"I'm sorry. I've tried to put this behind me, Detective…?"

"Dark, John Dark."

"I'm just a little overwhelmed as you…" He sniffled. Somewhere far away, Mr. Whitacre sat on his bed and cried. "As you can imagine. This has haunted me for decades. We were *destroyed* by this."

John said nothing.

"Who did you say did this? Who killed my daughter."

John looked up at Whitesands. *Richard Keyes. Richard Keyes, the man who was currently headmaster of Whitesands.*

"I can't say anything about that at this moment. We have some leads that will be investigated and the case will be reopened. Someone will be in contact with you, Mr. Whitacre, once more is known."

"Not you?"

"Sorry?"

"You said someone."

"I am not on this case, no. Someone else will contact you."

"So that's it?" Whitacre asked after a moment of silence.

"Sir?"

"I'm sorry. After all this time I hadn't expected to ever hear anything about her. My wife she… it drove her over the edge."

I know, John thought. He looked at the car driving away with Daniel. He thought of all the things he would never be able to tell anyone.

"They'll need you to come in for assistance with identifying your daughter, sir. Your DNA and some formalities."

"My DNA?"

"For genetic identification. Your daughter she… it's been three decades. The body—"

"I see. Yes. I'll come, of course I'll come. Thank you, Officer."

"Detective," John corrected.

"Yes, Detective. Thank you."

Two officers walked towards John.

"I have to go Mr. Whitacre," John said. "Someone will call you soon. I'm sorry about this."

"No, thank you. Will I be able to reach you at this number in the coming days, Detective?"

"Yes," John said. "I'm sorry they weren't able to find her sooner, Mr. Whitacre."

"You'll hear from me," Whitacre said and hung up.

John put his phone into his pocket and wiped his cheeks.

"You all right there, Dark?" The officer spoke with a heavy New England accent. *Dahk.*

"I've been better," John said and thought about what he'd accomplished that evening. "I've been worse. Can I call my wife?"

"You didn't just call your wife?"

"No. I had to call someone else first."

"Call her from the car," the other officer said. "Tell her you'll be staying in a nice warm bed at the precinct."

John did exactly that.

Chapter Thirty-Six

There are phases we go through in life, and we only know they are over when we look back and reflect. Graduating means that school is over as a time of our life. John Dark had spent the last few days going through a wringer of depositions and debriefings and knew, now, that he was looking back on a career in the police department that had ended. He had passed through a barrier and there was no going back.

He was sitting across from Lonei at their kitchen table, trying to find the words to explain all this when the call came. Lonei was trying to deflect and delay the discussion about what their lives were now, when all they had left was a thin thread connecting them. The search for Emily bound them together, but it was down to the scent of candle recently blown out, lingering, soon to disperse.

"The Vestigial Flock, John. It crops up a few times," Lonei was a better detective than he was when it came to using the tools of the new era. She would scour through parts of the internet John only ever heard mentioned by Lonei, at this dinner table. Message boards and blog comment threads, eBay listings and magazine archives. The past was being put online and Lonei knew how to search through it.

"I found one of their pamphlets listed with a used bookstore in Iowa but the owner doesn't answer email or phone. Probably it's gone out of business."

"Lonei," John said, stopping her. He drew a deep breath.

She was stalling. While John really *did* want to hear what she had found they had other matters to discuss.

"Lonei. They... I'm not a cop anymore."

"They suspended you again?" She was hoping. They had only his income now.

"No. Not a suspension. Badge and gun. No pension."

Lonei got up and poured herself a mug of coffee. The pot was not fresh and John couldn't see a light on. He sat still. A new reality was setting in for both of them. The loss of a child that kept taking more and more from them.

"Monique?" she asked.

Not ready to talk about the future yet, John thought.

"Monique stays on. She'll get a new partner and might get moved around but she was found to have performed well. Considering."

"And Raymond Miller?"

"Raymond will be fine. He's not suing and his recollection of what happened seems to match what I said at the shooting review board; he had an episode or a seizure or something. He doesn't remember what happened. The doctor who treated him found an incision under his chin and blood that matched Arthur Bartlett, so that lines up with how I told it."

John's phone rang. The screen flashed bright and the phone burred against the tabletop. They both looked at it and ignored it. Some number John didn't know. Both of them thinking *Is this it? Have they found Emily?* The same heartbreak every time.

"The schizophrenic's not going to come back here, is he John?" Lonei asked. Orlando had gone to stay with a friend and had not been home for a few days.

The phone kept vibrating on the table. John stared at it, eyes out of focus.

"Daniel is not dangerous. He *saved* my life."

"Attacked you with a knife."

"It wasn't him. It was…" He didn't finish. Not sure he would ever finish that sentence out loud.

"Answer that John."

John had no desire in the world to speak to anyone. He wanted to go to sleep and didn't really care if he wouldn't wake up. He selected *In a meeting, call you right back…* and sent it, without ever meaning to return the call.

"The pamphlet you found?" he said.

"John. What if he *does* come back?"

"Daniel Hope is harmless, Lonei. It wasn't him. And even if it was he's drugged up to his eyeballs now and locked away in a hospital. And that's part of what's fucking bothering me, Lonei, is that he helped me. I *made* him help me and in return he gets to probably spend the rest of his life locked away. They all do – him, Stillwater, Ortega, Wendy Bartlett, they all have to spend the rest of their lives alone in prison for things they didn't really do."

He had stood up and poured himself a cup of the overboiled coffee. It tasted worse than station-house ink and along with the injustice of the world John thought he might just choke on it.

"You think he's right?" Lonei asked. "The schizophrenic?"

"Daniel Hope, Lonei. And yes, I think so. But what does that mean? That ghosts are real? I can't hold both those things in my head, Lonei."

"What do you mean?"

"Either Stillwater, Ortega and Wendy Bartlett killed their spouses by coincidence in the same week and had a pact to claim not to remember it, or Daniel Hope is right and a ghost on a revenge mission possessed them and made them kill. Which sounds impossible. But how did he know where to find Alice's body?"

"He..."

"Don't give me that look, Lonei. He was ten years old when she died, he didn't do it. He couldn't know."

Their home phone rang. He should have gotten rid of it years ago, now it was only telemarketers and robocalls. It jarred the silence that had followed John's speech. It rang again and it was as if the house was a bell, amplifying the ring of the phone.

"John, get that."

They had set up a hotline for leads in the weeks after Emily went missing. All sorts of people called, with all sorts of leads. There had been a spate of psychics and mediums and John had spent many hours sitting on the sofa, listening to stories of what they thought happened to Emily. She had been abducted by two men, one of them on crutches and they were holding her in a loft in Minneapolis or she had gotten into a car with a tall woman with a wig and they were in Mexico. Sometimes they said she was with them, not physically but in spirit and wanted to let her parents know that she was in this place or that place. John came to hate that phone but also hoped it would never stop ringing because that was so much worse.

He almost didn't pick up.

"Dark residence," he said.

A silence. Pure silence, no static.

"John Dark?" the man said. He sounded familiar.

"Yes."

"My name is Graham Whitacre. I tried your cell phone."

John sat down. The sofa was old and soft and John sank deep into it.

"Mr. Dark. I wanted to thank you again for finding my daughter."

"My job, sir."

"Your job. There were many before you with the same job that failed. You didn't."

"I guess I got lucky, sir."

Lonei stood and stirred her cup of coffee. John wondered what she was stirring.

Whitacre seemed closer. The call was clear and his voice crisper.

"Do you know anything about me, Mr. Dark? I heard it is no longer *Detective* Dark. I saw a report in the paper."

"So you've arrived in the States?" John asked.

"Yes. Paperwork and procedures. I also want to thank you."

"Like I said, Mr. Whitacre, I had a job."

"I have an offer for you."

"Sir?"

"I want to hire you to find Emily."

"I'm not sure I—"

"Mr. Dark. I am perhaps not making it clear just how grateful I am to you. I have been lucky in most things in life and have more money than I really need. Alice's disappearance soured all things for me, as I am sure Emily's disappearance has for you. Maybe, one day I will come to terms with what happened. But I want to thank you."

"I am no longer a detective, Mr. Whitacre. I'm not sure how useful I can be."

"We'll see. The offer is this: I put you on the payroll. You get a credit card. I pay you a nice monthly salary and cover most expenses. I am a practical man."

"You want me to work for you?"

"No, not really. I want to thank you by making you an employee and your only job will be to search for your daughter. I know you have the skills and the drive, now you have the means. We'll meet later in the week to iron out details," and then Graham Whitacre hung up.

John gently placed the phone back and looked at Lonei. Relief and mourning and grief and anger twisted together within and he didn't know how to control it or even if he wanted to.

Lonei stood at the doorway to the living room and looked at him, and for the first time in two years John looked at his beautiful wife with a look of something other than grief in his eyes. John Dark looked at his wife with hope, and he saw it in her too.

He was going to find their daughter.

Epilogue

Uncaught

Whitesands headmaster Richard Keyes leaned against the open doorway leading out to his back garden in just his bathrobe, cradling a cup of tea. He had inherited a large country house and no neighbors and enjoyed looking out at the gloaming through the trees. A short-haired girl struggled against a thick rope that held her to a large tree in the yard. Her skin was pale against the night and she reminded Richard of a white balloon. Her screams did little to disturb Richard's evening cup of tea. There was no one else around for miles, and she wasn't nearly as loud as the last one.

It bothered him a little that the police had discovered Alice's body. He had thought of moving it, once, but with so much time having passed he had almost forgotten about it. Almost. You remembered your first very vividly.

That detective bothered him though. How had he managed to walk into the woods and find the body after all this time?

Richard sipped his tea and pulled his robe closer. He had just showered, as he always did afterwards. He would have to do something about that John Dark though. He might manage to figure out that *he* also knew Alice, and

Richard did not want Police Detective John Dark to pay him a visit to his home.

He took another sip of his tea and looked into the woods behind his house. He felt the faintest wisp of turned earth in his nostrils. It wouldn't do at all to have the police looking around out there.

He shivered, naked as he was under the robe, and closed the door, leaving the girl alone in the yard, screaming at the distant stars in the cold night.

Acknowledgements

My most heartfelt gratitude to the City of Exeter, The British Council and Literature Works for their hospitality. This book would not exist if not for the week I spent in Exeter in the summer of 2019 as the International Writer-in-Residence. I owe Heather Norman-Soderlind and Helen Chaloner a great debt of gratitude for their hospitality during my stay.

Richard Thomas for editing *Whitesands* and turning it from a pile of words into a book, and his encouragement throughout the process.

Troy L. Wiggins who provided much help on getting the voice of a black man right, or at least not completely wrong. Where John Dark is convincing, that is Troy. Any place where he sounds inauthentic is on me.

I'd especially like to thank early readers Barry Napier, Glen Krisch, Jessica Poteet and Kristján Atli for their patience with the book and their excellent critique throughout the writing process.

Finally, I'd like to thank my wife for her final tough-love critique-read of *Whitesands*. The book is better because you don't settle. Also, thanks for putting up with all the books around the house all these years, honey.